DAISY'S LONG ROAD HOME

1948: Daisy Driscoll is working as a qualified Sister in Brighton. The war may be over, but Daisy's heart is in turmoil. Abandoned in childhood and haunted by the experience of her first marriage, Daisy no longer trusts anyone. Convinced the roots of her identity lie in India, and desperate to find the truth, Daisy leaps at the chance to leave her lonely life behind when her friend Grayson Harte travels to the East on business. As she uncovers long-hidden secrets about the family she never knew, will she be able to put the past behind her and find happiness after all?

DAISY'S LONG ROAD HOME

DAISY'S LONG ROAD HOME

by

Merryn Allingham

Magna Large Print Books
Long Preston, North Yorkshire,
BD23 4ND, England.

British Library Cataloguing in Publication Data.

A catalogue record of this book is
available from the British Library

ISBN 978-0-7505-4374-3

First published in Great Britain 2015 by Harlequin MIRA,
an imprint of Harlequin (UK) Limited

Published in Large Print 2017 by arrangement with
HarperCollins Publishers Ltd.

Magna Large Print is an imprint of Library Magna Books Ltd.

Printed and bound in Great Britain by
T.J. (International) Ltd., Cornwall, PL28 8RW

This is a work of fiction. Names, characters, places, locations and incidents are purely fictional and bear no relationship to any real life individuals, living or dead, or to any actual places, business establishments, locations, events or incidents. Any resemblance is entirely coincidental.

To my father, who spent the happiest years of
his life in India, but who never went back

After a while, whoever you are, you just have to let go, and the river brings you home
–Joanne Harris, *Five Quarters of the Orange*

CHAPTER 1

Sussex, March 1948

Daisy ignored the doorbell when it rang. It had been a bad day and she'd no wish to entertain her prying neighbour. Half her nurses were down with influenza, but the ward was so crowded she'd had to order the few still on their feet to make up beds in the corridor. The row with Matron had been the last straw.

The bell rang again and she shut her ears to it. Until the third chime. Then she marched to the front door and flung it wide in exasperation. A man leant nonchalantly against the doorpost and she stared in amazement at him.

'Grayson?'

'It's nice to see you recognise me.' She didn't think he meant it as a jest. And why would he? It was months since they'd seen each other.

She tried to pull her thoughts together. 'But why are you here?'

'I needed to see you. Can I come in?'

'Yes, of course.' There had been a momentary hesitation and he was quick to notice it. 'Don't worry, I'm not staying. I have a train to catch back to London.'

But why had he needed to visit, and without warning? There had been no letter, no telegram. That was worrying and she wondered what was coming. She hadn't been wrong about the edge to his voice though. He was the man she'd loved, perhaps still loved, yet after so long apart, neither had made any attempt even to touch hands. He followed her into the small kitchen that gave straight on to the road and looked around him. She'd been here for nine months and this was the first time he'd walked through her door.

'It's cosy,' he decided.

'It's affordable.'

'Is Brighton so very expensive?'

He settled himself at the shabby wooden table. As always, he was completely relaxed. Only the slightly deeper creases around his mouth and the few grey hairs at his temple spoke the passing of years.

'Not by London standards, no, but salaries here are low.'

'And how is the job?'

She didn't answer immediately but put the kettle on to boil. She knew the job was a source of irritation to him, and she couldn't even boast that it was going well. Today had been the worst by far, culminating in a vitriolic exchange with her superior. For the first time, she'd answered the woman back and known immediately she'd done the wrong thing.

'Beecham's is a small hospital,' she said, arranging cups and saucers on a tray. She was prevaricating, but if she showed her true feelings, she'd have to acknowledge the mistake she had made in coming to Brighton.

'So?'

'It can be a little insular, that's all. Trifles can

become too important. And the work itself is hardly challenging.' She was willing to confess that much, but she wished she didn't sound quite so weary or quite so frustrated.

'I imagine the lack of challenge is inevitable. After the war, most nursing will seem humdrum.'

She poured the tea, trying to lose herself in the routine action, conscious she should fight a desire to confide in him. They were almost strangers now. Since she'd made the move to Brighton, they'd met only once. She'd gone up to London to spend the day with him just before Christmas. It had been a forlorn attempt to rekindle a love that had once burnt brightly. In determined fashion, they'd made their way around old haunts, exchanged opinions on the city's new landmarks, chattered a little too much, told a few too many silly jokes, but there had been a hollowness to the day that neither could ignore. They hadn't repeated the experiment. And now he was here, and she didn't know how she should feel.

'You could be right about the war,' she said, carrying the tray to the table, her finger jabbing at a small spill of tea on the plastic tablecloth. 'It was an extraordinary experience.'

She sat down opposite him and felt his eyes fixed on her. His gaze made her shift uneasily in her seat. He knew she wasn't happy, she thought. As always, he knew, and she could feel herself getting ready to confess the truth.

'Brighton might have been a mistake,' she blurted out.

There, she'd said it, but his eyebrows barely rose at the admission. 'I got the promotion I wanted, but the nursing is fairly basic, and though the patients are wonderful and most of my staff are well enough...' The words were tumbling forth now. 'It's the pettiness that gets me down. It's a small town and the hospital is a very small community.'

'And who is being particularly petty?' He was as perceptive as ever.

She allowed herself a small sigh. 'Miss Thornberry – the matron.'

'Ah!'

She read his exclamation rightly. A hospital's matron was always key. They could be fiercesome women, but most were dedicated to their work and fair in their dealings. This one, though, had beaten her. The woman was constantly niggling; sly remarks that suggested that Daisy, as a newly promoted sister, wasn't quite up to the job. For months she'd taken the criticisms in silence but today she'd had enough and let fly.

'I expect the latest trouble will blow over.' Her voice had a false brightness to it.

Grayson stirred his tea and waited for her to go on. He knew there was more to say and so did she. The job had certainly proved a disappointment, but the real heaviness in her heart came from elsewhere. For years, she'd lived a solitary life and felt proud of her independence. But a moment had come, and quite recently, when she'd had to accept the truth. She wasn't just alone, she was lonely. A thirty-year-old woman who still hadn't got life right. She missed the camaraderie of wartime, though it had taken her a while to realise it. And she missed the comfort of a good friend. If

Connie were here, she could have confessed her loneliness. But Connie was now Mrs Lawson and living a new life in Canada with her doctor husband. Together they'd decided the old Empire offered better prospects than a ravaged and debt-ridden England. And then there was Grayson. How long had that taken before she recognised how large a void he'd left in her life? But that was something else she wouldn't admit.

He'd been silent all this time and she felt impelled to speak, to fill the empty air with words, any words. 'I'm sorry. None of this is important and you haven't travelled miles to hear me moan. It's only that today has been particularly difficult.'

'Don't give it a thought.' His gaze finally relaxed. 'Why have friends if you can't complain to them?' There was a studied emphasis on the word 'friends', and she was trying to think how best to respond, when a loud burst of music clattered through the adjoining wall.

'Your neighbour?'

'She has a gramophone and she likes to play it.'

'Noisy as well as nosy then. She watched me as I walked along the road – every step of the way.'

Next door, Peggy Lee was delivering her final flourish, making it impossible for them to speak. But when the last strains of *'Mañana'* had died away, Grayson nodded his head towards the drab cream wall that separated the two cottages. 'I take it you've tried to negotiate?'

'I have, but it made little difference and unless I'm to have a stand-up row with her – look, Grayson, forget my neighbour, instead tell me why you're here. You said nothing about coming.'

He rocked back on the hard chair, his hands in his pockets. 'If I'd given you advance warning, you might have made an excuse for not seeing me.'

'I wouldn't have done that.'

He looked fixedly at her once more, and she found herself lowering her eyes. 'Things haven't been good between us, you must admit,' he said. 'And I wasn't sure I'd see you. It was important that I did.'

'You're seeing me now.'

She knew she sounded impatient. She hadn't liked the reminder of how bad things had become. And now she was over the first shock of his appearance, the first rush of pleasure at seeing again the face she'd loved so well, annoyance was uppermost. She was tired and hungry and, she thought confusedly, a little scared. Something bad was about to happen, else Grayson would never have made this trip.

He stood up and stretched his long frame. 'Can we talk somewhere more comfortable?'

She thought it unlikely. The cottage was rented and the landlord a skinflint. What furniture he'd provided had almost certainly been bought at auction at rock-bottom prices.

'Will this do?' She gestured towards the narrow sofa crouching beneath the windowsill, its red moquette worn so thin as to be almost colourless. Grayson followed and perched precariously on the seat's hard edge. He half turned so he was looking directly at her. 'I'm going back to India. Not permanently, but I've no idea how long I'll be. I thought it only courteous to a lover, or should I say a former lover, to bid her farewell.'

Daisy's mouth dropped open. She was stunned, too surprised to speak, too surprised to dwell on being demoted to a former lover. In any case, he spoke truly. Their love seemed to have gone missing somewhere along the way, and right now she hadn't the energy or the will to try to recapture it.

'But why?' she stumbled. 'Why go back? Why go now?'

She felt stupidly upset. Twice this week India had swum into her world, seemingly out of nowhere, and left her bewildered. Ever since the package from Jocelyn had dropped through her letter box, she'd felt it burdening her mind. And now Grayson had arrived with India on his lips and the burden had just grown heavier.

He leaned back against the unyielding sofa cushion and took his time to answer. 'Why now? Because there's trouble. And I'm needed.'

That did nothing to calm her nerves. 'Trouble? What trouble?'

'You must have read about the situation – what's been happening in India since Independence.'

'You mean the killings? Yes, I've read about them. It's been awful. But what have they to do with you?' An unspecified fear tightened her face, until she felt her skin drawn hard against her cheekbones. Her voice must have sounded panicked because he tried to soothe her.

'Most of them have nothing to do with me and, at the moment, the country is generally peaceful. It was the speed of Partition that caused so many problems – huge swathes of the population suddenly on the move, Hindus and Sikhs going east,

Moslems west. But people are more or less settled now. Most of them have got to where they want to be, and there are only a few areas where all the old horrors – murder, arson, rape – are still going on. But they're going on in one spot that interests me in particular.'

If he was trying to soothe her, he wasn't succeeding.

'And where's that?' Somehow she knew without asking.

'Yes, you've got it.' He'd read her mind, as he so often did. 'Jasirapur. At least not the town itself but an area of Rajputana some distance away – sorry, I should say Rajasthan now.'

'I still don't see what it has to do with you,' she argued stubbornly. 'The Indian authorities must be in charge.'

'Javinder has to do with me. Do you remember him?' Grayson smiled as he put the question to her. She knew he was recalling the time they'd spent together at the cantonment hospital.

'Of course, I remember.' Javinder Joshi had been Grayson's assistant in Jasirapur. She had helped nurse him back to health after he'd been badly hurt in one of the riots that had been frequent before the war.

'He's gone missing and, since he's one of our intelligence officers, London is interested in finding him. Which is where I come in. I was the SIS man in Jasirapur before Independence and a close colleague of Javinder's. They reckon I have the best chance of discovering what's happened to him.'

'I don't see that at all.'

Why was she so anxious to stop Grayson going,

she wondered, when she'd allowed herself to drift from him with hardly a backward glance? And what could he do if he went to India? The country was vast, Rajasthan was vast. If the people on the ground hadn't been able to find Javinder, why should Grayson be successful?

'Surely, someone in the local office must have searched for him?'

'In a desultory kind of way, I imagine. But they don't have the manpower and the situation is confused. Thanks to Partition, we've had the greatest migration in human history and that includes the civil administration. Add in the fact that the Europeans have all but disappeared, and India has been left running the show on a skeleton staff.'

'It still doesn't make sense. Why send you? It's years since you've been there. There must be someone else they could send, someone who's worked in India more recently.'

'Apparently not. The security service only ever had a small presence in Jasirapur and nearly all the ICS officers who worked alongside me have either retired or returned to England.'

'Javinder can't just disappear. He's probably taken leave of absence. Maybe someone in his family is ill and he's had to take off quickly, without notifying anyone.' She sounded desperate, she knew. And there was a part of her that was.

'Unfortunately, he *has* just disappeared. Javinder is responsibility itself. He would never simply take off. I've spoken to the current admin team and they're pretty sure he was investigating an unusual spate of violence that broke out a few months back. They think he had a lead as to who was behind it, but naturally as his work is secret, he told them virtually nothing. They were guessing, though they can't be sure, that he was travelling north.'

Daisy was silent for several minutes and, when she spoke, her voice was devoid of emotion. 'It's going to be dangerous, isn't it?'

'It could be. Javinder may have been a little too successful in discovering the culprits. That's why I wanted to say a proper goodbye.'

The threat hung in the air and her stomach cramped with tension. He had been in danger before and she knew how that felt. She didn't want to feel that way again but here she was, before he'd even left the country, feeling sick at the thought that he might once more be walking towards serious trouble. She swallowed hard.

'And you're going alone?'

'No.' His face had grown sombre but now it broke into a warm smile. 'That's the good thing. I'm taking Mike.'

'Mike Corrigan?'

'The very same.'

'But surely he's never had anything to do with India? I remember you telling me that he'd always worked in Eastern Europe.'

'True enough, but wherever he's worked, he's a good operative and a good friend. And the trip will be a kind of swan song for him.'

She tried mentally to calculate Corrigan's age. 'He's retiring? I wouldn't have thought him old enough.'

'Not retiring. He's being moved. New brooms are sweeping through the security service and his injury has made it difficult for him to work in the field. He's been seconded to another part of the organisation. To a section that's strictly admin – so no more adventures.'

'I know his leg was bad, but he seemed to manage.' Mike's limp hadn't appeared to impede him when Daisy and he had met during the Sweetman crisis. But that might no longer be the case. Sweetman had forced him into crashing his car and Mike had ended up with broken bones and a split head.

'He's managed okay, more or less,' Grayson agreed. 'But by the time you met him, he hadn't worked abroad for some years. And since the incident with that fanatic, his health has become more of a problem. His leg has always given him stick but now he's experiencing giddiness, fearsome headaches, that kind of thing. Smashing into a lamp post head on isn't to be recommended.'

'So why are you taking him? I know he's been a very good colleague, but if it's going to be dangerous, surely you need someone who's completely fit?'

'Mike will stay in Jasirapur. He'll be my man in the office while I travel further afield. I need someone back at base that I can trust absolutely. And it will be easier to hunt for Javinder on my own. That way, with luck, I won't draw too much attention to what I'm doing.'

It seemed a little too pat. It was unlikely Grayson would take a man who had no experience of India whatsoever, on a journey that could be extremely dangerous.

'Is that the real reason he's going with you, or is

there something else?' She knew how close the two friends were.

His blue eyes lit with amusement. 'You've got me well and truly taped, haven't you? I suppose I want to do Mike some kind of favour. He's been dealt a rotten hand and I feel sad for him. He makes the best of it, but there's no disguising that being forced out of ops and into pen-pushing has come as a real blow. He jumped at the chance of a last grab at the old life.'

'I imagine that having a close friend with you might be helpful.' She couldn't quite keep the doubt from her voice.

'Enormously helpful. With Mike in charge, I won't have to worry what's happening in Jasirapur while I'm up country. And he'll make sure I get everything I need, when I need it.'

He'd already planned his strategy. He was determined to go and nothing would dissuade him. But why that was making her so dejected, she couldn't understand. It was natural to worry for a friend about to embark on a perilous journey, but in her heart she knew there was more to it than that.

CHAPTER 2

She stood up and began mechanically to clear the teacups. She'd been too shocked before to think clearly, but now her mind brooded over the way in which India had once again assumed centre stage in her life. After months of silence, Grayson had appeared out of the blue and with startling news. And this just days after the package from Jocelyn had arrived, stirring recollections she would rather be without. It all seemed too coincidental and she didn't believe in coincidence. Was fate dealing her another of its ugly hands?

She felt him watching her closely again. 'Is there something else? Something bothering you?'

She tried to formulate the words that would make sense to him, but found it impossible. Instead, she swooshed the cups beneath the tap with unnecessary vigour. He came to stand behind her and she felt his warmth immediately. She wished she wasn't so susceptible. This was the time, if any, to have a hard head and a hard heart. He was launching himself into some insane exploit and there was at least a likelihood that she would never see him again.

'What's bothering you?' he repeated.

'Apart from your intention to go adventuring in a country swirling in blood?'

'A wild exaggeration. It's been bad, very bad, but these last few months, things have been relatively quiet. Gandhi's death seems finally to have brought Hindus and Moslems together. A paradox if ever there was one. A man who used prayers rather than guns to stir the masses, but then meets a violent death himself. Still, his murder seems to have clinched the peace, though it's the last thing his assassin would have wanted.'

'Gandhi's peace doesn't seem to be operating where you're going,' she said tersely, concentrating hard on hanging the tea towel square on the roller.

He linked his arms loosely around her waist. His breath was on her cheek and his voice in her ear. 'It's not just my journey that's worrying you, is it? So what is it? Be brave and tell me.'

She eased herself from his hold and began to stack the china into a cupboard. She was oppressed by a sense of impending trouble and the stirring of emotions she thought she'd lost, the memories she couldn't lose. But he deserved some kind of explanation, and she must find one.

'A few days ago a package arrived. It came from India and was completely unexpected. For some reason I found it upsetting and I haven't been able to forget about it. And now you've arrived and I wasn't expecting that either. Then, without warning, you tell me you're going back there...' She shook her head, the tears pricking dangerously. She was glad she had her back to him.

He took her by the shoulders and swivelled her around. 'Who sent this package?'

'It was from Jocelyn, Jocelyn Forester. Though that's not her name now, of course.'

'She's living in Assam, isn't she? I think you told me she married a tea planter.'

Daisy's eyes were stinging with unshed tears but she took a deep breath and said levelly, 'She did and Assam is miles away from Jasirapur. But she went back there recently. Her parents are leaving after twenty years – imagine – and they're returning to England. She travelled down to help her mother pack up the bungalow and clear all the unwanted stuff they've accumulated. It's amazing what you hoard over twenty years.' She felt on firmer ground now.

Grayson frowned. 'Is Colonel Forester leaving the army then?'

'Yes. Leaving or maybe retiring early. The Indian Army has been disbanded, I believe.'

'Well, there's a new Indian army. But you're right, the old regiments have been divided up.'

'Jocelyn said in her letter that as the 7th Cavalry was a mixed regiment, the Hindu soldiers had to join the new Indian army and–'

'–and their Moslem brothers-in-arms had to leave for Pakistan,' he finished for her.

'She said her father was very cut up about it and it made him decide to leave the military altogether.'

'I heard it was the same for most of the British officers and you can't blame them. Showing a preference for one faith or the other goes against the IA's founding principles. It's a miserable business though. You can divide equipment easily enough, but not people.'

He drifted away towards the window and seemed to be watching the small boy on the pavement opposite trying to launch his new kite on a near windless day. But she knew he wasn't seeing the child; in thought he was back in India and very soon he would be there in body too.

'Sorry, daydreaming,' he said apologetically. 'You still haven't told me what was in this mysterious package.'

She joined him by the window and, side by side, they stood looking out on the now empty street. She was back in control of her feelings and able to tell him calmly what she knew.

'When Jocelyn finished working on the bungalow, the colonel asked her to sort out the regimental stuff. Not the obvious things that were to be shared between the two countries – equipment, furniture, pictures, the mess china – those kinds of things. But the odds and ends that no one knew what to do with. It's not only bungalows that collect unwanted stuff.'

At the thought of those odds and ends, that unwanted stuff, the tight control she'd forced on herself began to waver and it was a little while before she could go on. 'Anish's belongings were there.' Even now it hurt to mention him.

'I see.'

She knew that he did. More than anyone, Grayson was aware of how Anish's death had haunted her over the years.

She struggled to find a lighter note. 'The adjutant was tired of trying to find someone who would take them, so he was delighted when Jocelyn put in an appearance. Apparently he'd spent a lot of time attempting to trace relatives, only to discover when he found them – I believe the mother's family live not too distant from Jasirapur – that they wanted nothing to do with it. Anish may have been a hero to his regiment, but he was someone his family wished to forget.'

'That's hardly surprising, is it? You told me yourself there was a deep rift between Rana and his uncle.'

'There was, but it's still painful to think of.' The silence stretched between them before she began again. 'After that, the adjutant looked for someone in the father's family. But that failed too. The Ranas are somewhere in Rajasthan, but he couldn't locate them. Captain Laughton sent several messengers around the region, but no one came forward. I don't believe Anish had any contact with his family, not after his father died.'

'So Jocelyn sent you his things?'

'Not things in the plural. Just one thing. The rest were auctioned for regimental funds. She sent me something she thought I might like. She said she knew how close I was to him.'

Her voice had dropped to little more than a whisper. 'It was a purse, a small pink purse made from the softest leather and fastened with a crimson drawstring. When I unpacked it, it smelt of India. The purse was very pretty,' she went on quickly, 'though not terribly practical. But I don't believe it was ever supposed to be. It must have belonged to Anish's mother, perhaps the only thing of hers that he kept.'

Grayson looked at her for a moment and then said gently, 'I can see that Jocelyn's letter has dredged up bad memories for you.'

She was grateful for his understanding. 'I've pushed them away, you know. The memories. All these years since I left India. Tried not to think what happened there, tried to keep those months separate from the rest of my life. But opening that package brought it rushing back.'

'It is just a purse,' he reminded her.

She shook her head. 'It's more than a purse, more than a keepsake. It's a jab in the ribs, a reminder that I always intended to go back. *To exorcise the ghosts,* wasn't that what you said?'

They fell silent, remembering the pledge they'd made to each other when their love had been new and intoxicating. 'But you chose Brighton instead,' he joked, trying to dispel the tension.

She turned away from the window and switched on the battered standard lamp that hunched in one corner. The small windowpanes let in little light and the day was already waning. Then she looked across at Grayson and spoke the thought that had been gathering in her for weeks. His arrival had only sharpened its edge. She knew she had to get out of this poky cottage, away from her noisy, nosy neighbour, away from Miss Thornberry and her constant carping.

'I'm thinking of going back to London.'

'Back to London?' He sounded bemused but angry too. 'You're going back to town the very moment I'm leaving?'

The light was dim but it didn't stop her seeing the bitterness in his face.

'But how convenient for you. I won't be in London, so you won't need to find an excuse for not meeting me. Did you plan this stroke of genius while we've been talking? I've got to hand it to you, Daisy, you can be utterly ruthless when you need to be.'

The injustice stung her. She stood back from him, her small figure stiff with outrage. 'That's unfair, dreadfully unfair. If you must know, the idea has been in my mind for weeks. I wasn't sure whether I should cut my losses and leave, but when I saw you today, I knew I had to.'

'Why?' His tone was pugnacious.

'I don't know. I came to Brighton for the wrong reasons, I guess. I knew my mother had nursed here and I had some stupid idea that if I followed in her footsteps, worked in a local hospital, lived close to where she'd lived, I would feel her presence. That somehow I'd discover more about her. More about me. But it was a crazy idea and it's been a wretched failure. I haven't felt her near me for one minute and I've found nothing to remind me of her, nothing to say she was ever even in the town. Except the entry we saw years ago in the Pavilion archives.'

He looked at her measuringly. 'So Brighton wasn't about promotion after all?'

'Only very slightly,' she confessed. 'And that hasn't worked either.'

The bitterness had vanished from his face and, in its place, there was the beginning of warmth. He reached out and took her hand and she felt it lying cold in his palm. 'You won't want to hear this, but it seems to me that your drive to uncover a past you can't know has brought you nothing but upset. I wish you'd get this identity thing out of your hair. It's messing up your life.'

'Not any longer. When I go back to London, that will be the end of the story.' But, even as she spoke, she knew herself unconvinced. The identity thing, as Grayson called it, was just too important. That was something he couldn't understand, would never understand, but it didn't make her need to discover the past any less compelling.

'You won't give up, whatever you say.' His contradiction was point blank and his blue eyes held a bleak expression. 'I can't see an end to it. It comes between us all the time, and it will go on doing so.'

'I don't see how.'

'Neither do I – at least not clearly. I just know

that it will. In your mind, it seems mixed up with India. The fact that an Indian purse can send you into a spin is proof of that. You talk about bad memories, but I think you've forgotten most of them. You've coped with being kidnapped, you've coped with Gerald dying – twice. You may even have coped with knowing that he betrayed you. But Anish Rana is a different matter and it's evident his death still troubles you. I've no idea how it's connected in your mind with parents you never knew, except for the fact of loss. But I do know it's a barrier between us and has been ever since Jasirapur.'

He let go of her hand and stood looking at her, his expression marked by disappointment. 'You shake your head, but I'm right. You were plotted against and you were frightened. Gerald died and you were angry. But this is different. This is something we can't seem to get over. I thought we had. I really thought we'd made a breakthrough. Right here in Brighton.'

'We had.' But she knew she sounded insufficiently certain.

'It didn't turn out that way though, did it? I accept the war made things difficult, but since then? Month by month, you've slipped away. Maybe not deliberately, but that's what's happened. Moving to Brighton might have been an attempt at reconnecting with your mother, as you say, but it was also a way of escaping.'

'It wasn't an escape,' she protested. 'It was a new start or that's what I thought.'

'Without me.'

'Without the pressure.'

'And what pressure would that be?'

'You wanted something I didn't.'

'I asked you to marry me. After years of separation, was that so unreasonable? I wanted you with me – for always. But before you answered me with a word, I had only to look at your face to know that a wedding was the last thing you desired. You made me feel as though I'd suggested something shocking. Yet marriage between two people who have loved each other as long as we have – surely that's the most natural thing in the world?'

She lowered her head, studying the worn carpet intensely. 'You have every right to be angry, but I was happy as we were. And you wouldn't let things be.'

'So you escaped down here – yes, it was an escape, whether you're willing to acknowledge it or not. And it hasn't worked out.'

'No.' She subsided onto the sofa, her complexion ghostly in the evening light.

He came to sit beside her and she smelt the sharp tang of his cologne. It was a smell she'd always loved and the urge to nestle into him was strong. But that was one stupidity she wouldn't commit. As he'd pointed out, she had made an escape of sorts and she should keep to it.

'So come back to London,' he was saying. 'Find a different job – something that challenges you in the way Beecham's doesn't. But don't cut me out of your life. If I promise no more persuasion, no more pressure, will that help? We could try it when I get back from Jasirapur.'

When she didn't respond, he got up from the

sofa and pulled her to her feet. 'I've missed you – enormously. And you're probably right about marriage. I don't really know why I was so keen. No doubt a reaction to having survived some very dangerous years.'

He kissed her gently on the cheek and picked up his coat to go. 'Until we met, I never thought I'd want to marry and I know very well that you've had your fill of weddings. So probably not my brightest idea. But if you come back into my life, I'm willing to sue for terms – whatever you decide.'

The offer was attractive. To be back in the hum and thrum of London again, the city of her birth. To be working in a busy teaching hospital, learning something new every day, growing in confidence again. And, once he was back from India, and he would come back she promised herself, Grayson would be there, close by. Nothing too heavy. Nothing too committed. Just there.

She thought about it and was still thinking when he reached the front door. He turned on the threshold, a wry smile on his face. 'If you do make the move back to town, leave your address at Baker Street. But be prepared to see me on your doorstep as soon as I get back.'

'There's no "if",' she said firmly. 'I'm handing in my resignation. Tomorrow.' She'd known for weeks it was the right thing to do but Grayson's visit had proved the spur.

'What good news to take away with me.'

She wondered if he'd think so when he knew what she intended. Her plans had just been radically revised and weren't quite as he imagined. A new job in London was certainly tempting, but something else was more tempting still. Something that could lay to rest her fears, her doubts. Her obsession, as he called it. Finally.

He was half in and half out of the door, when she said, 'I'll be giving in my notice, but I'm not going to London.'

He stopped in surprise. 'Why ever not? Surely, the pick of nursing jobs are there. Or have you decided to give work a miss altogether? I know what it is – the purse Jocelyn sent was a magic one and you have all the money you'll ever need.'

'It *was* magic,' she said slowly. 'But not in the way you mean. Magic because it's helped me discover what I really want to do.'

A deep crease cut across his brow. 'I thought we had a decision on what you wanted to do.'

'You had a decision,' she pointed out. 'I was still deciding. And now I have. Mine is to go back to India. I'm coming with you and Mike.'

CHAPTER 3

Bombay and Jasirapur, early April 1948

It was hot, scorchingly hot. After ten years, Daisy had forgotten the intensity of an Indian summer. She walked along the quayside to the waiting car, feeling herself wilt beneath the sun's glare and her limbs drain of energy. But it wasn't the heat that was bothering her most. It was memory.

Again. Memory that was sharp and painful and minted afresh. She'd guessed this moment would be difficult but she hadn't foreseen just how difficult. It was as though she were once more living through that long ago April day. She felt it all: bewilderment as she'd waited in the noisy reception, the one she could see now, just over her shoulder; her nervous smoothing of the silk dress for which she'd saved so hard but which the heat had crumpled to a rag; the sick uncertainty when the man she was to marry was nowhere to be seen. And then out into the crowd. The sheer overpowering energy of India, its people, its colours, its smells, met for the first time. Above all, the memory of Anish Rana. He had been the one who'd accompanied her to church, delivered her to a drunken bridegroom. This morning there was to be no church and no wedding. Instead a slow carriage drive, sandwiched between Mike and Grayson, through Bombay's congested streets to the Victoria railway station.

The journey to Jasirapur took as long as before and was almost as tiresome, the train bumping its way across a sprawling landscape on rails laid down when Victoria was Empress of India. But bump though the train might, travelling was not as uncomfortable as ten years earlier. This time first class meant a little more luxury. There were sleeping bunks and a courteous attendant who brought them food and drink, and bowls of water to wash with. It was badly needed, for heat was still the enemy. The sun hung huge and golden in the sky, burning through the dusty haze to broil the plain beneath, and, despite thick linen blinds, it permeated every crevice of the compartment. Handles on doors soon grew too hot to touch and the studded leather benches turned slimy beneath damp limbs.

Once again, the train stopped at every small station to allow the waiting crowds to clamber aboard, a noisy hustle accompanying every halt they made. Despite the clamour, and despite the heat and the dust, she felt sufficiently relaxed to fall asleep on her narrow bunk during the night's darkest hours. She was grateful to have the compartment to herself. It was impossible to keep from remembering but there was a solace in travelling alone for much of the journey. Occasionally, her companions would put their heads around the door, once or twice they drank tea with her, but otherwise she was left in peace.

And it *was* a kind of peace, she realised. The future might still be uncertain, but it was an uncertainty she could accept, a lifetime away from the wrenching hesitancy of her last journey to Jasirapur. This time there was no need to watch covertly a new husband's expression or examine every word she said before she spoke it. No need, in fact, to placate the man she had married but hardly recognised from their courtship in London. How callous Gerald had been. It was only now that she saw the depth of his unkindness. She'd been so desperate to fit in, desperate to please him and not do or say the wrong thing. Of course, she'd failed on every count. It was never going to be any other way. The odds were stacked against her from the very beginning.

But this time, when an hour after dawn Grayson

helped her down from the train at Marwar Junction – the station's sign was still crooked, she saw – she found she could walk to the waiting jeep with an untroubled heart. There was no man to tangle with her thoughts. Gerald was long dead and Grayson had kept the promise he'd made on that fleeting visit to Brighton. Not a word of marriage had come from him, not even a suggestion that he'd ever been her lover. The journey had brought them closer but closer as friends – three friends, in fact – bound together by their Indian adventure.

Though it was barely six o'clock in the morning, the sun was already burning a path through the platform's paving, its heat piercing the thin soles of her shoes. Creased and weary from the journey, she climbed gratefully into the stuffy jeep. In a few minutes, luggage had been loaded and directions given.

'Let's hope the house isn't too far. This heat is appalling.' Mike mopped a dripping forehead. 'I'm in desperate need of a shower.'

'Amen to that, but we shouldn't be long getting there,' Grayson replied. 'I asked them to put us within easy reach of the town.'

He had spoken truly. Within a blink, or so it seemed to a still half-asleep Daisy, they were coming to a halt outside a large, whitewashed bungalow, its trim garden stretching into the distance on either side of a long, winding drive.

'Our home for the duration,' Grayson announced. 'Number six Tamarind Drive.'

Her eyes were at last properly open. 'However did you manage to bag this?' She was used to living in cramped spaces and the house seemed extravagant.

He gave a shrug. 'It's government owned and currently empty, so why wouldn't they want to house us in style?'

A man, dressed in a long white kurta, came hurrying down the veranda steps to greet them. It was all so reminiscent, she thought. Except that this servant's smile appeared genuine. He tucked her bags under his arm and straightaway escorted her to the room that would be hers. It was refreshingly cool. Well kept, too, she noticed, with furniture that looked almost new. At first she'd thought the scene a replay of that earlier one ten long years ago, but she had only to remark the smile on the young Indian's face, the pleasant interior, the manicured garden, to know that it was not at all the same.

She plumped down on the bed and eased her feet from shoes that had tightened their grip. The house was as large as it had seemed from the road and there was plenty of space in which to lose themselves. Until now, she hadn't thought how necessary that might be. On-board ship, they had led carefully demarcated lives and seen little of each other. A few drinks, the evening meal, an occasional gathering in the bar of all three of them. But now they were under the same roof and would be thrown together far more often and far more closely. How awkward would that prove to be? So far Grayson had shown no inclination to resurrect their old relationship and that was a comfort. From tomorrow, too, his work would take him into town for most of each day and then no doubt he'd be on the road, scouring the countryside for Javinder.

'Ahmed will cook for us,' Grayson said, when they re-emerged from their rooms a short time later to a tray of cold drinks. 'Here, have some lemonade, Daisy. I'd forgotten how invasive this red dust is. I've a throat that feels like sandpaper.'

'Let's hope Ahmed proves a better cook than Mrs Hoskins,' Mike said dryly. Mrs Hoskins was Mike's turbulent landlady. He'd amused them from time to time on-board ship with anecdotes of Mrs H., as he called her, and her many tribulations.

'I'm sure he'll be excellent,' Grayson said easily. 'I think we've been given a cleaner as well and a man for the garden. So not too much for us to do.'

'Except concentrate on the search for Javinder Joshi.' Mike's tone was not hopeful.

'Exactly.'

Daisy felt Grayson looking directly at her. She knew he was wondering what she would be doing while he and Mike were involved in the search. She'd had trouble convincing him that it was a good idea she travel with them. There had been several angry spats before he'd accepted he wasn't going to dissuade her. He'd argued vehemently that it was unsafe for her to visit India at this time, to which she'd retorted that it must then be unsafe for him, doubly so since he was there to investigate a likely crime. He'd argued that it was the wrong time of the year, but she'd pointed out that it had been April when she'd landed in Bombay to marry Gerald. He'd argued that she would be bored, but she'd told him to leave that to her. She would find ways of filling her time. At that he'd looked suspicious. Then she'd had to play her ace, the wartime promise they'd made each other during that one wonderful weekend in Brighton, the promise to return to India together.

'I was wrong. I shouldn't have promised,' he'd said. 'I shouldn't have encouraged you to go back. You're going on an insane whim. Your mother had only the slightest of links with India and yet you're preparing to travel thousands of miles in the mad hope of discovering a few fragments of family history. The only thing you'll find in India is disappointment. And what then? You'll be launching yourself into the next search and the next one, and so it will go on. You'll never be at peace.'

'Even if I find nothing,' she'd reasoned, 'I need to go back. I need to lay the ghosts from my past. You said so yourself. And once I've done that, I'll be content. I promise. I'll have to accept that I'll never know who I truly am.'

'You're Daisy and that's all I need to know. It matters not a jot to me who your mother and father were.'

'But it matters to me.'

And so they'd argued, back and forth, until eventually she'd worn him down and he'd agreed to take her, as long as Mike had no objections. Mike hadn't. On the contrary, his friend appeared delighted to have her alongside. She would have to pay her own passage, Grayson had warned. She suspected that he hoped the proviso would put a stop to her dream. But she'd managed to pay for her ticket, though it had taken every penny of her savings. And she was glad she had.

She'd known for months that her life was going nowhere and Jocelyn's letter, Grayson's visit, had stirred her to action. She was ready to leave an unsatisfying job in an unsatisfying town, ready to throw her world to the winds. The practical choice was a return to London. Instead, a sixth sense had taken over and brought her this far from home. She'd found herself propelled like a compass point searching out its magnetic home, to where she knew she had to be. The strength of that compulsion was extraordinary. For years, she'd tried to stifle it, but finally it had broken free. It had been the moment that Grayson had picked up his coat ready to leave her small, drab cottage, that she'd been certain. Certain that how she lived the rest of her life depended on her returning to India, depended on her scrubbing her memory clean of the past and finding a future that was waiting to be found. And so she'd retraced the miles she'd believed she would never travel again, and now she was back, here in India, here in Jasirapur.

She glanced across at Grayson and noticed that the cool room and a glass of lemonade had given him a new energy. She wished she could say the same but her eyes were heavy with tiredness, and within minutes she had slipped away, back to her own room.

She lay down on the cool white counterpane and breathed in the newly familiar smells, tasted the warm, thick air and felt the heat suffusing her bones. With delight, she listened to the calls of the birds beyond the shutters. Later, she would go on to the veranda and see how many of the birds she'd grown to love inhabited this new garden:

cheerful little bulbuls with red and yellow rumps she hoped, hoopoe birds with their art deco plumage, and perhaps even paradise flycatchers with tails like long, white streamers, nesting in the trees that she'd noticed marked the boundaries of the property. After the monsoon, she knew, the garden would truly live again. There would be butterflies almost as big as the birds, dressed in their peppermint green and primrose yellow. Meantime there were months of the most incredible heat to live through. She would doze a while until the heat of the day had faded and then go on an inspection tour. Instead, she slept for the rest of the morning and most of the afternoon.

When finally she ventured into the sitting room, it was to find Ahmed setting the table for dinner.

'Gentlemen will be back very soon, memsahib.' He smiled at her. 'They begin work already.'

She felt a fraud. Grayson and Mike must have gone into Jasirapur to organise their office while she had done nothing but sleep. And, sure enough, minutes later, she heard the sound of the jeep's wheels crunching along the gravelled drive. She went out to meet them.

'Sleeping Beauty, I presume,' Grayson mocked. 'I looked in to say goodbye but you were well away.'

Mike followed several paces behind his friend and she noticed he smiled no greeting. Instead, he looked tired, defeated almost. She guessed the journey was beginning to take its toll.

'How were things at ICS?' she asked, as Ahmed finished serving the inescapable curried chicken.

'Everyone was very helpful,' Grayson replied, 'without actually being very helpful.'

She looked enquiringly at him. 'They're a nice bunch, the new officers,' he said, 'but they've no idea about Javinder's whereabouts and only the haziest notion of his work. So staying in the office is not going to get us too far.'

'I'm the one who'll be staying,' Mike said heavily.

Grayson looked across the table at his colleague. Mike's tone had evidently surprised him. 'Mike will be staying in the office,' he echoed, 'as logistical backup. And I'm certainly going to need some. They've given us Javinder's old room and we've made a start getting the place set up. Mike has three filing cabinets and a ton of files to sort through. Hopefully our man might have left some indication of where he was going. The first job, though, is to get the telephone company to install an extra line. One that doesn't go through the main switchboard. We need to be able to talk privately, once I'm on the road.'

Daisy felt a small sinking in her heart. 'When will that be?'

'In a day or so, I imagine. Tomorrow I'll begin making enquiries – someone may know something.'

'But where will you start?' It seemed to her that a search for a lone man somewhere in the huge expanse of Rajasthan would be more difficult than for the proverbial needle.

Grayson was undaunted. 'Where I always start. The town. The bazaar.'

She brightened. At least he should be safe for a

few days. And the idea of a visit to the bazaar and its delights was an attractive one.

'Can I drive in with you?' It would give her the chance to ask questions of her own under the guise of some innocent shopping.

'You can, but I have to warn you, I'll be leaving very early. You'll have to forgo the Sleeping Beauty routine.'

She smiled at his teasing. 'And what if my prince hasn't hacked his way through the forest by then?'

'I'm afraid you'll have no choice but to abandon him and make do with me,' he retorted.

She saw Mike frown and realised with a shock that they had come close to flirting. It would be too easy, she knew, to fall back in love with Grayson and she must guard against it. There was no such thing as a perfect man, any more than a perfect woman, but he came close. Nearly perfect men, though, had their own plan for life and she had hers, and the two were never going to fit. She must be careful. She had no wish to complicate this trip and neither did she want to upset Mike. This evening he seemed to be in a strange mood, his expression morose, his liveliness depressed. Not too many quips about Mrs H., she thought. It might be the effect of the country on him. She had loved India from the start, but she understood that it was not the same for everyone. And she knew, too, that Mike had worries back home. She would need to be extra vigilant in her dealings with Grayson. If Mike were forced to play an awkward third in their relationship, it was unlikely to make him any happier.

Grayson, too, had been surprised to find himself falling back into the easy relationship he'd once enjoyed with Daisy. He wasn't sure how he felt about that, though he had no illusions. The long months of absence had taken their toll on both of them. Once upon a time, she had given him her heart and given it completely, but that moment hadn't lasted. When he remembered those heady few months after the Sweetman debacle, months when they'd lived only for each other, he felt a pain that stung. And it was still there. He should have realised the truth then, of course. Daisy had saved his life and, in doing so, come close to death herself. Because of the Sweetman affair, they'd been living in an oddly heightened state and that very fact had encouraged them to step into a whirl of emotion they couldn't control. They had thought they couldn't live without one another. Except that the war had dragged on for another three years and they'd been forced to. Between Daisy's nursing shifts and his punishing hours at SIS, they'd met infrequently and, when they did, they were both exhausted from the pressure of work. He'd hoped that when peace came, things would be different. They would pick up the pieces and finally make a home together. He'd told his mother he intended to marry and she'd been content. She had met Daisy on several occasions and liked her. The girl's background hadn't been the stumbling block he'd feared, for his mother had proved far more open-minded than he'd expected. And she'd admired Daisy for the way she had made something of her life out of so very little. But even if that had not been the case, his mother would never have rejected the girl who had saved her son from certain death.

Mrs Harte had not been the problem. Mrs Harte's friends, clustered in their small, genteel enclave of Pimlico, had not been the problem. It had been Daisy herself. His proposal had stunned her. It was as though a stranger had asked to be her husband. After the first shock of rejection, he'd felt angry. Gerald Mortimer had died in dreadful circumstances but that had been seven years ago and, long before then, Daisy had come to know him for what he was – an adventurer, a liar, a betrayer. Memories of her dead husband could not be preventing her from saying yes, so what was? It was hard to swallow but he was forced to the simple conclusion that Daisy had no desire to marry. She was determined to stay a single, independent woman. She had no wish to share her life in any meaningful way. It was sufficient for her to see him from time to time, but she wanted no greater commitment. He'd told her plainly what he thought of that arrangement and the next thing he'd known, she'd taken a job fifty miles away and moved there without telling him. He'd lost heart then; it was better to let her slip away. His mother had been consolatory. She had begun to think that Daisy saying no was a good thing. The girl had been harmed by her harsh upbringing and would never settle to married life. After all, she had never known a family had she, so how could she create a successful one of her own?

Grayson hadn't accepted his mother's logic, but a part of him acknowledged there was some small truth in what Mrs Harte had said. He'd seen for himself that Daisy had not escaped her life unharmed. She'd fought the fight well and to all intents and purposes, she'd come through, but there remained a large void in her which she'd been unable to fill. And he'd been unable to help her. This was why she was here. This was what she was chasing by coming to India, a chase that, in his view, was doomed to failure and could mean only more heartache. He understood how the gaps in her story tormented her, but he couldn't for the life of him see how coming here could help fill them. His best hope was what he'd always believed – that coming back to India would help her deal with the very bad memories she still carried.

The next morning she was already eating her *chota hazri* when Grayson made an appearance. He looked at her and she saw him smile.

'Lovely dress, Daisy. But much too good for the bazaar.'

'On the contrary. I have to compete with some very beautiful women and some very beautiful saris.' Her polka dot sundress was young and fresh but against the richness of Indian materials, she knew it would go unnoticed.

'No competition. You'll win hands down.' She felt herself flush beneath his gaze. She *would* have to be careful.

She buried herself in the plate of small, sweet cakes that Ahmed had left to tempt her.

Grayson said no more and made no effort to join her at the table, ignoring the customary small breakfast and downing two cups of coffee while he stood by the window.

'It's going to be hotter today, if that's possible,' he opined. He was looking out at the garden, which was already shimmering in the heat. 'We'd better get going unless we want to fry in the jeep.'

There were few other vehicles on the road. Several bullock carts passed them, heading out of town, and for a while they were caught behind a small boy who was driving his flock of goats to the fields. Eventually, he peeled away from the main thoroughfare and, with loud yells and brutal whackings of his stick, herded the beasts down the narrow lane leading to their barren grazing.

Grayson picked up speed again and they were halfway to the centre of town when he said suddenly, 'Would you like to take a look at the old place?'

He meant the old bungalow, she knew, the one she'd shared with Gerald and his malevolent servant, the one that had stored stolen guns for a group of outlawed fighters and nearly cost her her life. She felt beads of perspiration on her forehead.

'You don't have to put yourself through it,' he said quietly. 'But I thought it might help.'

Would it help? She didn't think so, yet she knew she had to see the house again. For years, she'd hoped she could break free of its frightening shadow. Grayson seemed certain that she had, that she'd coped with the past far better than she realised. But she knew differently. She hadn't coped with it. Not really. Not deep down. She'd muffled it in bandages, layer upon layer of them. And though she'd wanted to come back to India, secretly she'd been sceptical that a return could act as any kind of purification. But here she was, and she owed it to herself to take whatever chance offered to lose the millstone she carried.

'Yes, let's take a look,' she said, as casually as she could.

It was a shock when she saw the place. The garden had always been unkempt, Gerald having little interest and even less money to keep it under control. But now the *alfalfa* grass had grown almost to the roof line and a weed she couldn't put a name to had started its inexorable colonisation, gripping the whitewashed walls in iron tentacles. Rajiv's quarters to the right were almost submerged beneath the wilderness. As she looked across at the rooms he'd inhabited, she could conjure no clear picture, no clear vision of him emerging from his door, sullen-faced, suspicious, hostile. That was good. That particular image was rubbed clean.

'It looks pretty dilapidated,' Grayson said.

'It never looked anything else.'

'Not quite as bad as this though. In the ten years since you left, I don't think it's had a lick of paint. And see, several of the shutters are off their hinges. They won't afford the house any kind of protection – *and* there's a hole appearing in the thatch. Come the monsoon, the rain will pour through that roof and drown the interior. I imagine rot has already set in. A few more years and the house will crumble inwards.'

'A waste of a bungalow,' she remarked, though privately thinking that crumbling was exactly what was needed. If the house lay in ruins, she would be happy. It had only ever been the garden that she'd loved and that was beyond saving.

'It is a waste. It would have made someone a good home. I made a few enquiries.' That was news to her. So this unscripted visit wasn't quite so unscripted. 'The army tried to sell it as soon as they knew the regiment was to disband – they must have acquired the property years ago – and they were willing to sell at a knockdown price. But there were no takers. No one would even move in for free. The locals won't come near the place.'

'Because of what happened here?'

'That hasn't helped, certainly. The gang has become notorious in the district.'

Anish, too, she imagined. He would be just as notorious. 'But they're all in prison.'

'That makes no difference. India is a land of superstition and superstition ensures that the gang will return to haunt the place. It doesn't help either that the house was built on an ancestral burial ground. That in itself would be reason enough for the locals to avoid it. Far too many ghosts.'

Ghosts, she thought ironically. The ghosts she was supposed foolishly to have seen when she tried to talk to Gerald of her fears. Those particular spirits had turned out to be entirely flesh and blood, and criminal flesh and blood at that. But she'd had other phantoms to face and they were still with her. She turned away and walked back to the jeep. If she'd hoped the visit might prove an exorcism, it had been unsuccessful.

CHAPTER 4

Grayson dropped her at the edge of the bazaar and then disappeared in a swirl of dust, intent on a mission that would take him deep into the network of narrow alleys and hidden courtyards. For most of that morning, he would be only a few hundred yards from her but she was sure she would see nothing more of him. He would keep a low profile and so must she. She'd had second thoughts about asking questions today. It might be better to postpone them until a second visit and in the meantime, learn or relearn her way around the sprawl of shops and traders.

She spent several delightful hours wandering between brilliantly coloured stalls and, despite her best intentions not to buy until she left for home, she came away with a bolt of the most beautiful emerald silk and a stock of coloured glass bangles. They would be small presents for any patients she had in the future, when or if she found another post. Miss Thornberry's reaction to her resignation had been typically ill natured and she wasn't expecting a glowing reference.

In the last few minutes, her skin had begun to burn, even as she stood in deep shade. It was time to turn for home and she headed for where she remembered the tonga drivers used to gather. Weaving a complicated path through the jumble of stalls, she edged her way through one narrow space after another, skirting the sweep of craft workers who plied their trade at ground level. Very soon she spied the tall plumes of a horse's bridle and saw them move with the shake of the animal's head. She felt pleased with herself that she'd managed to find the place unaided.

The sun was now directly overhead, its rays arrowing through the thick air and hitting the ground with such force that they bounced upwards and slapped her in the face. She felt sandwiched between two opposing armies, both brandishing fire, and it was a relief to climb into the first carriage she came to. She lay back in the shade of the faded cloth canopy and watched its decorative bobbles jump to the rhythm of the wheels, as the tonga swerved out into the traffic and made for Tamarind Drive. She was looking forward to home, to a cold shower and an even colder drink. And then a long rest on the cool counterpane. It was a guilty pleasure, a sheer indulgence, when at this very moment she should by rights be directing the activities of a busy ward.

But when she walked up the veranda steps, her plans received a setback. Mike was sitting at the dining table surrounded by paper, and she felt disconcerted. She had expected him to be at the office. He looked up when she walked in and she thought he seemed irritated. That was probably her imagination, for his face relaxed quickly into a smile and he folded the map he'd been studying and asked her how her first day's return to Jasirapur had gone.

'Don't clear the table for me.' She gestured to the stack of papers he'd begun to load into his ancient briefcase. 'I'm ashamed to say the bazaar has tired me out and I think I may take a sneaky nap.'

'I don't blame you. This heat is a killer. But I have to go back to the office in any case. I just needed a few hours' peace and quiet to go through some difficult correspondence.'

She went to the table and poured herself a glass of water and drank it down thirstily. Mike's words surprised her. She remembered Grayson saying that the administration team was short staffed, and it seemed odd that his friend had been unable to find a quiet haven in which to work, but perhaps the offices were in more of a mess than Grayson realised. His passion lay in fieldwork, she knew, and he was more than happy to leave the paperwork to someone else. But Mike must feel just the same and she felt sorry he had the unenviable task of trawling an endless succession of files in the meagre hope that he might uncover a clue to Javinder's whereabouts.

He tucked his briefcase beneath one arm and walked to the door. 'You look a trifle hot still,' he said. 'Ahmed is ordering me a tonga. Shall I ask him to bring you some tea?'

'You're right. I am hot, and tired too. I'd forgotten how tired you get – I've no energy left. But I'll settle for water, thanks. I don't want to delay you. *I* may be utterly lazy but I know the wheels of industry must keep turning.'

'Not much industry going on, I'm afraid. We're on a bit of a wild goose chase.'

'Grayson doesn't appear to think so,' she said carefully. 'He's expecting to leave in a few days.

This morning, when we drove into town, he was talking about the equipment he needs to order.' It had been news to her that he needed to prepare so extensively for his travels. 'I wasn't sure what exactly he had in mind.'

'I imagine he'll be camping, so a tent, cooking utensils, that kind of thing.'

'Then he must be anticipating a long journey.'

'Who knows?' Mike shrugged his shoulders. 'It's a crazy idea, a crazy trip and fraught with danger, but you know Grayson.' His smile was a little off centre. 'He's no idea where Joshi could be, except a vague notion that the man travelled north, but he's setting off come what may. He's too stubborn for his own good. For all he knows, the chap could be dead by now.'

'So there's been no more news?'

'Nothing. We haven't a clue, but I sure as hell wouldn't start traipsing through Rajasthan in this excruciating heat. Not to mention the restive natives. And all on the off chance that I might come across a missing man. He's probably gone walkabout to see his family. I've been told they come from an adjoining state, so it's more than likely.'

'I suggested that to Grayson, but he said Javinder was far too conscientious to do such a thing.'

'He would, wouldn't he? He trained him. But whatever the truth of the matter, I haven't been able to persuade him out of this fool's errand.'

She took another long drink of water, then looked up to find that Mike had left his case by the door and walked back into the room. He was standing very near, his face serious, and when he spoke he leaned towards her to emphasise his words. '*I* haven't persuaded him, Daisy, but you could. And I hope you'll try.'

She felt herself grow hot with embarrassment. 'I doubt I'd be any more successful. I don't have that much influence.' Maybe once, she thought, but not any more.

'You underestimate yourself. You mean a lot to him and he'll listen to you. There's still time to get him to think again.'

She felt trapped. She didn't want Grayson to walk into unknown dangers, any more than Mike did, but neither did she want to do or say anything that might unsettle their new relationship. At the moment, it seemed to be working. It was affectionate but mercifully uncommitted. If she pleaded with Grayson too hard, she might raise expectations she couldn't fulfil.

Mike walked back to the door and picked up his briefcase. 'Talk to him tonight,' he urged. 'He can still be made to abandon this wild project.'

'Tonga here, Mister Corrigan.' Ahmed had come quietly into the room and she was spared from answering. Mike gave her a brief nod and strode towards the veranda.

'See you at supper,' he said over his shoulder.

The sound of hooves on the gravel signalled that Mike was on his way to town. The house was within easy reach of Jasirapur, just a short tonga ride away. Unlike the lonely bungalow she'd visited this morning. That had been a thieves' den, but had also been her prison, and she could never think of the place or what happened there without her heart beginning to trip and her stomach to knot.

So she wouldn't think of it.

Ahmed had returned, this time bearing another large jug. 'For you, memsahib. Water is very cold. I think you are still feeling bad.'

'I'm afraid so.'

She smiled her thanks and allowed another glass of the liquid to slide icily down her throat, then sat for some while simply enjoying the feeling. It was strange how uncomfortable she'd felt when Mike was in the room and it made her pause. He'd seemed so insistent that she intervene with Grayson. Perhaps that was it. But when she thought more, she realised she hadn't felt entirely easy with him during the whole journey. Even on the ship, his heartiness had seemed a little forced. She hardly knew him, of course, whereas Grayson and he had been colleagues, good friends too, for many years. But in the short time she'd spent with him during the war, he'd seemed almost a different man.

He'd driven her to the safe house in Highgate, except that it had turned out to be anything but safe. At least not for her. He'd been easy-going, she recalled, pleasant, chatty. He was still friendly enough but she had the sense of it being purely a surface emotion. He'd lost the genuine warmth she remembered, that was it. She wondered if he resented her being here. Grayson might have voiced his doubts but Mike had seemed happy to include her in the trip. He'd welcomed her effusively, perhaps too effusively. After all, she'd invited herself, imposed herself on what had been an all-male adventure. He'd probably been looking forward to working closely with his friend – a last grab at the old life, Grayson had called it. In London, he might have been easy with her decision to join them but now her presence in India had begun to feel intrusive. Even worse, he might have started to suspect that Grayson and she were trying to rekindle their romance and he'd be dragged unwillingly into the situation. He really needn't worry on that score; it was the last thing she intended.

What she did intend was very different and, when the sun began its slow fade to the horizon, she roused herself to wash her face, brush her hair and don a fresh dress. Her wardrobe was severely limited, as much by money as by space, but a plain linen button-through seemed ideal for the lady she was about to visit. If Edith Forester still espoused the exotic flowing robes she used to love, it would be the perfect foil. The Foresters would be starting on their journey back to England any day now, but she had discovered from Ahmed, who seemed to know the ins and outs of every military deployment, that at the moment at least, they were still at the civil station.

The cantonment was subtly changed from the first time she'd seen it. Most of the army had moved out only months before but already she could see the signs of neglect. The clipped lawns were no longer quite so neat, the whitewashed walls of the bungalows not quite so white, and the road which ran a straight course through the spread of houses arranged in military precision had fractured into potholes every few yards.

The tonga had barely pulled to a halt outside the Foresters' official bungalow, when Edith came running out onto the veranda. As soon as she realised who her visitor was, she ran down the wooden steps and greeted Daisy ecstatically. As though she were a long lost sheep, Daisy thought. A black sheep, perhaps.

'It's so lovely to see you, my dear. After all this time, too. Of course, Jocelyn has kept us up to date with all your doings but it's not the same, is it? To actually meet again, face to face, is quite wonderful.'

Over the intervening years both she and Jocelyn had proved poor correspondents and Daisy thought it unlikely that Edith knew much about her life, but she smiled sweetly and returned the compliment. 'Thank you, Mrs Forester. It's very good to see you too.'

'Edith, my dear. Surely we know each other well enough not to stand on ceremony. And you're back in Jasirapur?' It was a question that answered itself. Daisy could see the older woman was agog with interest. And why wouldn't she be? After what had happened here, Jasirapur would be the last place anyone would expect her to return to.

'A friend of mine, Grayson Harte – you'll remember him, I'm sure – kept in touch when we got back to England. He mentioned he had to make a short trip here. Something to do with his work, I'm not sure what.' She had better give nothing away, she thought, though Edith was unlikely to pose a danger to the security service. 'At the time I'd just resigned from my job and thought that for old times' sake I'd like to come back. Just once more.'

The 'old times' stuck in her throat but she tried to sound indifferent. Mrs Forester was unlikely to believe such a feeble explanation, but she had no intention of disclosing why she was really here.

'The Colonel will be so sorry to have missed you. He's just this minute gone back to barracks. Goodness knows what the problem is now. There's always something. But come in, my dear, and Salim will fix you a drink.'

She led the way into a large but bare sitting room, her dress streaming behind her. It was the same floating, exotic garment that Daisy remembered, but this time a little faded, a little limp.

'You see what a state we're in. Most of the house has been packed up, but there's still so much unfinished business left for the regiment that I'm beginning to doubt the Colonel will ever be through. The boat will most likely go without us.'

She smiled as she made the little jest but Daisy could see the sadness behind the smile. India had been Edith Forester's world and her husband's. Daisy had never herself known a settled life, but she was sensitive enough to imagine how frightening this new experience must be for them.

'He'll be sorry to have missed you,' Edith repeated, 'but we must have that drink. We must drink to your return.' She clapped her hands and a white-coated servant obediently appeared at her elbow. 'A gin and lime, my dear?'

She remembered Edith's fondness for gimlets. She had never grown to like the drink, but at least she'd learned to swallow it without grimacing, and she accepted the glass that Salim held out to her.

She'd made this call for a very particular reason and she would need to be patient and allow Edith time to tell her sorrowful tale. And she did, at length. Of how dreadful it had been seeing the Indian Army divided in such a cavalier fashion, how bitterly sad its dismemberment was after two hundred proud years of service.

'Two hundred years to build, my dear Daisy, and three months to destroy. And these are men who fought side by side in two world wars.' The older woman's voice shook very slightly. 'Every caste, every creed and colour – all united in a common cause. Countless numbers of them have died for Britain, yet with just one stroke of a pen, they've been divided forever.'

'I heard,' was all Daisy could say.

'Everyone's heard,' Edith said a trifle scornfully, 'but they don't know *how* it's been. Soldiers, tough men – Moslems, Hindus, Sikhs – wept on each other's shoulders when it happened. Can you imagine? And look how it has left *us*.' Edith waved her hand at the nearly bare room. Daisy saw the marks on the walls where their treasured pictures had hung.

'Jocelyn came home to help you pack, I believe.' She needed to interrupt this flow of gentle complaint and get to what she wanted to know.

'Yes, she's a wonderful daughter. She travelled across, all the way from Assam. It's not an easy journey, but she was such a help. So quick, too. I've become a little slow these days.'

For the first time Daisy looked at her hostess closely. Edith was showing signs of age that she hadn't noticed before. Her skin had always appeared toughened from years in the sun, but it was more papery now, and the luxuriant hair she'd always worn in a disorderly bun was sparser and showed more grey than brown.

'Jocelyn sent me a keepsake from among the things she sorted,' Daisy began.

'Did she? She was always a kind, thoughtful girl. It was something nice, I hope.'

'A purse, a very pretty little purse. It was among Anish Rana's possessions, I think she said. It must have belonged to his mother.'

'Ah.' There was a pause while Edith decided how best to approach the difficult subject. Daisy helped her out. 'The regiment was still holding Lieutenant Rana's belongings?'

'Yes, indeed. Dreadful business. The Colonel didn't know what to do with the stuff after the poor man died. There wasn't a great deal of it, of course. He was a single officer living in barracks. But it was still right to return his personal possessions to his family.'

'It doesn't seem the regiment was able to.'

'The adjutant tried. He tried very hard. He managed to trace the family, I believe, well, part of the family. I think it was the relatives on the mother's side. But the man he spoke to simply didn't want to know. He was quite rude, Dennis said.'

'So the family was local?' Daisy asked carefully, holding her breath a fraction.

'I imagine so. Dennis did tell me where he found the man – I think he was Lieutenant Rana's uncle – but I can't remember the name of the place. I doubt you'd know it anyway.'

'But quite near Jasirapur?' Daisy persisted.

Her hostess was looking at her oddly. She supposed her questions had become a little too particular. 'Yes. It wasn't far. In fact, the adjutant even thought of driving there and pushing the stuff through the gate. But, in the end, he decided it wouldn't look very dignified.'

Her companion said nothing for several minutes and seemed lost in thought. Daisy felt disappointment seeping through her. The Foresters had been her most certain hope, but it appeared she would discover little here. She felt flustered and unsure of what to do next and the heat of the room began to overpower her. A small electric fan was churning in one corner but it succeeded only in stirring the heavy air anew. She glanced up at the ceiling. The punkah was still there, she saw, but now there was no man to work it. She hoped that Independence had given the punkah wallah a less wearisome job.

'Amrita – that was the name of the house,' Edith announced out of the blue. 'I remember thinking what a pretty name it was, far too pretty for the rude man who lived there.'

'Amrita,' Daisy repeated. 'You're right – it is pretty.' But would she ever be able to trace the house? There were bound to be a hundred Amritas in the district.

'Something's coming back to me. Let me see. Yes, the Colonel had once to visit nearby – I can't recall why. My memory worsens every year, but I do remember going with him. The village was quite attractive, as Indian villages go. Yes, that's right. It was a place called ... Megaur ... or perhaps it was a village near Megaur. I know you turned left at the station, Marwar Junction that is, and not straight ahead as though you were going to Jasirapur. Then you simply followed the road. It can't be more than twenty miles from here. Less, probably, if we drove there quite easily.'

Amrita, Megaur. It was enough. Daisy wriggled in her chair, barely able to contain her excitement. 'It's good to know where my purse might have come from,' she murmured. The remark was inane, she knew, but she had to say something. Hopefully, it might distract Edith's attention from the strange behaviour of her guest.

'I suppose it is good to know,' the lady said vaguely. 'But do have another gimlet.'

'I won't, thank you ... Edith. I should be getting back, or I'll hold up dinner. And the tonga driver has been waiting for me all this time.'

'That's his job, my dear,' Mrs Forester said dismissively.

She wondered anew how the Foresters would cope in the very different world of post-war England. Edith and her husband had devoted their lives to the Raj and no doubt loved India passionately. But, whatever their benevolence, they were blind to the truth that Britain had no lasting place here. She was remembering the words of a patient she'd had at Bart's, a retired colonial officer. He'd taken a keen interest in her travels and he'd talked a good deal about India. At one point he'd said rather wearily that no foreign power would ever succeed in mastering the country. *You can order them about a little,* he'd said, *introduce new ideas, even dragoon them into accepting the unfamiliar, but then you must go away and die in Cheltenham.*

She wasn't sure where in England the Foresters were bound, but the old man's words had an unsettling truth to them.

'Thank you again,' she said, and rose to leave. 'Please give my best wishes to the Colonel and to Jocelyn.'

Her hostess rose with her and escorted her to the front door. She stood watching as Daisy walked down the veranda steps to the waiting tonga, her face gaunt and slightly bewildered. 'Do come back when you can,' she called out. 'I'm sorry you have to go so soon.'

Daisy looked back and saw the older woman desolate against the naked interior of the house. Her parting words seemed a fitting elegy.

CHAPTER 5

That evening, she made a decision. She was going to Megaur, she was going to find Amrita. But she knew she would face stiff opposition from both Mike and Grayson. She must keep her plans to herself and, if possible, keep silent too, on her visit to Mrs Forester. She was lucky. Both men assumed that after she'd returned from the bazaar, she'd spent the rest of the day at Tamarind Drive. The talk over dinner turned instead to the papers Mike had unearthed that day, with Daisy a silent listener. She was surprised to hear for the first time an edge creeping into their conversation.

'I can't for the life of me see why Mountbatten

had to be in such a hurry,' Mike grumbled. 'He pushed Partition forwards ten whole months and completely destroyed the government's own schedule. Why rush such a delicate operation? The more I read, the more I realise how close India came to annihilation. His decision was totally reckless. But then what do you expect from an aristocrat who fought a bit in Burma but knows nothing else of the world.'

'He won a grand victory in Burma and I don't think you can blame all the violence on Mountbatten's decision,' Grayson said mildly.

'Don't you? Well, try reading some of the reports filed by the civil admin teams from around the country.' He saw Grayson looking quizzical. 'Copies of their records were sent to every regional administration. And yes, I know, it's unlikely to lead to any useful information on Javinder, but I have to go through everything.'

'I'm glad you're being so thorough,' Grayson said, but Daisy thought that he didn't look that glad.

'Well, I am, and it's often frightening stuff. Endless disputes over the anomalies caused by carving up the country. If people were lucky, disagreements were settled peacefully but if not...' He wagged his head dismissively.

'There were bound to be anomalies, Mike, whenever Partition was done and however long it took.'

Grayson was trying for calm, but his friend hardly heard him. 'Ludicrous situations, too, which make the so-called Raj a laughing stock. Canal works on one side of the border while the embankments protecting it are on the other. Loads of instances like that. The border even runs down the middle of some villages, would you believe, with a dozen huts left in India and a dozen more in Pakistan. One poor devil had his house bisected – his front door opened to India but his rear window looked into Pakistan. It's laughable but it's also terrifying. No wonder there's been such trouble.'

'I know. I've read some of the accounts. But you could argue that rushing through independence was the best way to prevent even more violence.'

'There surely couldn't have been more. And what about the huge refugee problem it's created. That has to be down to Mountbatten.'

'Like I said, whenever it was done, Partition was always going to mean chaos.' There was a forced patience to Grayson's voice now. 'India has known centuries of integration. It's a mass of different cultures and traditions and beliefs. The entire country is a cultural compromise. However you divide it, there will always be people who don't fit a particular "box".'

'Let's hope they like the boxes they've ended up in then.' Mike laid down his knife and fork and pushed away his half-eaten meal. 'The only positive I can see is that no matter how bad the current situation, it's got to be better than the Raj.'

'Maybe.'

Daisy was surprised to hear Grayson sound uncertain. He had always been a firm believer in Indian independence. Perhaps the dreadful violence had made him reconsider, or perhaps he was simply antagonised by Mike's truculence.

'No maybe, my friend. The Raj made Britain wealthy and self-confident but at the expense of millions of Indians.'

'I'd agree that some people made a lot of money out of the country,' Grayson conceded, 'but not the vast majority of those who worked here. The ordinary little people who actually ran India.'

'That was their job.'

'True, but they also did it because they loved the country and its people. They built roads, hospitals, looked after forests, joined the Indian Army. People like Colonel Forester and his wife.'

He looked towards Daisy as he said this, but thankfully Mike had the bit between his teeth and she was spared having to respond. She would surely have given herself away.

'You're talking like an imperialist, Gray.' Mike's lips thinned. 'I'm surprised and, as an Irishman, I have to say it grates.'

'I'm just trying to give the other side of the picture.' Grayson stretched his long legs beneath the table. 'You could argue that it was Britain who first introduced the idea of liberty, albeit indirectly.'

Mike threw back his head and laughed, but it was a peculiarly joyless laugh. 'You're saying that Britain encouraged independence? Someone should have told the poor devils banged up for years for being nationalists. And perhaps I hadn't heard but did Britain maybe help to set up Congress?'

'Of course not. But sometimes ideas percolate without there appearing to be any definite agency. The need for progress, for instance. And, in a sense, being against Britain united India. It created the concept of patriotism, of a nation. Indians started to talk of Mother India. That was new, and look where it's led.'

Mike shook his head. 'I never thought I'd hear you justify a colonial regime.'

'I'm not justifying it. Merely playing devil's advocate.'

'Be careful you don't turn into the devil while you're doing it,' Mike said sourly.

'Don't worry, I'll take care.' Grayson got up from the table and pulled back Daisy's chair for her. 'You're very quiet this evening, Miss Driscoll. Have we overwhelmed you by the brilliance of our arguments?'

'I really don't know enough to say anything sensible,' she excused herself. 'Overall, though, I think I'd be with Mike on this.'

Mike smiled at her with genuine warmth and she realised how much that had been missing during their trip.

'I've clearly lost out,' Grayson said, 'and before you two gang up on me any more, I'm off to bed. There's a lot to do tomorrow and I can't imagine it will be any cooler to do it in.'

It was the signal for a general breaking up of the party and Daisy was able to slip away to her room with a murmured goodnight. The slightly bad-tempered conversation had ensured that she'd escaped interrogation, not just about how she'd spent today, but how she intended to spend tomorrow. There had been a price to pay for it though. An unaccustomed divide had opened up between the two friends and she hadn't enjoyed seeing them disagree so starkly.

Once Mike and Grayson had left the house the following morning – together, she noted, and that felt a good deal better – she set off for Megaur. It took an hour's driving along a road which wound northwards and across a landscape crackling with heat. In this first searing blast of India's hot season, there was no sign that when the rains came, bushes and trees, fields and ditches would burst into new, green life. For now she looked out on a land shrivelled into crisp parchment. Beneath the sun's white glare, the bright trees on either side sent sparks flying heavenwards. Clouds of dust mushroomed over the tonga as they drove, covering horse and driver and passenger with a fine red sheen. Yesterday she'd been foolish enough to venture out bareheaded and Grayson had taken her to task. Today she'd been careful to unhook the last remaining *topi* from the corner stand, but it proved only a flimsy defence. Even beneath the tonga's fringed canopy, she had continually to adjust the helmet to cover as much of her neck as possible, and it wasn't long before she was feeling hot and gritty.

In just under the hour, they were driving through Megaur.

It was a sizeable village, with several narrow streets of whitewashed houses, a variety of shops and stalls and a large and ornate temple set back from the road. It was cleaner and tidier than most of the smaller villages they'd passed through and she wondered if Anish's uncle was the main landlord of the district. If so, Megaur did him proud. Mrs Forester had called him a rude man, but

Daisy hoped she'd been mistaken. Edith's relationship with Indians was mediated through long experience of living under the Raj and she was likely to interpret any show of pride as discourtesy.

The tonga drew to a halt outside a pair of elaborately decorated iron gates and the driver said something to her in Hindi. This must be Amrita. She went to alight and then realised with a sinking feeling that the colonel's wife had not mentioned the name of the man who lived here, and she had no idea how to address him. Not that it mattered, it seemed. She had barely rung the bell, when a white-coated servant emerged from the house and waved at her. It took her a while before she realised that he was waving her away.

She peered through the gate and tried to explain her arrival. But the man wasn't interested in listening. Either he spoke no English or he'd been sent to frighten her away. The latter it appeared, for he picked up a large wooden stave from the side of the drive and walked purposefully towards her. At the sign of this aggression, the tonga driver took fright and began to back his horse up the lane they had just travelled.

Daisy didn't blame him but neither did she intend to be intimidated. 'Tell your master that my name is Driscoll and I have travelled some miles to see him. Be sure to say that I won't intrude for long but I would be grateful to speak with him for a short while.'

A loudspeaker attached to one of the gateposts crackled into life. She hadn't noticed it before but evidently it relayed speech back into the house. The voice that emerged from its depths was smooth and urbane.

'Good morning, Miss Driscoll. Please, do come in.'

And the gates swung open.

Grayson had spent another frustrating morning. For nearly two days he'd questioned members of the administration team, telephoned old contacts and walked the town's streets, but only the haziest of whispers had been of any interest. It was a most unusual situation and it took him some time to realise that it was a reluctance to speak, rather than ignorance, that was keeping people silent. When yesterday he'd made an abortive visit to the bazaar, he'd thought the stallholders in those narrow, ancient streets might be holding out for more money than he'd so far offered. He knew them to be a canny bunch. But when today he'd cast his net wider, visiting every business, every professional office in the town, and received the same response, he became certain his potential informants were scared. Everywhere he met with the same reception – a warm greeting, a chair pulled out, *chai* brought, but when the conversation turned to the troubles in the north of Rajasthan, there was a deafening silence followed by an apologetic smile and more *chai.* It must be precisely what Javinder had faced, and yet the young man had discovered enough to send him hotfoot to – to where? The region was huge and Grayson could be travelling for days and still find himself nowhere near his young colleague. He needed to have some sense of where he should be heading, particularly as it seemed his journey was likely to be every bit as dangerous as he'd feared.

After hours of useless talking, he walked into the office he shared with Mike to find his companion looking equally disheartened. The room was sticky with heat, a ceiling fan stirring the sluggish air to little effect. Mike looked up as he came through the door, a slow trickle of perspiration running down the centre of his forehead and stopping short at the bridge of his nose.

'Did you have any luck?' he asked.

Their last evening's clash seemed to have been forgotten and Grayson could see his colleague was trying hard to look cheerful. That made him feel a little better. He hadn't enjoyed being at odds with Mike, who was a good friend, an old friend. And he needed the man's help if his quest was to have any chance of success.

'Not a scrap. How about you?'

'Much the same. I've been trying since early this morning to get these files into some kind of order.' He waved a damp hand towards the tottering piles of paper which all but covered the surface of both desks. 'I'm sure Javinder Joshi was an excellent worker. I can see he kept his paperwork more or less up to date, but he's been gone several months, and since then the filing has turned into a paper Everest. I reckon every person in the building has slung something in here over that time. Probably anything they didn't know what to do with.'

Grayson slumped down in his chair, putting his feet up on the desk and dislodging several files. He surveyed the mass of paper glumly. 'It certainly looks that way. But you shouldn't have the bother of going through every document in detail. For now, just stack the stuff as tidily as you can and someone else can decide later where it all belongs.'

Mike shook his head, then fished around on the floor for an errant pair of reading glasses that had somehow jumped from the desk. 'I've been reading everything closely in the hope that amid this mound of frustration, I might come across something that would help you. But I haven't.'

He straightened up and looked across at Grayson. 'You won't want to hear this, but I've got to say it.' His voice was cautious but determined. 'My advice is seriously to consider calling off the search. I know I've urged it before and you decided not to listen. But the problem is pressing now. We've found nothing and you haven't a clue where Javinder's gone or where you'd be going.'

'You're right, I haven't.' Grayson yawned, dazed by the soporific atmosphere. 'Not an actual clue, at least. But I've been thinking about the conversations I've had these last few days. Nothing very specific, but I'm getting a feel for where I might start.'

His colleague looked decidedly sceptical. 'A feel? You mean you'll point your compass and *feel* where the needle leads you?'

'Not quite so haphazard. It's just that certain comments, certain ideas have stuck in my mind. Almost as though they've been blown towards me in the breeze and then lodged deep in my consciousness.'

'Very poetic, but pure fantasy, Gray, and hardly likely to get you very far. What comments by the way?'

'I can't be certain and I shouldn't say too much for the moment. But the idea of a princely state is beginning to ring bells.'

'But surely they don't exist any longer? I thought they'd been incorporated into India.'

'Most of them. Mountbatten managed to persuade nearly all of them to sign the Act of Accession but some held out. Some are still holding out – the larger states particularly.'

'But not Rajasthan?'

'Rajasthan has always been a collection of princely states. Some large, some very small. Most have signed up, but a few haven't, and they're the ones I should be looking at, I think. It's the smaller ones to the north where there's trouble. And one or two of the ICS officers are convinced that Javinder travelled northwards.'

Mike's expression made it clear that he wasn't equally convinced. 'Have you thought that the problems you're talking about might have nothing to do with Javinder's journey? They might be nothing more than the usual disputes.'

'How is that?'

'From what I gather, tension between the different communities is long standing. If there is aggression, it could be the same old trouble rearing its head. Why should it be anything new?'

'Because disaffected people cause trouble. And that's what we've got. There are rulers who refuse to accept the new dispensation. For them the fifteenth of August last year was a day of mourning. That was when they lost their privileges, lost the world of pomp and splendour they'd expected to inhabit for the rest of their lives.'

'You're saying these chaps might be responsible for the violence? That they're deliberately organising it? That seems pretty far-fetched to me. What on earth would they gain? In any case, there must still be pockets of unrest around the country. The odd disturbance is still happening elsewhere in India, isn't it, so why not in the north of Rajasthan?'

'It is happening,' Grayson conceded wearily. 'And you could well be right. I don't honestly know what to make of the reports. At the moment I'm just going on a hunch.' He swung his legs off the desk and got to his feet. 'I think I'll miss the tea break. I've had enough *chai* today to float me to the Indian Ocean. I'd feel better if I went back to the bungalow and stood under a shower.'

Mike walked with him to the door. He laid his hands on either side of Grayson's shoulders and shook him gently. 'You can't plunge through Rajasthan on a hunch. You have to have more to go on than that. The country isn't properly stabilised yet and God knows what kind of mishap you could meet with. That's if you're lucky and it's not outright danger that you face.'

'I appreciate your concern, Mike, but I've been asking questions for two whole days and I'm still none the wiser. A hunch, I fear, is all I'm going to get.'

'So the answer is don't go.'

Grayson's expression was mulish. It said quite plainly that Mike was making needless difficulties and he wished that he wouldn't.

'Your place is in the town,' his companion ploughed on, undeterred. 'Send scouts to wherever you think best, but stay in Jasirapur and manage the search from here. Think man, you've brought Daisy with us. I'm not saying she's a problem, at least not at the moment. And I like her well enough. But she's here against my advice, I'd remind you. And you need to keep a closer watch on her.'

Grayson's eyes opened wide in astonishment. 'Whatever do you mean?'

'Let me ask you this. Do you know what she's doing right now?'

He felt mystified. Of course, he didn't know exactly. And did it matter that he didn't?

Mike looked satisfied at having startled him. 'I thought not. You have no idea what she's up to and neither have I. But I'd bet a pound to a penny, it's something you wouldn't approve of.'

CHAPTER 6

Grayson wouldn't have approved, Daisy was sure. She was following a uniformed retainer down a long hall of polished marble and feeling very slightly intimidated. She wondered whether after all she should have mentioned her plans to him, or at least left word with Ahmed. It was too late for that now. The hall which had seemed unending finally came to a halt, and she was ushered into what she supposed was a drawing room. She had a brief glimpse of sumptuous walls lined with red and gold silk before a man glided towards her. He offered her his hand in greeting.

'Miss Driscoll? I am Ramesh Suri.'

Her host wasn't a large man, no more than average height and of slender build, but Daisy still felt a qualm when she looked at him. She wasn't sure why. He gestured her towards one of the several thickly brocaded sofas and sat down opposite. The servant who'd escorted her toured the room, pulling the satin blinds fully down at every window and plunging the space into near darkness. For a short moment, she was blinded but then her eyes regained focus and she was able to take in her surroundings. There was richness everywhere, from the wall coverings to the embossed ceiling to the Indian silk rugs on the floor. What she took to be antiques were scattered at random throughout the room. Ramesh Suri was evidently a very wealthy man, but one who chose to live isolated. She wondered where his money came from and had a premonition that it might not be too sensible to enquire.

'You have come far, Miss Driscoll?' he asked in a soft voice.

'From Jasirapur.'

'That is far enough on a hot day. And in an open tonga.'

Her skin was doing an unpleasant thing, sending short, sharp prickles around her body. There was nothing in his speech to make her wary, so why did she feel this disquiet? She sensed his gaze on her, hard and impervious. Yes, it was his gaze, she decided, or rather his eyes that were so disturbing. They were coal black and, at a certain angle, they appeared opaque, as though a screen had descended. As though their owner could look out but no one could look in.

'Have you happened at my gate by accident?' he asked.

He must know that she hadn't. He had clearly heard her tell his aggressive servant that she had come to speak to the master of the house. But she answered him tranquilly enough, ignoring his pretence. 'Not by accident, Mr Suri. I came to see you.'

She heard a slight shuffling behind her and saw Suri beckon to whoever had come into the room. From the corner of her eye, she caught sight of two young men, one not much more than a boy. They hovered discreetly to one side until their father beckoned to them again.

'You must meet my sons, Miss Driscoll. This is Dalip.' The older of the two came forward and bowed. He didn't offer his hand, she noticed. He was dressed less ostentatiously than his father but there was the same opaqueness to the eyes. 'And this is Daya.' The boy moved awkwardly forward. He was barely out of his teens and had not yet lost the innocence of boyhood. His face was open, friendly. Quite unlike his brother or his father.

A second servant, dressed in the same red embroidered livery, brought small bowls of sweetmeats and a tray of clinking glasses. Gratefully, Daisy sipped the iced lemonade. Ramesh Suri had been right in saying it was hardly a sensible day to come travelling in an open tonga. Another misdeed for which Grayson could scold her. Right now, though, she must banish him from her mind. He had his own business to attend to and she had hers. And hers was here, in the home of Anish's uncle.

'So how do you find Jasirapur?'

'It's an interesting town,' she said neutrally, and then with more enthusiasm, 'and India is fascinating.'

'But this is not your first trip to India, I believe?'

How did he know that? If she were a stray traveller who'd stopped at his house – to ask for directions, to seek refreshment – he would surely know nothing of her. But she wasn't a stray traveller, was she? He knew her, he knew who she was. She had a frightening feeling that he'd known even before she'd said her name at the gate. The prickling increased.

'And are you here for long? This is not the best time of the year to visit our country.'

'I'm not sure when we're to return to England. We may stay for the cooler weather.'

'You mention "we". So you are here with companions?'

She was sure that he knew that too. And just as sure he was aware of who her companions were. Suddenly, the thought that Grayson and Mike belonged to the Intelligence Service carried meaning. It had always seemed a strange way of life, Grayson's career, nothing to do with the real world as she knew it. But, in that instant, she realised it had everything to do with it. And this man with the opaque eyes knew that better than she. 'I'm here with a friend and his colleague,' she said, continuing the bluff. 'They have business in Jasirapur.'

'And have left you to your own devices today, I

see. You have come adventuring alone.'

She didn't like the way that sounded. 'I left a message to say where I was going. They won't be worried.'

'How very sensible of you. But to come all this way – Megaur must be more famous than I realised.' He lounged backwards in the heavily embossed chair, his head resting on cushions weaved in golden thread. The slightest smirk touched his mouth. He was playing with her, she decided.

'It's not Megaur I came to see, Mr Suri, but you.' She was fed up with this cat and mouse game. She would state what she wanted and he could make what he would of it.

'Dear me. Now why would you wish to see me?' He swatted lazily at a passing fly.

'I knew your nephew.' She was bold now, refusing to look at the black eyes.

'You must be mistaken. I do not have a nephew.'

'No longer, it's true,' she said even more boldly, 'but you used to. His name was Anish, Anish Rana. I'm sure you cannot have forgotten him. He died only ten years ago. His mother, Parvati, was your very own sister.'

'I know none of these people, if they ever existed.'

She felt the elder son begin to move towards her, but his father's glare flashed at him to stay where he was. Suri's eyes were as hard as agate and he sat poker straight in the imposing armchair. His mouth was a thin, tight line, his expression no longer lazy. If she were to find out what she wanted, she would need to be more conciliatory.

In a gentler voice she said, 'I understand this subject may be painful for you but–'

'You understand nothing,' he interrupted, and there was no doubting his hostility.

'Forgive me if I've angered you. I've come only to ask one question and I hope you will answer it for me. I think you can. It's something that is entirely personal but very important to me. I believe Anish's father may have been a patient in the hospital where my mother was a nurse. If your sister left papers belonging to her husband and you still have them, it's possible that my mother is mentioned in them.'

He said nothing but his face was chipped from stone.

'I know it sounds most unlikely,' she went on, 'but it's the only lead I have. I'm sure Anish's father must have written to his wife while he was recovering in England from the wounds he'd received, and it's just possible that your sister kept his letters. I hoped you might still have them.'

'I know not one person you speak of.' The voice brooked no argument.

It didn't stop Daisy though. 'Karan Rana was your brother-in-law and you don't know him?'

Ramesh half rose from his chair, his body taut and his stare dagger sharp. 'I know nothing of this man.'

'And nothing of your sister, Parvati?'

'I have no sister. Can you not understand that? I have never before found the English to be quite as stupid as you appear to be.'

'Is it stupid to ask for information?'

'There is none to have.' He clapped his hands

as if to underscore the finality of his words. 'Now I think it is time for you to leave.'

'But–'

He pointed to the door. 'Leave, Miss Driscoll, unless you wish to be helped on your way.'

She became conscious that the retainer who had served them drinks had returned and brought with him several companions. Together they flanked the doorway.

The glowering elder son walked forward, his steps marked and deliberate. He took up a position at his father's shoulder. He was a clone of the older Suri, she thought. It was Daya who was different. He remained standing at a distance, half in shadow, but she could see the smooth skin of his face creased with worry lines.

Unhurriedly, she stood up. She was determined not to betray alarm and fought to keep her voice level. 'Thank you for your hospitality.' She hoped the irony would not go unnoticed.

Her legs felt flimsy but, without a backward glance, she strode to the door. It swung open before she reached it, and she realised that yet another servant had been lingering on the other side. Suri appeared to need a battalion of retainers to protect him, any one of them eager to eject her if she'd shown a reluctance to leave. His voice followed her as she began to walk back along the long ribbon of marble.

'You would do well to forget your questions, Miss Driscoll. For your own well-being. Enjoy India but forget the questions.'

She stopped in her tracks and retraced her steps to the door, facing her host across the flurry of silken rugs. His threat was too important to ignore.

'I *will* enjoy my stay in your country, Mr Suri, but it won't stop me asking questions.' And, with that, she turned and marched proudly back along the hall, through the huge carved wooden door, which stood ajar, and out into the hot midday sun.

'You won't get any answers, you know.' It was Dalip who had followed her out to the iron gates. 'That woman brought humiliation on our family. A woman from a princely house who should have brought only pride. Her belongings were burnt. Every item. There is nothing left. Whatever you hoped to find no longer exists.'

Daisy climbed into the tonga without replying.

Her pride was bruised. The visit had been a disaster. She'd been all but thrown out of the house and had learned nothing for her pains. As the tonga bounced its way back to Jasirapur, Dalip Suri's parting shot echoed in the rhythm of the wheels. His words had hit home. Everything his aunt had owned had been burnt, he'd said, and she believed him. His father wasn't just angry, he was malevolent. Ramesh's insistence that he'd never had a sister, never had a nephew, disclosed the cold fact that he'd wiped these two close relatives from out of his life. The burning of Parvati's small stock of possessions was consistent with her brother's frightening pretence that she had never existed. And consistent with his refusal to accept any of Anish's belongings when his nephew died. The adjutant had described Ramesh as rude. Daisy would have said vindictive. But there was little point in name calling. If Parvati had ever possessed papers that in anyway referred to her husband's time as a patient in England, they were long gone. And, after all, it had been the most tenuous of clues.

The more she thought of it, the more she realised that today's visit had been foolish. Karan Rana had been wounded in France and sent to England to recuperate. She knew that to be the truth, since she'd had it from Anish's own lips. But where in England, she didn't know. It was her own wild hope that he'd been sent to Brighton where her mother had nursed Indian soldiers back to life. A wild hope that Karan had known her mother and, even wilder, that he had known her mother's lover and therefore her own father. Grayson had warned her it was an impossible quest and she must learn to accept that he was right. She had discovered nothing; more than that she had received a warning not even to try. Suri had been a little too knowledgeable about her and the thought made her deeply uneasy.

His warning was still reverberating in her head when she walked up the veranda steps of number six Tamarind Drive and bent her mind to the next problem: how to explain her long absence this morning to Grayson and Mike. The expedition had taken much longer than she'd expected and they would have returned for lunch an hour ago and be worried to find her gone without a word of explanation.

As she came through the door, Grayson's face lit with relief.

'Thank God, Daisy. We were just about to send

out a search party. Ahmed had no idea where you'd gone.'

'I thought I'd take a drive in the country.' Her tone was airy, as though this was the most natural thing to do in the middle of the day in the middle of an Indian summer. If she'd hoped to deflect disapproval, she'd hoped wrongly. But it was Mike, rather than Grayson, who appeared the most annoyed.

'A drive in the country? In this weather? If that's so, you need your head examined. Grayson wasn't joking when he said we were about to launch a search. We could have had the entire Jasirapur police force looking for you. And why exactly?'

She was taken aback by his vehemence, but put it down to genuine concern. 'I'm sorry, Mike. Truly, I never meant to worry either of you. I hadn't realised I'd gone so far or that it would be quite so hot. I had to take shelter for a while, that's why I'm so late.'

Grayson looked at her steadily. 'You know Rajasthan better than that, Daisy. It's April. It's hot. What could be so important that you'd risk driving under a burning sun for so long?'

'It wasn't important,' she said quietly. 'I was mistaken.'

She was relieved when he walked to the table and rang the small brass bell to tell Ahmed they were ready to eat at last. He wasn't going to pursue the matter, not in front of Mike she thought, but she was sure that once they were alone he'd want to know just where she had been.

They ate the entire meal without speaking a word. It was clear that Mike was still furious with her, while Grayson seemed lost in his own thoughts. But when Ahmed had cleared the plates and set out three individual dishes of crème caramel, he broke his silence.

'This may be the time to tell you both that I've decided to leave tomorrow.'

She saw that Mike looked shocked, as shocked as she felt.

'I think I've worked out the general direction Javinder took,' Grayson said coolly, 'and I don't want to waste more time hanging around Jasirapur.'

'But all you know is that he took off travelling north, and you're not even sure of that.' She was amazed that he would try to follow the young man on such meagre information.

'I think I can probably narrow it down a little more now.'

'But how?'

Grayson spread his hands wide and gave a rueful smile. 'It's taken a while but, over the last few days, odds and ends have come my way. You know how it is.' That was the problem; she didn't know.

'More instinct, Gray?' Mike put in, a grim look on his face. 'What you're proposing is madness.'

'You'd be surprised at how helpful instinct can be. It's often more reliable than paid sources.'

'You can't really be serious.' Mike's face had turned blood red.

But, when Grayson didn't reply, he appeared to make an attempt at swallowing the anger he evidently felt and, when he spoke, it was in a coaxing tone. 'Look, the paperwork can go hang for a few days. In any case, I'm not finding anything in the office that's remotely useful. Let me come out and about with you – we'll dig around locally together. With both of us on the job, we're more likely to uncover something.'

'I appreciate the offer, but I've waited long enough. At this very moment Javinder may be hurt, ill even. And definitely in trouble or he'd have found a way of contacting us. So speed is important. I'm pretty sure I'll pick up other intelligence as I go.'

When his friend gave another impatient shake of the head, Grayson held up his hand as if to stem the flow of condemnation coming his way. 'I know you're worried, but you shouldn't be. I'm going to be fine and don't forget, I'll have you here, back at the sharp end. That gives me confidence.'

She could see that Mike wasn't convinced, and neither was she. The thought that Grayson would be leaving the next day filled her with mild panic. She didn't want to be left behind in Jasirapur with only an irate Mike for company. She got up and began clearing the bowls onto the tray that Ahmed had left. Out of the corner of her eye, she saw Mike's hand reach out and seize one of the spoons from the table. As she looked up, he rapped it loudly against the wooden surface to gain their attention.

'Aren't you going to make any attempt to stop him going on this mad journey, Daisy?' The angry red flush had died but Mike's lips were compressed into a thin line. 'It's the least you could do. After all, you must be here for some reason.'

She was astonished. The attack had come from out of nowhere and it was a struggle to defend herself. 'I'm here for my own reasons,' was all she managed.

'That's clear enough,' he said bitingly.

'I don't understand. Just what are you accusing me of?'

'There's no accusation, though if you choose to interpret it that way, you can. Put simply, I'm unsure just why you thought it a good idea to gatecrash this trip. It certainly wasn't to help. In fact, judging by the scare you gave us today, just the opposite.'

'Mike, please...' Grayson began, but his colleague had pushed his chair roughly back from the table and picked up the battered briefcase he never seemed without. 'I'm going back to the office. I've work to do.' And he banged out of the door.

Grayson stood for a minute, watching after him, then turned to face her, his dark blue eyes troubled. 'I'm sorry. I don't know what that was about. He's not himself, it's clear enough.'

She cut his apology short. 'It's fine. It really doesn't matter.'

And it didn't. She'd wondered before if Mike resented her coming on this journey and it seemed that she'd been right. He resented her badly. She was sorry for it but there was little she could do. In time, his antagonism might soften. She certainly hoped so. Living with that degree of animosity would be far from easy. But other than being open and friendly in her dealings with him, she could do nothing to improve matters. What she must do, though, was to make this trip to India count. Over their silent lunch, she had begun to toy with a new idea, and when Grayson followed in his colleague's footsteps and she was left alone in the house, she set to thinking it through.

Anish's maternal family, in the guise of Ramesh Suri, had been no help. Indeed just the opposite; there had been threats and she took them seriously. But what of Anish's paternal relatives? There must be someone left in the family that she could talk to. And now she was thinking more clearly, she realised it would be far more likely that Karan Rana would have contacted his birth family rather than ask Parvati to keep his few possessions until he returned to India. By that stage in his life, she calculated, he would have written the letter his son remembered. The letter Anish had spoken of ten years ago. She could still see his face, clouded with emotion – fury, grief, disillusion, all there. As a child, he said, he had worshipped his father, made a hero of the soldier who had died on a First World War battlefield. But then he'd read his father's letter, the one Karan had written to his wife to say that he'd fallen in love with another woman. *He wasn't a hero after all*, Anish had said, *he was a little man capable of deserting his wife and child for a prostitute.* And when Daisy had protested that it might not have been that way, Anish had rounded on her angrily. *What else could she be? He was married with a small child and the woman must have known that. What else can you call it but prostitution?* She should have remembered that letter before she began playing detective. After writing it, Karan would hardly have sent his belongings back to a now abandoned wife. If those papers or letters or even a journal existed, he would have sent them home to his father for safekeeping when he knew he was to fight a second time in France.

But the Rana family had proved elusive. As far as she knew, no one in the regiment had managed to find them, and she had little idea where to look. She thought it likely they lived some distance from Jasirapur. Another complication. But she couldn't let that stop her. She'd found Anish's uncle on his mother's side, hadn't she, and, if she tried hard enough, she could find his father's family. It was not going to be easy though. According to Mrs Forester, the adjutant had tried but failed to make contact, and that in itself was strange. One thing Daisy had learned from her previous stay was that most Indians knew not only where every member of their own kin resided but also where their neighbours' friends, colleagues and relatives hailed from too. Yet Dennis Laughton had been unable to discover a single clue. No, it wouldn't be easy, but it was the last hope she had of finding out what she needed to know. Quite simply, who she was.

She was Daisy Driscoll, of course. Illegitimate child, penniless orphan, a widow of almost seven years. But also a servant, a shop girl and now a professional woman. She'd occupied all these boxes, but who she really was remained a mystery. Over the years, she'd tried to fill the void with work, even with marriage, but nothing had succeeded. The void hadn't always been there, at least not obviously. For much of her life she'd been only vaguely aware of something missing, had deliberately refused in fact, to think of her roots. But from her first step on Indian soil, things had changed. It was as though, out of nowhere, a secret spring had bubbled into being, and, as the months and years passed, had become wider, fuller, and fiercer flowing. Now she was helpless against its tide, and could do nothing but allow herself to be borne aloft to wherever it took her.

So what to do? Someone in this town must know something. She would start by seeking out anyone willing to talk. She could do the trivial stuff, the weather, her bungalow, the town itself, anything to get conversation flowing. If she could gain the confidence of her chance-met acquaintance, she might gradually steer them towards the subject that was uppermost in her mind. It would take time and patience but it would be worth it. And if she wanted people to talk to, where better to start than in the bazaar.

Grayson didn't broach the subject of Daisy with his colleague. That afternoon, he was in and out of the office and Mike was busy on the telephone, or in the bowels of the basement, searching for documents he'd decided were temporarily lost but worth finding. He might be vociferous in his opposition to this journey, but Grayson was conscious that his friend still clung to the hope that he might come across something in Javinder's records that would give them a more definite path to follow. Mike was a frustrated man, he knew. Frustrated by his inability to work in the field and no doubt, too, frustrated by the pain he suffered. For years that had been a constant in his life, his legs smashed in an earlier adventure in Eastern Europe and, more recently, the head-on collision engineered by that fanatic, Sweetman.

Still, his attack on Daisy had been startling. It was so unlike the Mike Corrigan he'd known and though he tried to make excuses for his friend, it picked at him like a sore place. He hadn't wanted to bring Daisy to India. True, he'd made the suggestion a very long time ago that she return some day, but he'd felt strongly that now wasn't the right time. His reluctance, though, had stemmed from the worry he'd felt at bringing her to a country that was still unsettled and placing her close to a mission that could be dangerous. It hadn't been because of any likely tension between his two companions. That was unexpected. But Mike was hardly his old self and Daisy was finding him heavy weather. And since they'd arrived in India, she'd become far more tense herself, and that hadn't helped matters either. It was this identity thing, the old, old problem. She was a great deal more exercised about it than she ever revealed. He could understand, or at least part of him could understand, why she was so intent on discovering the true story behind her birth. He felt sympathy, but he could never fully enter into her feelings. His own experience of childhood had been a million miles from hers. It did mean, though, that he was more objective, and could see how badly the search was disturbing her, how badly it was distorting her life.

Each time she had a lead or even the smallest possibility of finding one, she ended disappointed and it cut her deeply. He wished she would accept that she would never know her father's name and that her mother's story would remain a mystery. Only then would she gain peace of mind. But she wasn't going to let it go, he knew. She would worry away at it until there was nothing left. And maybe nothing left of her. She'd looked so lovely that first morning here. A new dress, her dark shiny curls brushed back and held in a smooth band. She'd been happy, smiling. Looking forward. Something had happened to take the smile away and he wished fervently that he could restore it. He had no illusions about her feelings for him. She was unlikely to fall back in love, but that didn't stop his own heart having other ideas.

Tomorrow he must leave her behind in Jasirapur and he needed Mike and she to be good friends, to look out for each other until he returned. She hadn't appeared badly upset by the attack, but he knew she was good at hiding how she felt. Before he left, he must try to mend fences between them. It would have to be this last evening, he decided, somehow he would have to get them talking together. Not at the bungalow. It needed to be neutral territory, where whatever had flared between them could be forgotten. He would take them both out to dinner, that was it. And it would be a chance for all three of them to raise a toast to the success of his journey.

CHAPTER 7

The afternoon was long, most of it spent gathering equipment for the next day's journey, and when he finally got back to the bungalow, they were both at home. It had taken him a while to prise rope, torches and a shovel out of the hardware store. He'd ordered them two days ago, in fact as soon as he'd arrived in Jasirapur, but at the counter the proprietor had shaken his head in astonishment that a customer could be making such an extraordinary request. In the end, Grayson had marched through the shop into the storeroom beyond and helped himself. A first aid kit was already stowed, along with two jerry cans of fuel and two huge plastic containers of purified water.

He parked the jeep out of sight in the shadow of the jambul trees that lined one side of the drive. The vehicle was a reminder of what lay ahead in the morning, and he had no wish to provoke another angry exchange. Crunching his way towards the house, he felt the first softness of evening. It was sufficiently cool now for Daisy to have ventured onto the veranda and he found her looking out over the trimmed grass. He sauntered up the wooden steps, hearing the rustle of bushes in the whisper of a breeze. The garden was deeply peaceful, and he sat down beside her to enjoy it. She looked up and smiled a silent greeting.

'You always loved the old garden, didn't you?'

he said at last.

'It was hardly a garden, more a wilderness. But yes, it had life, vitality. At night when the stars shone so brightly, it was magical. Like a theatre set made out of silver.'

As they watched, the sun dipped slowly from sight and, when he spoke again, it was into the gathering dusk. 'Has it been tough coming back?'

'At times,' she admitted, 'but I still have that feeling – it's very strange – that somehow I belong. And after all that's happened to me here.'

'So maybe I was right to suggest you return – despite all my qualms?'

She reached across and squeezed his hand. 'You were. You usually are – about me.'

He got up from his chair and stood facing her. Then bent his head and kissed the top of her hair. It was as soft and sweet smelling as he remembered. One of her curls tickled his nose.

'I wish we could stay like this,' he said. He didn't know what he meant by that, only that he was happy, and for the moment so was she. She stirred in her seat and he remembered that he was in India on business and that the serious stuff was about to begin.

'I was wondering if we should try the local cuisine tonight?'

'We usually do.'

'Not Ahmed's cooking. A restaurant in town. What do you think?'

She didn't answer immediately but followed him into the bungalow. Mike was coming out of his bedroom as they walked through the door. 'I thought we'd go out to dinner,' Grayson said. He had the two of them together now. When better to put his plan into action?

'Ahmed will already have prepared a meal,' Mike returned.

'I rang him earlier and warned him we wouldn't be needing anything tonight.'

'You shouldn't have done that, Gray. I'm not going out.' Mike went over to the table. The usual clutter of papers was spread across its surface.

'There's a new restaurant opened at the Paradise. It's supposed to be the smartest place in town. Let's give it a go,' Grayson urged.

Mike hunched over his paperwork. 'I don't think so. Thanks for the invite, but you go. I've brought some work back that I need to get through before tomorrow.'

'All work and no play...'

'Gets things done,' his friend finished for him. And when Grayson began an attempt to persuade, he interrupted with a curt, 'To tell the truth, my leg is playing up and I'd rather stay here.' Then, seeming to regret his abruptness, he added, 'You and Daisy go and enjoy yourselves.'

It wasn't what Grayson had wanted. The reconciliation he'd planned was not about to happen. On the other hand, Mike had not been unfriendly, merely gruff, so perhaps a threesome wasn't strictly necessary. And he wanted to go. He hoped Daisy did too. She was looking at him waiting for a decision.

'Go and get your glad rags on,' he said. 'The Paradise Hotel awaits.'

She decided to wear the very best frock she had

brought. From memory, the Paradise Hotel was badly misnamed but tonight was likely to be the only opportunity she would have of wearing it. Once Grayson had left, most of her evenings would be spent alone in the bungalow. And the dress deserved an outing. It was yellow, a bright yellow satin cotton, and she loved it. It was the colour of sunshine and striking against the creamy olive of her skin. The tightly cinched waist flared to a full skirt, not ridiculously full like some of the 'New Look' images she'd seen in magazines, but full enough to swish and swirl very satisfyingly. The bodice sported a row of neat buttons and finished in a double peplum to accentuate her small waist, while the collar – another double peplum of material curved its way around a deep neckline. It was the most stylish dress she had ever owned. Hair and make-up were swiftly done, but, when she looked at her reflection in the mirror, she wondered if she'd indulged herself too much. She didn't want Grayson to think she was dressing for him. She'd simply wanted to dress up. For just one evening. Should she change? No, she decided, she felt too happy. She would wear the frock.

But then she saw his face as she walked into the sitting room. He tried to alter his expression but she knew she had stunned him. It had been foolish after all to wear the dress, but it was too late to change her mind. The tonga was at the door and, in minutes, they were on their way. They sat side by side on the cracked leather seat, listening to the muffled clop of hooves and feeling the softest of breezes in their hair. It felt right not to speak; it was enough simply to enjoy the ride together.

The Paradise Hotel, when they arrived, was lit as though for a coronation. Every floor blazed. Grayson helped her down from the tonga and tucked her arm in his. She wished she didn't feel this happy and tried telling herself that they were merely friends now, that it was only one dinner and, in any case, he was leaving in the morning. Leaving at dawn, he'd said.

The Peacock restaurant was in full swing, splashes of light spilling warmth out on to the street and a low hum of music and chatter trickling through the open windows. The hotel, she knew, had once housed tea and indigo planters who'd travelled from their estates to do business in Jasirapur, but it was happy now to host anyone who could pay its optimistic prices. The Peacock was its newest venture and the management had gone for opulence. The restaurant exclaimed the exotic loudly. Lavish murals of brightly coloured peacocks covered each wall and tall vases stood in every corner, filled with flowers and girdled with what looked like headdresses of jewelled beads. Each table sported a cluster of candles in peacock hues and even the menus had a fan of brightly coloured feathers splayed across their covers.

They were escorted to a table by the window. There was a lot of bobbing and bowing – the staff had been over-drilled in courtesy, Daisy guessed – but drinks were brought and menus distributed with only a little delay.

Grayson studied his closely. 'What do you think?' he asked.

'You choose.'

'If you're sure...'

She was. Most of the dishes listed were strange to her and she would have the time to look around and take in her surroundings. Instead, she found herself looking at Grayson. India suited him, she decided. But then it always had. His skin had already acquired a light tan and his hair danced with sun-given highlights. He had put on a crisp new shirt and its vibrant blue echoed eyes that, in the candlelight, were close to navy. He looked up at that moment and caught her glance and she quickly busied herself flicking through the unread pages of her menu.

A delightful smelling cloud drifted past. 'The cooking seems to have improved since I was last here,' he remarked.

'When was that?' She was grateful to lose herself in a mundane topic.

'At least ten years ago. At the time we were both in Jasirapur. An old acquaintance from Uttar Pradesh, United Provinces as it was then, came to town on business and took the trouble to look me up. We had lunch together in the hotel's old restaurant. I have to say, it wasn't the most exciting meal I've ever eaten.'

'Then let's hope we're luckier tonight.'

Grayson lifted his glass and clinked it gently against hers. 'Let's hope. We'll call it a good luck dinner – for both of us.'

'I could certainly have done with some today.'

She hadn't intended to mention Megaur, but this evening she'd been plunged afresh into an old intimacy and was beginning to feel her feeble defences crumble. Grayson's glance was shrewd and she knew she wouldn't be able to hide from him. He would home straight to his target.

'Did you have a disappointing day? I've been wondering where you went. Speculating on it.'

She wondered how much she should say, but he'd already jumped ahead of her. 'No, don't tell me. Let me guess. You found Rana's relatives.'

'I found his maternal relatives,' she corrected. 'A Ramesh Suri. He was Anish's uncle.'

The arrival of their first course, plates of dainty samosas and lettuce wraps, put a temporary stop to the conversation. But, once they were eating, he wanted to know more. 'And where did you run Mr Suri to ground?'

'He lives on the outskirts of a village called Megaur.'

'I know it. It's a fair distance from here.'

She wiped her hands on the stiff white napkin. 'It was.'

'No wonder you looked exhausted when you got back. It's hardly the best time of the year to go exploring.'

'I know,' she said quickly. 'But don't scold. The visit turned out to be a disappointment, and definitely not worth the exhaustion.'

The waiter had reappeared at Grayson's shoulder. He swept away their empty plates while a second man trundled a covered trolley towards them. In a few minutes their table was drowning beneath an enormous array of food. She peered into the large tureen the waiter had just served: a luscious vegetable curry. She could smell the dry fruits, the spices and the yoghurt. And scattered haphazardly around the table, a number of small bowls filled to the brim and looking equally delicious.

'It looks as though we'll be eating for England.'

'No curried chicken, though, I hope you notice.' Grayson smiled.

'No indeed. But what are they all?' She waved her hand over the table.

'The one to your right is *dahiwale aloo* – basically potatoes. The one next to it is *keerai dal.* You can see the cucumbers. And these are *missi rotis.* You must have eaten them before.'

'I don't think so. Rajiv might have been an excellent gun runner but his repertoire in the kitchen was fairly limited.'

'Then you're in luck. They're a marvellous Indian bread – made with wheat flour and gram flour and seasoned with spices.'

'And the rest of the dishes?'

'No idea. I just pointed to the menu. Let's find out.'

They set to with sharpened appetites, the memory of dreary years of rationing dwindling fast. She thought of what Connie would have made of the laden table and smiled. Even in the leanest times, her friend had battled with her weight and Canada's plenty must be making her life difficult. In Brighton, Daisy had been too depressed to put pen to paper, but once she was back in England, she promised herself that she would write to Connie again. She would have a lot to tell her.

Once they'd made inroads into the feast, Grayson picked up the conversation where he'd left it. 'So why wasn't Megaur worth the effort? You said your luck ran out.'

'It was me that was run out,' she said ruefully. 'Ramesh Suri refused to talk to me. He denied he'd ever had a sister or a nephew, denied they had ever existed. And when I kept on questioning, he threw me out. Or at least he ordered me off his property which comes to the same thing.'

His eyebrows rose. 'That doesn't sound at all like Indian hospitality.'

'I don't think he's a proper Indian.'

'What do you mean?' Grayson was looking amused.

'He's a very rich man, but it's not that he's wealthy. And he's ostentatious – everything in his house is showy, but that wasn't it either. It was the way he treated me. Right from the outset. He wasn't hospitable, he wasn't even indifferent. He was threatening. Even before I began to ask him about his relatives, I could feel it. And he seemed to know about me. He knew who I was and the fact I'd been to India before. I found that disconcerting.'

Her companion frowned. 'I hope this visit of yours hasn't roused a rats' nest, Daisy.' It seemed that Grayson was finding it disconcerting too. 'Were you alone with him?'

'There was a mass of servants, but apart from them, his two sons were there. The eldest – Dalip, I think his father called him – felt just as threatening, in his own way. He followed me out to the tonga and told me I would never find anything. That all his aunt's things had been burned.'

'Not a nice family then. No doubt they have secrets to hide. But at least you learned something.'

'I can't see what.'

'That Megaur is a dead end.'

Her face must have shown plainly that she considered it hardly worth learning, because he leant forward with another question, trying it seemed to soften her disappointment. 'Was the younger boy any more helpful?'

'He was pleasant enough. I don't remember his name. I do remember he smiled at me. He had a nice open face.'

'So that's one member of the Suri family who is a proper Indian.'

'It doesn't help me though. The boy is too young to know much of what happened all those years ago.'

Grayson said nothing more but sat staring at the tablecloth for what seemed an inordinate time. She wondered what he could see there.

'I wish I weren't going,' he said suddenly.

'I wish you weren't. You have no idea what you're walking into. It could be very dangerous.'

He'd continued to make light of his journey but it worried her greatly. In recent months India had become vastly more tranquil, she understood that, but there were always tensions simmering just below the surface and the nearer Grayson travelled to the areas that were most disturbed, the more risks he ran.

'There's no cause for you to worry on my behalf. I'll be fine. It's leaving you here that I don't like. If this Suri chap decides to call on you, for instance, to return your visit, it could be very unpleasant.'

She hadn't thought of that. But Grayson was right, it would be unpleasant. She would be alone. Alone except for Mike.

'Mike will be at the bungalow.' He'd spoken aloud the words running through her mind. 'And you can always get hold of him at the office if you need to.'

'Yes,' she agreed, but her tone was uncertain.

He pushed his empty plate to one side. 'What is it?'

'Mike doesn't seem too well,' she said diffidently. 'He finds the heat difficult, I think, and maybe he's in pain.'

'He often is – it's nothing new.'

'He seems changed though. Of course, it's nearly seven years since I last saw him and a lot can happen in that time.'

'He took a drubbing in the Sweetman affair. Not just the busted head and ribs. You know about those, but what you might not know is that he still blames himself for what happened. If he'd been more alert, he wouldn't have let Sweetman overhear the code to your safe house and so put your life in danger. Or pretty much hand him his own security pass.'

'But he couldn't have known the man was going to smash him unconscious and steal his pass.'

'He should have seen he was being followed and taken action. I can understand why he feels so bad about it. But it's water under the bridge. You both survived, and thanks to you, so did I.'

He reached across the table and covered her hand with his. 'I wouldn't worry about Mike. He's got a few difficulties right now, but he'll be there for you. I'm sure of that.'

'I'm sure he will. It's just that he doesn't seem

to be enjoying the trip very much.'

'Like you said, he's finding the heat a great trial. I did warn him, but you can never really make people understand just how obliterating it is.' He tightened his grip on her hand. 'You seem to be holding up pretty well though.'

'Second time round, I guess. I *did* know what to expect.'

He looked across at her and she knew what he was thinking. Tonight she looked the picture of health, her eyes bright, her hair shining, her skin not yet tanned but a creamy silk.

He lowered his eyes and picked up the menu, shuffling its pages. 'A dessert?'

'Not for me,' she thanked him. 'I always find them too sweet and we've eaten loads already. Perhaps we should be getting back? You've a very early start.'

'You're right. We should get moving.' The awkward moment had passed and he was quick to summon the waiter to bring the bill.

The street outside was hushed and deserted. The hotel's restaurant was still the only one in Jasirapur that opened at night, but local people rarely visited. A blanket of stillness covered the town and, apart from the small line of tongas opposite, they were alone in the world. They began to cross the road and were several yards from the pavement when a car roared out of nowhere and hurtled towards them. Its headlights were so powerful that they were temporarily blinded, but though they couldn't see, they could hear the thunder of its engine as it bore down on them. Grayson reached out and grabbed her by the waist, at the last minute jumping her to one side. The car seemed to miss them by inches.

'What the hell,' he muttered when he could get his breath back.

Daisy was trembling and he held her close until she'd recovered sufficiently to cross the road to one of the waiting tongas.

'Who would do such a thing?' he asked of nobody in particular, once they were settled in the carriage. 'It must have been some crazy drunk. I'll leave a note for the police. They need to investigate before he mows someone down.'

She had been too shocked by the incident to utter a word, but now she said in a small voice, 'It wasn't a drunk.'

He twisted round to face her. Then grabbed her by the arm and held it very tightly. 'Why do you say that?' It was clear that she'd worried him.

'Because I'm a hundred per cent sure that it was deliberate.' She tried to keep her voice from shaking. 'I recognised the driver, you see.'

'Who was it, in God's name?'

'It was Dalip Suri.'

There was a long pause. 'Ramesh's son. The eldest boy,' she reminded him, as if he were likely to have forgotten.

Grayson didn't reply immediately, but tapped his fingers hard against the side of the tonga. When he spoke, his voice had a weariness to it but there was a note of anger too.

'What kind of trouble have you stirred up, Daisy?'

CHAPTER 8

Her fright melted in the heat of indignation. She was blameless. She had done nothing but try to discover something that mattered to her, something she believed herself entitled to know. A secret that was there to be found.

'The only thing I'm guilty of is asking a question,' she said tautly.

'It seems it was a big enough question for the Suris to consider murdering you.'

She started at the harsh words. Until now, she'd thought the runaway car a tactic to scare her, bad enough in itself, but now Grayson was giving it a very different complexion. The pulse in her wrist began a rapid beat.

'Do you really think they wanted to kill me?'

'Well, they certainly didn't want to escort you home. My guess, though, is that it wasn't so much murder on that young man's mind but accidental damage. Enough damage to put you out of commission and stop you asking questions the family don't want to answer.'

Dalip had certainly been hostile towards her, but would he do such a drastic thing? She found it difficult to believe, yet under orders... 'His father must have made him do it,' she decided.

'No doubt. But it would never have happened if you hadn't sought the family out. You were stupid to go to their house. Stupid to start this hare running. If you'd told me what you intended, I would have stopped you. You knew that, of course. It's why you sneaked off when I wasn't around.' His anger was palpable now. It was a reaction to the fright they'd both had, she knew, but that didn't make it any easier to swallow.

'What do you expect me to do?' she retorted. 'Sit around and twiddle my thumbs while you go breezily about your investigations?'

'What I don't expect,' he said in the coldest of tones, 'is for you deliberately to court disaster. There's enough trouble surrounding this assignment already. You've found out nothing for your pains and tonight you might have been severely injured. Leave it be, for God's sake. This search for a history that in all probability doesn't exist is getting out of hand.'

It was a familiar refrain and she had to bite back a response. The intimacy of the evening lay in pieces around them and they made the rest of the journey in silence. But when they pulled up outside the bungalow, Grayson was swift to help her down from the tonga. She saw him wince as he did so. He turned to pay the driver and she walked away into the garden. She was feeling jangled and unsure and she craved its quiet solitude. A moon had climbed high in the sky and its ghostly sheen blanketed bushes, trees and grass in an arc of silver.

'I'm sorry.' He had joined her on the grass and he sounded regretful. 'The last thing I want to do is quarrel with you. I guess this business has shaken me up a trifle.'

She turned a softer face towards him. She had

no wish to quarrel either and she knew she'd involved him in more danger, when he already had enough of his own. 'I'm sorry, too,' she said. 'I had no idea when I went to the Suris that this might happen.'

'How could you? It was unfair of me to suggest otherwise. But I think we should take this evening's little foray as a warning and heed it. While I'm away, please don't go asking questions of anyone.'

She made no promise but she thought she would do as he asked. If tonight was anything to go by, he was right about her stirring a rats' nest. They stood for a while drinking in the quiet coolness, then slowly retraced their steps through the garden and up the stairs to the veranda. She noticed he used his left hand to open the door. 'You've hurt yourself,' she said. 'How did that happen?'

'That young maniac's car caught me on the wrist, that's all. But nothing too bad – it's a very slight injury.'

She paused on the threshold, 'I'll try to forget what happened tonight and I promise not to mention it again, but don't you think the Suris' reaction was extreme?'

'Extreme it might have been, but whatever nerve you hit, you'd better not hit it again.' He followed her into the empty sitting room. Mike had evidently gone to bed early. 'Give it some serious thought. You've upset them sufficiently that they're prepared to injure you badly. My advice – no, let's make it a command – is that you keep clear of them. I want you in one piece when I return.'

She gave a small sigh. 'I'll keep as low a profile as I can, but you don't even know when you'll be back.'

'I'll be as swift as possible. In the meantime, you must be doubly careful. And when you see Mike tomorrow, tell him about the Suris. You needn't mention what happened this evening, just that you made a mistake in going to see them. That way, he'll be prepared in case there's any further trouble.'

She nodded her agreement though she wasn't convinced she should burden Mike with her problems. He seemed to have enough of his own. She picked up one of the jugs of water that Ahmed had left for them, and walked with it towards her bedroom. At the door, she paused. 'I suppose I should bid you goodbye now. You'll be gone by the time I'm awake.'

He walked up to her and took her face in his hands. 'Keep safe,' he insisted, and kissed her fully on the mouth.

For a moment, she was breathless. Shocked by the turn of events. He shouldn't have done that and he must know it. Had the impulse been too strong for even such a controlled man as Grayson? In a daze, she watched him go back to the table for the remaining water jug. As he did so, there was a soft scratching at the front door. He looked across at her and his eyes widened. She felt fear begin its insidious creep once more and wished she were braver. Putting the jug back onto the table, Grayson walked quietly towards the door. Then he turned and held up a finger to signal to her not to speak. A pistol appeared in his hand and she could barely contain her gasp. She had no idea he carried a gun, but after their narrow escape in the street, she could see that it might be needed. He gestured her to crouch down behind the cane sofa. Then he flung the door wide.

A pair of soft brown eyes looked into the room. The young man on the threshold gave a startled glance at the gun and backed away, muttering his apologies. 'So sorry to disturb you. I will come back another time.'

Grayson stepped through the door and pulled the boy roughly into the room. 'Who are you and what are you doing here?'

'I have come to see Miss Driscoll,' the boy faltered, 'she is here?'

Despite Grayson's warning hand, Daisy emerged from her hiding place.

'Yes, I'm here. It's all right, Grayson. I know this young man. He's Mr Suri's youngest son.'

The boy gave a small grateful smile. 'I am Daya Suri,' he confirmed.

Somewhere in the bungalow, a door closed. Mike, Daisy thought. He wasn't asleep after all, wasn't even in his bedroom, but he'd made sure to avoid them. At the sound the boy's head shot round, peering beyond them and into the dark corners of the room.

'That was my colleague,' Grayson said in a gentler voice. 'There's nothing to fear.'

The boy tried a smile, which didn't quite reach his eyes. 'I shouldn't be here.'

'I'd gathered that. But what are you afraid of?'

He didn't answer but instead repeated, 'I shouldn't be here.'

'So why are you?'

The boy looked across at Daisy who stood silently to one side. 'Good evening, Miss Driscoll.' She nodded an acknowledgement. 'I have come to apologise. I wish you to know how sorry I am that you were treated so rudely at my home today.'

The formal courtesies jarred with the cloak and dagger atmosphere and made Daisy want to giggle. That was nerves too, she imagined.

'And you travelled all the way from Megaur to tell me that?'

'Yes. No. Not entirely. I wanted to speak to you at Amrita but there was no chance.'

She sank limply into one of the cane chairs. This evening was proving just a little too exciting.

'I'm sorry.' The boy seemed to need perpetually to apologise. 'I have upset you by coming.'

Before she could answer, Grayson said, 'Miss Driscoll has had a narrow escape this evening and she is naturally feeling a little weary.'

'An escape? But from what?' The scared look was back.

'From a car driven deliberately at us. Do you know anything about it?'

The boy shook his head vehemently. 'I know nothing. But why would you think that I did?'

Grayson's voice was at its laziest. 'Only that it was your brother who was driving.'

She thought the young man was going to faint. His face turned ashen and she saw his thin legs begin to tremble through the narrow trousers he wore.

'You seem shocked, Mr Suri,' Grayson said.

The boy stuttered into life. 'I am shocked,

terribly shocked. But are you sure it was Dalip who was driving? It is dark. It could have been anyone.' His speech galloped ahead in desperation. 'It might have been an accident. Perhaps the driver did not see you. Perhaps he was drunk...' His voice tailed off.

'He saw us all right,' Grayson said grimly. 'And Miss Driscoll will vouch for the driver's identity.'

Without being invited, Daya sank into a second chair. What life he'd had in him had melted away and left him an empty husk. He remained slumped there for some while until Grayson poured him a glass of water and pushed it into his hand.

'This is news to you then?'

The boy hung his head and muttered into his shoes. Daisy could barely catch his words. 'I did hear something,' he admitted, 'but I did not think for one minute such a terrible thing would happen.'

'What did you hear?' Grayson was going to squeeze him for all the information he could.

'My father ordered Dalip to make sure that Miss Driscoll never came back to the house. Or any of her companions.'

'And why would that be?'

'He does not want anyone asking questions about our family,' the boy mumbled unhappily.

'And is that the only reason?'

'What else could there be? He is very protective of our honour.'

'Honour?' There was a derisive note to Grayson's voice. 'Is that what you call it?'

'It is of the utmost importance to him. When I

was very small, we owned a large estate in Sind province,' the boy rushed on, 'but then my father was deposed and lost everything and we had to start again in Rajputana. It has been hard for him. Humiliating. But I didn't... I had no idea... I thought he meant that Dalip would speak a warning.'

'He did a little more than speak.'

'Yes, yes. It is most terrible.' He gulped down more water.

Daisy leaned forward in her chair. 'What did you come to tell us, Daya? It wasn't just to apologise for your father's behaviour, was it?'

He shook his head. 'My father would not speak of the people you mentioned. But I saw that for you it mattered. He thinks that his sister was a very bad person. My mother was an honourable woman, you see. She suffered much to give my father two sons and she died when I was born. But my aunt lived and brought disgrace again to our family.'

'And do you think she was a bad person?'

'No.' He shook his head in a bewildered fashion. 'I don't think so. I was too young to play with Anish but Dalip did. And when Anish came to our house, my aunt did too. I was a very small boy but I liked her. She was kind. That was before the trouble.'

'What trouble was that?'

'Before her husband cast her away. Before he died.'

'So you never met her again? Not after her husband died?'

He hung his head, the picture of guilt. 'Once. I

met her once but for a few minutes only. She saw me in the bazaar. Dalip had taken me there. He wanted to buy a kit to make a model aeroplane. He used to build very many of them and it took him ages to find one he didn't already have. I got bored and wandered off. Then she was there, in front of me, with a man I'd never seen before. I knew I was not supposed to speak to her, but I didn't understand why. She was smiling and she was kind, still. She bought me sweets,' he remembered. 'They were wrapped in silver paper.'

Daisy felt the slightest shiver of excitement. 'Do you know who the man was with your aunt?'

'I am not to speak of him.'

'You can speak of him to us. What you say will stay within these walls.'

Daya twisted in his seat, evidently uneasy. He had been brainwashed, Daisy thought, into seeing Parvati's lover – and the man must be her lover – as a force of evil.

'He was a friend,' Daya said finally. 'Not our friend, you understand. A friend of my aunt's.'

'I understand, but do you know his name?'

'He is an important businessman, I believe. Or he was. Here in Jasirapur.'

'His name?'

If it was possible, the boy looked even more guilty. 'It's best that you don't look for him.'

'I doubt that I would find him.' She didn't doubt it, but she could see the alarm in the boy's face and she wanted that name.

'Mr Bakhul Bahndari,' he muttered with reluctance.

'And then what happened?' she prompted

gently. 'After you saw your aunt in the bazaar?'

'Then nothing. We were not to mention her at home. I never saw her again and when she died, my father forbade us to go to her funeral.'

He saw Daisy's shocked expression and tried to explain. 'You see, in India it is a big disgrace to lose your husband to another woman. And if you are a widow–'

'I know about widows,' she interrupted. Anish's words were still with her. *A woman has no status of her own and, when her husband dies, she becomes nothing. Years ago a widow was required to throw herself on her husband's funeral pyre. Now she dies a more lingering death. This is her punishment for losing a husband.*

'Then you will see how it was.'

'And your aunt's belongings. Were they really burned?'

'They were brought to the house by the woman who rented her a room. My father ordered everything to be burned. He said they smelt of her and must be destroyed.'

'But her son was in Jasirapur. Was nothing given to him?'

'Only what my aunt Parvati may have given him when she was alive.'

And that was probably just one small pink leather purse, Daisy thought. Other than the name of Mr Bahndari, it seemed that Daya's visit had provided nothing more than another dead end. She was still unclear, though, exactly why he'd come and she leaned towards him now, inviting a final confidence.

'There's something else, isn't there, something

you came here tonight to tell me?'

Grayson shifted uneasily from foot to foot and she knew he was unhappy with her probing. He'd already decided that they'd got from Daya everything worth getting and to prolong the interview could only heighten her disappointment. He wanted to protect her but he couldn't. For him, this search was an unhealthy obsession; for her it was a visceral need to uncover the truth.

'There was something,' the boy murmured.

She felt her face relax, the tightness dissolve and her skin soften.

He put his hand in his pocket and pulled out a battered postcard. 'This was in my aunt's things. I stole it,' he said shamefaced.

'Why?'

'I liked the picture. It was so pretty and so strange. It had come from England – I could see that by the stamp – but it looked like India.'

Daisy stretched her hand to take the card. It shook only a little as she gazed down on the faded image.

'It's the Pavilion,' she said aloud. 'It's Brighton Pavilion!'

'Now I know what it is,' Daya put in, 'but then I was just a child and knew nothing about England. I was fascinated though, so I sneaked it away and kept it hidden.'

'Until now. So why have you brought it to me?'

'You looked so nice, Miss Driscoll. And sad. I thought you should have it. It is the only thing I have of my aunt's.'

'I can keep it?'

'Of course. I think it must mean more to you

than to me.'

When the young man had gone, slipping quietly into the darkness, Daisy sank back into the chair. Her body was limp with tiredness but her face told another story. It blazed excitement. She had been right to think that finding Anish's family was key. She held the postcard delicately between finger and thumb and waved it at her companion.

'It's the Pavilion, Grayson.' He nodded without enthusiasm. 'But you see what this means?' she continued. 'Anish's father *was* in Brighton and the postcard proves it. He must have sent it to his wife when he first arrived. I can just make out the date on the postmark.' In the dim light she could barely trace the faded printing, but it was there all the same. 'May 1916,' she said in triumph. 'He sent it to Parvati to let her know where he was.'

'Of course he could always have been on a day trip to the seaside. An outing for wounded soldiers.' Grayson's gentle mockery passed her by.

'The only reason Karan Rana would be in Brighton was to convalesce from the wounds he received in France, to convalesce at the Pavilion hospital where my mother was nursing. He would have known her, he had to have. And I'm sure he would have known the name of her lover. Hospital gossip would have seen to that. Was it someone on the staff, do you think? Or a visitor, a patient even? He must have known.'

Grayson sat down opposite her, putting the postcard gently aside. 'What you say is quite possible, but I don't see how it helps you in your search. Karan Rana is no longer alive and neither is his son. The trail goes dead after them.'

'But Karan may have left papers behind, letters he wrote, a diary, anything that spoke of his time in Brighton and the people he met. Maybe *they* haven't been burnt. Maybe they're still sitting somewhere.'

'Sitting somewhere? You thought they were sitting at Ramesh Suri's house but they weren't. All you have from there is one solitary postcard. Where else do you expect them to be – even if they still exist?'

'I agree it's a gamble. But this–' she pointed to the faded postcard '–this is a strong clue. And there will be others, I'm sure. If Karan's papers are still intact, they'll be at his family home. I'm convinced of it. That's what happens when people die – their possessions are returned to their home. Parvati's were until that brute of a brother destroyed them.'

'Just supposing there are papers and they're where you say they are – the Rana family home – you have no idea where that is.'

'And you have no idea where Javinder is.'

'I don't see the connection.'

'If you can look for Javinder on only the flimsiest of evidence, I can look for the Rana house.'

'At least I have a vague notion of where to look.'

'And so do I. Anish's family comes from the north of Rajasthan – Jocelyn said so in her letter.'

'That covers around four hundred square miles.'

'But that won't deter you from your search, will it?' She was newly energised. 'And it's not going to deter me either.'

CHAPTER 9

Grayson went to bed that night deeply troubled. The boy's intervention had made a bad situation worse. Without the postcard of Brighton Pavilion, he might have persuaded Daisy to abandon her search. He'd been in a fair way of doing so, he thought. But now she knew that Karan Rana had been a patient there, the bit was firmly between her teeth. He worried that she was courting danger, but he knew Daisy and tonight's incident was unlikely to stop her. He suspected the situation was a great deal more complex than she realised, that there were reasons for Dalip Suri's attack she knew nothing of. It hadn't yet occurred to her, but he'd been in the driver's sights as much as she. At the moment, he couldn't fathom what the connection might be between Suri and his own interests, but he was fairly certain that the young man had driven at them for reasons other than the questions Daisy had been asking. That thought was something he intended to keep to himself. But if he were right, it would be foolish to report the incident and involve the police, when his success at finding Javinder alive depended on working silently and alone.

And he must find him. Javinder was a senior man, responsible, professional, highly conscientious. He was a guardian of secrets, a possessor of crucial knowledge. And he was a friend. Grayson had worked with him on and off for months and they had grown close. It had been Javinder who'd aided his masquerade as a district officer when he'd first come to Jasirapur, Javinder who'd supported his evidence at the trial of the nationalist gang that had threatened Daisy's life, and Javinder who'd helped him pick up the pieces when he'd been forced back to India to take temporary charge of the station after its chief officer fell ill. The young man had been a staunch ally throughout and, when India gained her independence, Grayson had been delighted to see him promoted and put in charge of liaison with SIS in London. He had to find him. But after this evening's events, he was doubly unhappy at leaving Daisy alone in Jasirapur. Whatever grand plans she was hatching, he wanted her safe and he wished very much he wasn't going away.

When he woke in the morning, though, he realised he was going nowhere, at least not on that day. During the night his wrist joint had swollen to the size of a golf ball and was extremely painful. There was no chance he would be able to drive with such a savagely throbbing hand, and certainly no chance of driving safely over rough terrain.

Mike was already up and about and noticed Grayson's clumsy efforts at lacing his shoes. 'Let's have a look.' He turned the wrist gently over and then back again. 'I don't think there's anything broken, but it's nasty,' he opined. 'How did you do it?'

'I stumbled coming out of the restaurant and fell against a brick wall,' Grayson lied fluently.

'It looks as though your hand lost out to the

wall. How much did you drink last night?' Mike seemed to have recovered his spirits this morning. Ironic, Grayson thought, when his own were plummeting.

'Not guilty. But it's a wretched nuisance. I can't drive like this.'

'Someone should look at it. You'll probably end up in a sling. I doubt you'll be going anywhere for at least a week.'

His friend's pessimism didn't come as a surprise, but Grayson wasn't going to argue. He had every intention of setting off the following day, however painful his wrist. He would get it strapped, that was the answer.

'There's a medical unit at the cantonment,' Mike advised. 'You could call in there. They might even have an X-ray machine.'

'I didn't realise the hospital was still functioning. I wonder if Dr Lane has stayed. I doubt it – it's been ten years.'

'Only one way to find out,' his friend said cheerfully and, for the first time since they'd arrived at the bungalow, he sat down to eat the *chota hazri* Ahmed had prepared.

Grayson didn't follow suit. The pain was making him feel too sick to eat. 'Can you drive me to the military lines, Mike, before you go into town?'

'Sure thing. I'll be with you in two ticks.'

He was as good as his word and dropped his colleague at the hospital less than thirty minutes later. The last time he'd been here, Grayson remembered, was to collect Javinder after his young colleague had received a dangerous head wound from the rioting in Jasirapur. At first sight, he was surprised to see the place looking no different. But when he observed the building more closely, he saw its paint was peeling and rampant weeds had breached the walls at random intervals. The bicycle racks by the main entrance were slowly rusting into a pile of red crumbs.

He pushed open the familiar green door and peered into the dark interior. He was about to call out when footsteps sounded and a slightly shabby white coat appeared at the further end of the waiting room.

'Dr Lane!'

'The very same. And I recognise you too.' The elderly man's parched skin crinkled into ever deeper creases as he tried to recall the man who stood on the threshold.

'Grayson Harte, District Officer.'

'Ah yes, now I recall. Grayson Harte. Supposed District Officer, wasn't it? Well, well, who would have thought it. Have you come back to Jasirapur to put away more villains?'

'Not exactly.'

Grayson opted for vagueness on the subject of why he'd returned. But he was genuinely pleased to see the older man, now grey-haired and a little stooping. 'I had no idea you were still here, Doctor. But it's lucky for me that you are. I've come hoping you or your nurse might do something with this.' He stretched out his hand.

'There's just me. No nurse. No anybody in fact.' Grayson heard the tinge of bitterness. 'The 7th was disbanded some time ago, you know, and the hospital will close in two weeks. I'm the very last remnant.'

'It must be a difficult time for you,' Grayson conceded. In an attempt to lighten the mood, he said, 'But you'll be returning home, I imagine?'

'Home?' The doctor almost barked the word. 'Where is home do you think? This is my home.' He shot Grayson a swift glare and then promptly forgot his grievance. 'You're looking decidedly sick. Pasty-faced. Come into the surgery.'

Once there, he carefully examined the swollen wrist, turning it this way and that until Grayson thought he would pass out at any minute.

'Not broken,' the doctor eventually pronounced. 'You're fortunate. But it will need binding pretty securely.' And he marched off into one of the small anterooms and brought back a large stack of padding and bandages. Enough to wrap an Egyptian mummy, Grayson thought.

'The last time we met, I had that young girl helping me,' Dr Lane said conversationally. A ploy, Grayson could see, to distract him from the newly exquisite pain. 'You remember, the one who nearly came to grief the night the monsoon broke.'

'I remember,' he said between clenched teeth. 'Daisy Driscoll.'

'Yes, Daisy, that's right. But not Driscoll ... no, it was ... Mortimer.'

'It's Driscoll now.'

'How come?'

'Her husband died.'

'Yes, of course he did. Drowned, wasn't he, trying to save her from those blaggards?'

'That's the story,' his patient said noncommittally.

'But why Driscoll?' The doctor swathed the last

of the bandages tightly across the wrist bone and clamped a large safety pin in place.

'It's the name she was born with. She's working as a nurse and I imagine she felt it would be more professional to revert to her unmarried name.'

'A nurse, eh? Splendid. I always thought she would make a good one. I'm glad she did it – train, I mean.'

'She did – at Bart's and during the Blitz. A pretty rigorous training too.'

'You seem to know a lot about her.'

'I still see her occasionally,' he said casually. 'This looks a very solid job. Thank you.' He rolled down his sleeve. 'She's here now,' he offered. He saw the doctor looking thunderstruck and said, 'For some reason or another she wanted to come back to India and, when I told her I was headed here on business, she decided to tag along.'

He purposefully made it sound as though Daisy's decision had been a last-minute whim and his own business nothing out of the ordinary.

Dr Lane shrugged his shoulders as though to free himself from the inexplicability of people and went to fetch a linen sling. He tied it around Grayson's neck, then stood back to observe his workmanship. 'That should stand you in good stead. But no weight on the wrist, mind. And rest it as much as possible. I'll check it over for you if you come back before they finally evict me.'

'I won't be able to keep the sling on for long. I need to drive.'

'That would be stupid.'

'I'm afraid I don't have a choice.'

'Then you're likely to damage yourself further

and your wrist will have to go in plaster. Is that what you want?'

'I'll have to risk it.'

'What's so urgent that you have to drive?' the doctor enquired. 'And if it's so desperate that you go somewhere, why not employ a driver?'

No, Grayson thought, the job was far too secret to share with a driver. He wondered how much to tell and then decided on at least a small degree of honesty. A doctor gets to hear all kinds of things and who knows, Lane might have heard something that could help his mission.

'Do you remember a chap called Javinder Joshi?' he began.

'Javinder? Of course, I remember him. Had him in here a few months ago. He needed a check-up, he said. He was going up country and wanted to be sure he was fit for it. Rugged terrain up north, I gather.'

The small hairs on Grayson's arms stood to attention. Here, quite unexpectedly, could be the breakthrough he'd been seeking and so far had failed to find.

'Do you know where Javinder was headed?' he asked, trying to keep his voice as devoid of interest as possible.

'One of the princely states,' Dr Lane said distantly. 'One of the smaller ones.' It was looking better all the time. He had been thinking on precisely those lines. 'Let me see...' The doctor pondered. 'No. I can't remember the actual name. There are so many of them.'

'It's not important,' Grayson reassured him, while a deep well of disappointment opened within. 'But thanks for patching me up so neatly.'

'Much good it will do if you're intent on driving for days.'

'I'll try my best to keep your handiwork intact,' he promised. 'And I'm glad I found you today. Wherever you decide to go, I wish you the best of good fortune.'

And he did, sincerely. He could imagine what a tremendous wrench it must be for the doctor to leave after being so long a medical man in India. Forty years or more, it had to be.

'Time moves on,' Dr Lane said gruffly and opened the door for him. 'Need a tonga?'

'No, I'll walk. The sun is still on its climb. I should be able to reach town before disappearing in a pool of sweat.'

The older man permitted himself a slight smile and waved his patient off. Grayson heard the door close as he began to walk down the main thoroughfare of the cantonment towards the gates that led to the Jasirapur road. But he'd travelled only a few yards when he heard a shout from behind. Dr Lane was standing on the hospital threshold, his hands flapping wildly in the air.

'Sikaner,' he yelled.

Grayson frowned and cupped his hand to his ear. 'Pardon.'

'That was the name. Where Javinder was bound. Sikaner.'

When she heard that Grayson was unable to leave that day, Daisy felt a small pinch of guilt. It was because of her that he'd been injured and had to seek medical help. He'd gone to the hospital, Ahmed told her. She wondered if by any chance he would meet Dr Lane there. When she'd first arrived in town, she'd been tempted to drive to the medical centre, but almost immediately had thought better of it. Her old mentor was most likely retired and, in any case, it was sensible not to stir the past any more than she was already doing. Her guilt did not survive long; instead a strong sense of relief took over, relief that Grayson was still in Jasirapur. It meant he was close at hand and that gave her the confidence she needed after the frightening events of the last evening. She needed it this morning in particular. There was one more thing she had to do, one last visit she had to make.

The tonga dropped her a few streets from the bazaar, where, according to Daya Suri, the Bahndari house was situated. It took only minutes to learn from a passer-by the precise address she needed. She was lucky to find Mr Bahndari at home that morning, luckier still that his servant appeared unfazed by a stranger on the doorstep and ushered her into the house without question. Her name would mean nothing to his master, she knew, and she had to hope that curiosity would drive the elderly man to meet her.

The servant left her waiting in a large, airy room, its wide windows overlooking the river and open to any chance breeze that blew. It was clear her host was another wealthy man, but one with elegant and understated taste. She felt immediately at ease in the cool, quiet space, filled with jewel coloured hangings and the most delicately wrought porcelain. Between tapestries, the walls of the room were a soft white but, here and there, washed the palest green from the water's dancing reflection. The only sound was a gentle ripple from the river below.

A quiet footfall and an elderly gentleman, band-box smart, entered the room and walked towards her. Mr Bahndari, she presumed. He bowed his head in greeting and, without speaking, waved her towards a silk-covered ottoman. When he clapped his hands for the servant to bring cold drinks, Daisy had the curious feeling that she had already lived through this scene; it was an eerie echo of the visit she had paid to the Suris. Except that it wasn't. This man appeared courteous and un-threatening, and even at an advanced age, made a fine figure. It was hardly surprising that Parvati Rana had sought his protection all those years ago.

'You are a visitor to Jasirapur, Miss Driscoll?'

She agreed with the proposition but was careful to add, 'A returning visitor.' His eyebrows rose slightly. It was evident he thought Jasirapur an unlikely place to revisit. 'I was here ten years ago.'

'And did we meet then? Forgive me if I have forgotten our encounter.' He was clearly per-plexed at her appearance in his house, but far too well mannered to mention it.

She hastened to reassure him. 'We've never met before, Mr Bahndari, but I believe that we have acquaintances in common.' It was only fair to him to get to the point as soon as she could.

'Really? So you or your family are in business?'

'No, indeed not. My husband was a soldier in the 7th Cavalry. He had a very good friend in the regiment. His name was Anish Rana and I believe you knew him.'

A little breathlessly, she waited for her host's reaction. The man's face appeared suddenly much older and his eyes, though fixed on her, seemed to be looking elsewhere.

'Yes,' he said at last. 'I knew Anish well.'

There was a lengthy pause in which he seemed unwilling to add to this sparse statement. She began to think that, despite her host's gentle manner, she would discover nothing. Unless, of course, she was willing to trespass in what could be difficult territory.

'I believe you knew his mother?' No doubt she was breaking every rule of Indian hospitality but she had to find out what he knew.

He didn't answer. Instead, he asked his own question. 'Why are you here? Anish has been long dead.'

'I know, and I realise that to talk of him might distress you. I find it difficult too – I considered him a friend. We used to ride out together and he spoke of you. He told me how kind you had been, his benefactor, he said. Without you he could not have become an officer in the cavalry.'

Mr Bahndari gave a long, sad sigh, which whispered around the airy space and fled through the open window. 'That is true enough. His family refused him any help.'

'So he told me. But you were good to him and good to his mother.'

The man's eyes were once more distant, his gaze drifting through time. A gentle smile played on his lips. 'She was a most beautiful woman, you know. Kind, gentle. A loving person.'

Then, as he returned to the present, his gaze sharpened. 'Do you believe in *karma*, Miss Driscoll?'

'I know what it means.'

'It is a concept in Buddhism, in Hinduism too. I believe in *karma*. I believe that everyone makes their own. Sooner or later, your deeds catch up with you. *What goes around, comes around*, isn't that the Western phrase? Perhaps not so poetic but it expresses much the same idea. Parvati will be revenged, you can be sure.'

The words shocked Daisy. They seemed so out of keeping with the conversation, with the quiet room, the gentle river, the courteous old man.

'You look upset. You don't consider revenge a suitable emotion for a man of my age? But if you had known Anish's mother, you would understand.'

'I'm sure I would,' Daisy made haste to say. 'Certainly I understand her brother was not kind to her.'

'That is to express his misdeeds mildly. Ramesh Suri was brutal. When Parvati's husband died in the mud of the Somme, she was cast from her family. She was a widow, useless to them and helpless to defend herself. Suri seized her husband's assets, such as they were, and she was left with nothing. Then he had the hypocrisy to judge her when she took my protection. What else was she to do? Shroud herself in white and beg at the temple in order to stay alive?'

She noticed his fists clench. The conversation was headed in a troubling direction. After all these years, it was clear his pain was still raw. She felt ashamed. She hadn't intended to stir such unhappy memories for the poor man and sought hard to find another tack.

'I imagine that her husband's family were not able to help?'

He made a soft tutting sound between his lips. 'They had no interest in a poor widow once their son was killed. That is not the way in India.'

Daisy sipped from the iced glass and tried to decide how best to approach what she needed to ask. At length she said, 'It can't have helped that the Rana family lived some distance away.'

He looked blank and she tried again. 'I believe their family home is miles from Jasirapur.'

'The Rana family?' he repeated.

'Yes. Anish's grandparents. He told me once that his grandfather wanted to adopt him when his father was killed, but his mother insisted he stay with her. That couldn't have helped the relationship, I imagine.'

'That may well be true. I know very little of the family. I do know, though, that their name is not Rana.'

She felt confused. 'But Parvati, your friend–'

'My lover,' he insisted. 'I am proud of the fact.'

'Parvati's name was Rana.'

'It was the name she took when she married. It was the name that Karan took.'

She shook her head, mystified. 'I don't understand.'

'Why should you? To understand you must have experienced the overbearing nature of Indian family life. Parvati told me about it many years later, told me that Karan had wanted to break free. And to do that, he changed his name. I believe his father ruled some small princely state to the north of the region, and the boy's destiny was to succeed him.'

Anish's grandfather must have been a princely ruler and he a direct heir, she thought. No wonder he'd been such a proud man. Perhaps a little too proud. Was it partly pride that had driven him to such murderous action?

'But it wasn't what Karan wanted,' Mr Bahndari continued. 'There were many quarrels, I think, before he escaped and joined the Indian Army. He enlisted under a new name and that ensured he could not be traced. Unless he decided otherwise, he would never have to return home.'

'I see.' That was one small mystery solved, but elsewhere the mist was still clinging thickly. 'You mentioned that Parvati's husband came from a princely state. I suppose you have no idea of its name?'

'No idea, Miss Driscoll. I am sorry to disappoint you if that has been the purpose of your visit. I did not know of Karan Rana's existence until after his death. Then over the years, I heard something of his story, but not all, from Parvati.'

'Did she know his real name?'

'But naturally. They were married, a couple, even though he turned out to be the wickedest of husbands. You know, of course, that he betrayed her?'

Daisy nodded. The conversation was veering towards the awkward again. 'I would love to know Anish's real name.' She hoped her voice wasn't too eager, hoped it didn't betray how much the information meant to her. 'He was a dear friend, you see,' she went on, 'and I've always thought of him as Anish Rana. Now that I can't, it doesn't feel quite right. It seems as if I no longer know him.'

'His real name? That's simple enough. Verghese, that was his father's birth name. Verghese.'

CHAPTER 10

She was back on the street again, having thanked her host profusely and left him to his bittersweet memories. She had the clue she sought, the clue that might lead her to Anish's paternal family. Verghese was an unusual name in Rajasthan, and surely one she could trace. Mr Bahndari had said the family came from a princely state in the north; it was odd that, one way or another, the north of the region had become a constant refrain. It was where Grayson was bound as soon as his injured wrist permitted. But she would need something more tangible than a simple compass point. If she could identify exactly where the Vergheses hailed from, she might be able to persuade Grayson to take her with him. She must ask as many people as she could, and since the Bahndari house was a stone's throw from the bazaar, she would start there. She would follow Grayson's advice. If you wanted information, he maintained, head for the bazaar, in this case a jumbled collection of shops and stalls that filled the centre of Jasirapur. With a few questions here, a smile there, and several purchases on the way, you would almost certainly find what you were looking for. It was true that it hadn't worked for him recently, but she was sure she would be more fortunate.

She started with Sanjay. His shop, the *Johari Bazar*, had expanded to twice the size she remembered, but was still a treasure trove of colour and touch. She could have easily spent the rest of the morning in aimless wandering among its stacked shelves, losing herself in the beauty of the silks, the laces, the organzas, but she had serious business to conduct. Sanjay himself came hurrying forward, eager to serve a European customer with money to spend, but, when he drew close enough to recognise her, his footsteps lagged.

'Mrs Mortimer. A very good day to you.'

His eyes fell and he seemed to be studying the sanded floor closely, unsure she imagined of how best to address her. She had been Mrs Mortimer when he'd last seen her, but Gerald was dead and in the most abject of circumstances. The name of Mortimer had a history in Jasirapur and Sanjay would know every line of it. Not the sanitised version of events espoused by the military and endorsed by the ICS, but every true line.

'It's good to see you again, Sanjay,' she said a little too heartily. 'How have you been?'

He had learned some English since she last saw him but it seemed to have done little to make him comfortable with his English customer. Natural good manners, though, forced him to continue the conversation.

'I am well, Mrs Mortimer.' The name was slightly slurred as if he still couldn't decide what to call her. He had never known her by her single name and to use her first name would be desperately impolite, but he seemed relieved at her cheerfulness. He must have concluded rightly that she was not about to resurrect dead events. 'My shop is doing well.'

'I can see that. I think the choice is more dazzling than ever.'

Sanjay brightened even further. 'And how can I interest you this morning?'

'I'm looking forward to buying another length of silk – for the sari I've always wanted. But it won't be today.' The shopkeeper's face fell a little. 'I'll be back, I promise. But first I have a job to do.'

He looked intrigued. 'And what would that be, memsahib?' He still used the familiar term of respect. Old habits die hard, she thought, and independence will change things only very slowly.

'I'm trying to find someone,' she began. Sanjay continued to look interested. 'You might remember Anish Rana – he was a lieutenant with the 7th Cavalry?' Sanjay's expression changed. His face clouded and she was sure he took a step back.

'I know there was trouble.' That was putting it mildly. 'But I need to get in touch with Lieutenant Rana's family – his father's family, that is. Have you any idea where in Rajastahan I should start looking?'

'No, no, memsahib. I know nothing of the lieutenant.'

He sounded scared, she thought. If he did know anything, he was reluctant to tell. She tried another approach.

'I know that Anish had some old friends – they lived close to his family, I think, and I'd love to meet them. Their name is Verghese. It's not a common name, I think. You might know them or at least where I might find them.'

At this idea, Sanjay shook his head so violently that she feared it would twist from off his neck. She could see that she might have to accept defeat since there was little point in harassing the man. But she would try just one more throw. 'I suppose you don't know anyone else who–'

'No.' The negative could not have been more emphatic.

'That's a shame,' she said easily. 'But not of any real importance.'

He seemed relieved at her willingness to drop the subject. 'And the sari, memsahib?'

'I'll be back, Sanjay, I promise.'

She turned to go out of the shop and was surprised when he hurried after her. 'Memsahib, Mrs Mortimer, please, you are nice lady. Please to be careful.'

'I will be, Sanjay, don't worry.'

'No more questions then, memsahib. They will be bad for you.'

It was plainly a warning, a friendly warning this time, but the second she had received in just a few days. For an instant she wondered whether she should heed it, but if she did, she would discover nothing. A renewed sense that something bad was being hidden strengthened her determination. She gave the shopkeeper a sunny smile and walked out into the street. Slowly, she sauntered along the main thoroughfare, sharply aware of averted eyes and turned backs, then took one of the many narrow alleys that housed the poorer stalls. Something had happened since the morning she'd taken a lift with Grayson and spent a few happy hours buying trinkets here, but what it was she had no idea. She walked on, the stallholders in these meaner streets staring through her as though she did not exist. Their glance was not hostile, not even suspicious, but simply impassive.

She paused at a stall selling fruit. Should she buy some and try to strike up a conversation? For a moment after she came to a halt, she thought she heard footsteps, footsteps that stopped when hers did. That decided her to walk on, though it was most likely her imagination, unruly at the best of times. And this wasn't the best of times. Coming back to Jasirapur had turned into a troubling experience and quite different from what she'd imagined. She'd expected memories to come thick and fast and braced herself to face them, but it was clear that far more than memory was at play now. These last few days had seen the past itself resurrected. At least it felt that way. She had known wickedness before here in this town, thriving beneath a veil of normality. Now another corner of the same veil had been lifted and she sensed there was a new wickedness that had taken its place. But what it was or why it was happening, she could not guess.

She had reached the end of the second alley and was about to turn back when she felt it. A decided tug at the hem of her dress. She looked down, nervously scanning the dirt path to right and left.

The faint outline of a man glimmered in the dust. He was crouching in the shadows between two abandoned stalls and he was beckoning her to follow him. Had they been his footsteps she'd heard? Had he been stalking her all this time? Common sense told her to walk away and quickly, but instinct tantalised her with the thought that here might be what she was looking for.

It took courage to follow the stained white kurta, but Daisy had never lacked courage. The man led her further and further into the maze of small back streets, twisting and turning their way – to what? To a blank wall. There was no exit from this alley, which was barely a yard wide and had high walls of windowless houses on either side. No exit except by retracing her steps and who knew what now lay around the corner she had just turned. Her courage began slowly to seep away. It looked as though she had walked into a trap.

'You have money?' the man asked in a guttural whisper.

'Some.'

'Show,' he demanded.

She was being robbed. Really she shouldn't be surprised. She fished in her handbag and took out a handful of crumpled rupee notes, hoping he wouldn't snatch the purse and find what was left of the small amount of money she had brought to India. But he nodded, satisfied with what she had offered.

'I tell you.' So the money was for information. Not a robbery then. She became alert to the harsh tones of his voice.

'Verghese family very important,' he gasped

out. 'Rajah too important. Nobody speaks.'

Her instinct hadn't lied and excitement tangled her breath, but she tried to keep her voice calm. The man could flee at any moment. 'I'm beginning to realise that, but where does the family live?'

He gave a swift, furtive glance behind him, as though he expected an army of men to come tearing around the corner. 'Many miles away.'

'Yes, yes,' she said impatiently, 'but where? In Rajasthan? In the north?'

He nodded, his eyes wide with fear. He was more scared than she.

'Sikaner.' His voice was barely a whisper. 'Kingdom of Sikaner.'

There was a sudden noise of running feet and three or four thickset men – it was difficult to tell their number, since they were thundering towards her so quickly – appeared at the end of the narrow lane, wielding long wooden sticks. Her informant let out a yell of terror and, before her eyes, disappeared into fresh air, or so it seemed. The house on her immediate left had an odd-shaped door and, for an instant, she saw a chink of light illuminating its wooden rim. It must be a kind of trapdoor, she thought, and the man had vanished through it. Goodness knows where it led, but he must deliberately have brought her to a place where he knew he could make his escape.

She turned to face the men who had stopped only feet away. Shoulder to shoulder, they filled the narrow space. 'If you will excuse me, please.' She went to push through them, but a hand came out and barred her passage.

She pulled herself up to her full height and once again wished for extra inches. 'Allow me to pass this minute,' she commanded, feeling slightly ridiculous. With a heft of one of the *lathis* they carried, she could be despatched instantly and for ever.

The man who appeared to be leading the posse stood looking at her stonily. 'You ask no more questions. You go back to England.'

'I shall certainly return to England, but only when I'm ready.' She tried to sound unconcerned while her stomach was somersaulting.

'Now. You go back now.' He rasped out the words.

'I'm afraid that won't be possible.'

The men continued to stare at her in a tense stand-off that lasted for several minutes. Finally, their leader took a step towards her, so close that she could feel his hot breath on her face. He looked down at her and spat contemptuously to one side, missing the skirt of her dress by inches.

'Go–' the voice was brutal '–or you will suffer.'

He said something to his compatriots and they turned and walked back up the narrow alley, swinging their *lathis* from side to side. For some minutes, Daisy remained where she was. Her heart was beating wildly, her pulse uneven and her forehead beaded in perspiration. She was scared, thoroughly scared, but she hoped she hadn't shown it. It had been yet another random moment of terror, she thought, in a recurring theme that made no sense. Surely the questions she'd asked were innocuous enough, yet now she had received threats from both sides of Anish's family – she had to presume the men with sticks had something to do with the Vergheses. Were they employed directly or indirectly by Anish's grandfather? But whoever was behind this intimidation, it was vastly puzzling. Why was she being threatened?

And why was everyone else? She wasn't the only one to have been scared. Sanjay had tried to warn her and none of the stallholders in the bazaar would meet her eye. Her poor, scruffy informant had risked his life for a few rupee notes. She felt bad that she might have put him in danger and could only hope that the gang of roughs would not catch up with him. Slowly, she walked back through the main bazaar, past line after line of stallholders who busied themselves at her approach. Silence followed her every step. For the first time in India, she felt alien. An exile. It was a horrible feeling.

A desperation to see Grayson took hold and, despite the heat, she almost ran towards the building which housed the civil administration. She burst through the door of his office, her hair a limp tangle and her cheeks two scarlet stains. Mike Corrigan was at one of the twin desks and barely visible behind the ever familiar piles of paper. Of Grayson, there was no sign.

Mike looked up as she bumped her way across the room, overturning several boxes of files and finally coming to rest opposite him.

'What on earth's happened, Daisy?' He'd started up from the desk and was staring at her dumbfounded. She must look a mad witch, she thought, stepped from the pages of a child's fairy tale.

'Nothing,' she stuttered. 'At least–' then

changed her mind and finished weakly '–nothing really.'

'Here, you'd better sit down.' He hauled himself from behind the desk and found a wooden chair. Then limped to the small refrigerator that sat in one corner of the office and poured iced water into a glass. 'Drink this. You don't look at all well.'

'I got confused and lost my way in the bazaar. I'm finding the heat too much, I suppose, but I'm fine really – silly of me.'

She knew she sounded mindless, but if it stopped him probing, she was content. She didn't want him asking questions. That would mean confessing what she'd rather keep to herself: her visit to the Bahndari house, the enquiries she'd made in the bazaar, the gang and their threats. Right now she wasn't equal to explaining any of it, and certainly not equal to enduring the inevitable lecture. For some reason, too, she wanted to share her information with Grayson alone.

'Is Grayson around?' She tried to sound as though his whereabouts was unimportant.

'No,' he said curtly, his concern for her welfare forgotten for the moment. 'He's taken the jeep for a drive.'

'But why?'

'Why do you think? He needed to see how his wrist would hold up. He's determined to leave tomorrow, no matter what I say.'

She wondered if he was about to begin a new harangue, forcing her to join his hymn of disapproval, but instead he said, 'Why, was it important? Did you need to see him particularly?'

'Not really, no. I was in town – taking a break

from the bungalow. And then it got very hot and I got very confused. I thought I might travel back with him.'

'I've no idea how long he'll be but it's probably best not to wait. Why don't you grab a tonga and get some rest before dinner?' It was clear that Mike wanted her out of the office, but he couldn't help adding, 'If Grayson's got any sense, he'll park the jeep up and not touch it for the next few weeks.'

'I don't think that's likely.'

'You know what *I* think – if you chose to, you could persuade him to stay.'

'I don't wish to make you angry,' she said quietly, 'but you've misjudged the situation. I've no influence over Grayson.'

'I'm not angry, and I'm sorry I bit your head off earlier. But you're underestimating yourself.' He held up his hand to stay her protest. 'Look, I know things have been rocky between the pair of you. I'm his friend after all. He doesn't tell me much, but I can see for myself. Nevertheless, he listens to you. He respects you. If you wanted, you could stop him.'

'I wish that were true. I don't want him going into danger any more than you do.'

'It's surely worth a try, particularly now he's injured himself. And that was pretty stupid – walking into a wall.'

She did a quick think. Grayson evidently didn't want the true nature of last night's escapade to be known, and she wondered why. Mike was a close friend and the colleague he was depending on.

'It was a silly accident,' she said, 'but it won't

stop him. You know Grayson. He's come to India to do a job, and he'll do it.'

'And, while he's doing it, he'll come off badly, if I'm any judge.'

'But you'll be here to support him?' She realised as she asked the question that she wasn't entirely sure.

'Of course, I will. Haven't I always been?'

A memory, hideously graphic, flashed into her mind. Mike had taken a dreadful beating in the Sweetman affair and she felt ashamed to have doubted him. 'Yes,' she said warmly, 'you have, and suffered for it.'

'So did Sweetman, if that's who you're thinking of.' He grinned across at her, looking much younger and far less intimidating.

'Running him to ground was quite a feat.'

'It was an adventure. I know I got mashed up, but it was worth it.' He relaxed back into his chair, still smiling. 'Wartime in London had real excitement, didn't it? The IRA sending spies over from Ireland in droves, and Germany constantly trying to infiltrate our network and just as constantly failing. Then those Indian chaps your husband...' He trailed off, no doubt remembering, she thought, that one of those Indian chaps had murdered Gerald. 'Anyway, they had an agenda of their own. So plenty to keep us busy,' he finished briskly.

'And you're still busy. You've travelled halfway round the world for *this* adventure.'

He pulled down the corners of his mouth in a gesture of disgust. 'To find a missing employee, who will no doubt walk back into the office at any time?'

'Grayson doesn't think so.'

'Then Grayson is wrong. Just this once, he's wrong. Javinder Joshi will turn up sooner or later, you'll see, and we'll have spent precious time and energy looking for him. And Grayson will have spent far more – his safety, for instance.'

It was difficult to counter Mike's pessimism, but she tried. 'He told me this trip was a last chance for you to work together, and that has to be a good thing surely.'

'But we won't be working together, will we? Grayson will be in the field and I won't. He's about to charge off into the unknown, while I'm stuck in this stuffy little box, weighted down by a ton of paper and sweating hour upon hour, with nothing to show for it.'

He had a point and she wondered why Grayson hadn't ordered things more agreeably. 'Perhaps if you told him how you felt, he'd change his mind. There must be someone who can staff the office while you're both away, someone you can rely on.'

He was looking at her queerly. 'That wouldn't do at all.'

'But why not? You haven't been able to discover anything useful, have you?' She wanted very much to see the old, happier Mike back. 'Why not go with Grayson? You have the perfect excuse now that his wrist is injured. I'd feel much happier if you were alongside.'

'Thank you, Daisy. That's nice of you. But he's made up his mind. He's travelling solo and really I shouldn't expect anything else.'

'I don't see why.'

'Don't you?' His face had an ugly twisted look

again. 'I didn't come to India for one last adventure, whatever Grayson likes to think. I came because he needed me and, in recent years, I've always been at his shoulder. But, once we're back in London, that will be it. He won't need me any longer. No one will.'

'What do you mean?'

'Put simply, I'm a has-been, my dear. The service thinks it and so does Grayson, though he's too polite to say so.'

'I'm sure that's not true.' She wasn't sure, but she felt his hurt acutely and words were all the consolation she had.

'And I'm just as certain that it is. They've pushed me out. And for what? To make way for men returning from India. That's a neat irony, isn't it? They're younger, you see. Not quite so battered. The fact that I've been injured in service is unfortunate. I've played my part and now I can be abandoned.'

His bitterness went deep, very deep. It went a long way to explaining his erratic moods and the fact that he'd turned on her so fiercely. In his view, he was doing all he could to support Grayson even as the axe hovered over him, while she was too busy with her own petty affairs to do the same.

'I can see how difficult it must be, when you've devoted your life to the service,' she ventured.

'Can you? I wonder... A lot of bad things have happened to you, I know. But you're still young and you've time to turn your life around. You'll marry again – yes.' He nodded his head, as she started to protest. 'You might not think so now, but you will. You'll marry and have a family and live a whole different life. I've never had a wife, never had children. You don't miss a family, you see, not while the work keeps coming. People who love you would be a burden when you're putting your life on the line. It's when the adrenaline stops humming that you realise what you've given away.'

'But you've enjoyed your work. You've enjoyed it hugely – you said so. There are bound to be good memories,' she reminded him.

'How good are they really though? How much do they compensate? I can live without a wife and children. God knows, I've done it for long enough. But without a country – that's a whole different matter.'

'Without a country?' she echoed.

'I'm Irish, or hadn't you noticed?'

She knew, of course, that he was Irish. The pale Celtic skin, the red hair, would have blazoned it clearly enough, even if Grayson had never told her.

She was perplexed. 'But you have a country – Ireland.'

'It's no longer mine.' The stern certainty robbed the words of their tawdry flourish. 'I've betrayed my country, didn't you know? That's what many of my fellow countrymen think. I've betrayed Ireland by working for Britain. And for what exactly? Where has my loyalty to a foreign land actually got me?'

When she said nothing, he muttered, 'Not a reciprocal loyalty, that's for sure. My so-called employers didn't think twice. When the need came, they jettisoned me like some worn-out piece of machinery. That's why they call it the scrap heap, isn't it?'

He gave a bark of angry laughter, then shuffled the papers about on his desk and looked towards the door. He seemed to be regretting his outburst and hoping she would leave. She couldn't fight such coruscating feelings, no one could, and she'd no wish to continue their argument. But she still wanted to speak to Grayson. Perhaps if she waited a little longer he would return, and she could tell him of the trouble in the bazaar. She was calm enough now to do it sensibly.

She wandered over to the far wall where a map of Rajasthan spun its colours in the bright light, and stood studying it for a while. She couldn't find what she was looking for. Did she dare ask Mike in his present mood? She dared.

'Where is the Kingdom of Sikaner?'

Her voice shattered what had grown into a forbidding silence. Mike's head shot up and he dropped his pen. 'Why do you want to know?' His voice was filled with suspicion.

'No real reason. I heard the name today and it was new to me.'

She tried to sound casual but didn't entirely succeed. He was looking askance at her, on edge and probably wondering what she meant to do next.

'I liked the sound of it,' she added lightly.

She was lying and he knew it. But if she were honest with him, it would spell disaster. She needed to keep Mike ignorant if her plans were to have any chance of success. It was better she left now. She'd never been adept at game playing and the longer she stayed, the more likely it was that she would blurt out what was in her mind. There was no hope for it; she would have to wait until evening before she saw Grayson.

When she said as much, Mike agreed a little too quickly. 'I'll see you back in Tamarind Drive,' he said, his voice oddly flat.

'Let's hope it isn't curried chicken again.' She was trying to lighten the mood, but his sole response was a brusque nod.

CHAPTER 11

Grayson came in halfway through the evening. Ahmed had left them a cold meal and Daisy had put hers aside, preferring to wait rather than eat with a glum Mike. She saw the bandaged wrist straight away.

'Dr Lane hasn't lost his skill,' Grayson said. He was smiling, despite the fatigue that shadowed his face. 'A pretty good job, don't you think?'

'It's good enough, but not for driving any distance.' She felt an urge to put her arms around him and keep him safe.

'Whether it is or not, it will have to do.'

He skimmed his *topi* across the room to land perfectly on one of the curling branches of the coat stand. It was pointless to remonstrate, she thought. When he'd made a decision, he was the most stubborn man on earth. Instead, she walked over to the table. 'I'm starving and you must be too. Come and eat.'

He took a seat opposite her and lifted the top plate. Curried eggs sat on a large bed of salad with a basket of spiced crusty bread waiting to one side. 'Hey, this looks good. Is it all for us?'

'Mike has already eaten. I think he's reading in his room.'

Grayson nodded. 'I'll go and see him later. I need to hand over several keys.'

'So you really are going tomorrow?' Not that she'd had any doubts.

'I must, despite a few bad moments at the wheel. I have to admit the wrist hurt like hell this morning, but thanks to the doc, it's now more or less stable.'

'How is Dr Lane?'

'Looking a little older, but then aren't we all? I was lucky to catch him – the hospital is closing next week for good.'

'I'm surprised he's still there.'

'He seems just as surprised. He expected to leave months ago. This last year there have been huge changes, of course. I don't know what will happen to the cantonment – the site is enormous. But virtually all the soldiers have left and most of the officers too. The colonel still seems to be knocking around but not for much longer. I think the Foresters have a berth reserved on the next P&O.'

'Where will the doctor go?'

'I don't know. I don't think he knows. There's nowhere else he calls home.'

'Poor Dr Lane. I can't imagine him living anywhere else but India.' It didn't matter who you were, she thought, the new dispensation had turned lives upside down.

Grayson poured two glasses of juice and handed her one. 'Here try this. It's pomegranate. Ahmed's speciality.'

'I expect the doctor counselled you against driving,' she said, 'but you're going to disobey him.'

'I am. But don't despair. I know better now where I'm going. I won't have to blunder around, driving miles out of my way and getting nowhere.'

Daisy stopped eating, half a curried egg speared on her fork. 'You've found out where Javinder was headed?' She was amazed. The mystery had seemed insoluble.

'I've found out where he intended to go – not quite the same thing. He may never have got there. He could have branched off at any point. But at least it gives me somewhere to start. If he never arrived, I'll find out. Then I can probably pick up his trail by asking around – working backwards, as it were.'

'But how–'

'Good old Dr Lane again. He sends his best wishes by the way. He was delighted when I told him you'd qualified as a nurse and become a sister no less. If you've got time while I'm away, you might want to call and say hello. I'm sure he'd love to hear about your time at Bart's.'

She had been busy weaving very different plans and for a moment, the suggestion that she visit the hospital distracted her. But only for a moment. Grayson's news could be of the utmost importance.

'What did Dr Lane tell you?' She tried to keep her voice unconcerned.

'Apparently Javinder went to him for a check-up before he set off travelling. He told the doctor he was heading north – to a small, princely state.'

'How strange.' Grayson's eyebrows formed a question mark. 'It's just that the north of Rajasthan keeps being mentioned,' she explained. 'And small princely states keep appearing too.'

'And when did they appear to you today? You've been playing detective again, and after I told you to walk away.'

His face had clouded and she tried to mollify him. 'I did listen to what you said – honestly.'

'But then went your own way in any case,' he said roughly.

'It was worth it though. *I* made a crucial discovery too. The Ranas aren't the Ranas.'

He pushed his plate away in an exasperated gesture and she hurried on. 'Karan Rana changed his identity when he ran away from home. He joined the Indian Army under a false name. His real name was Verghese and his family came from a princely state in the north of the region. Well, they still do. It must be Anish's grandfather who is the ruler there. He's a rajah, I think.'

Grayson's frown deepened. He was expecting something bad, she could see, something he wouldn't like one bit. 'And why is this important?' He was still trying to fend off the inevitable.

'I know where the family home is. Exactly where it is. You said I'd never find it,' she reminded him.

'And where is it?'

'Where was Javinder bound?' she parried.

He scraped back his chair in a gesture of impatience. 'I doubt you'd recognise the name.'

'Tell me.'

He groaned. 'It's a small state called Sikaner.'

'Bullseye!'

At this shout of joy, his deep blue eyes clouded. He had half risen, but now sank back onto the chair. 'Let me guess. Sikaner just happens to be where the Verghese family home is situated.'

'Right first time.' She couldn't quite keep the crowing from her voice.

'And so...'

'And so when you leave tomorrow, I'm coming with you.'

'That's one thing you won't be doing.' Several minutes had passed before he spoke. It had taken him time to digest what she was telling him.

She got up and marched around the table to stand at his elbow. 'And why not?'

He looked up at her, genuinely perplexed. This identity business had gone beyond obsession, he thought. 'You're not seriously suggesting you come with me? To the back of beyond through God knows what dangerous territory – and for what precisely?'

She didn't move an inch and he could feel the warmth of her body very close. It was disturbing but it wouldn't change his mind.

'Why ask the question when you know the answer?' Her voice was unfaltering.

He slewed round in his seat. 'For once, Daisy, think about this rationally. What possible clue could there be, even if we were to find the Ranas, or whatever their name is?'

'But that's the nature of clues, isn't it? You don't

know what they look like until you see them. I would know what I was looking for when I saw it. I shouldn't have to tell you that, you're an intelligence officer.'

It was said in a teasing tone but he knew very well it masked an iron determination. He was equally determined.

'I'm glad you can joke about it,' he said easily, 'but consider. Anish's father died in the First World War. By my reckoning, that's at least thirty years ago. What of his could have survived that length of time?'

She shook her head in silent disagreement and he went on, trying to reason with her. 'Let's say for argument's sake that some of Karan's possessions did remain intact, why would they have found their way back to his father's house? And if just possibly they had, why would his father keep anything? The boy abandoned his home, abandoned his name and his inheritance. Once he left, his father never saw him again. The old man might have discovered his son's new identity, probably did as you say he wanted to adopt the child Karan left behind, but that offer was rejected, wasn't it? So he had nothing of his son. Karan had ceased to exist for him – like Parvati for her brother. Why then would he keep anything of his, *if* there had been anything to keep in the first place?'

'People do,' she said stubbornly. 'People do keep things. He's an old man and you can't say how he'd behave. It may be that he felt betrayed, let down, but he may also have grieved at Karan's death and part of that grieving may have been to treasure what he had left of his son. Particularly when it became clear that he'd never know his grandson.'

She was unyielding and he began to despair that he would ever make her see sense. But he must keep trying. 'So the old man retains a few keepsakes to remind him of his son. But how likely is it that any of them relate to Karan's time in Brighton? And even if they did, how likely is it that they would refer to your mother?'

He stood up as he spoke, and took her firmly by the shoulders, trying to impress on her the futility of the quest. 'Think about it. Is he likely to have written home with hospital tittle-tattle? Nurse Driscoll is walking out with Joe Bloggs, or Nurse Driscoll is sweet on Tom Smith?'

'It wouldn't be Joe Bloggs though, would it, and that's why I think he may have mentioned it in his letters home.'

He could feel his face going blank. He had lost her.

'Have you noticed the colour of my skin, Grayson?' she went on.

Of course, he had noticed. It was quite, quite beautiful – a light olive that looked as though it had been spread with cream.

'And my hair,' she continued. 'So dark it could almost be black. My mother's photograph shows her as an English rose, so where did my colouring come from? Another Englishman? Somehow I don't think so. I believe my father was Indian.'

He felt his jaw slacken. The thought had never occurred to him.

'Do you see now?' she asked triumphantly. 'If my mother had an affair with an Indian soldier,

Karan Rana would have taken notice. He would have written about it because it was so out of the ordinary. It was shocking, in fact. Even today it would be shocking, but at the time it would have been an enormous transgression.'

He let his hands drop from her shoulders and walked towards the open door. The veranda and the fresh night air beckoned to him. He needed to clear his head, needed to get some purchase on reality. He was a long way from accepting the leap of faith Daisy had just made. Then he saw her face, drawn and uncertain, and realised with a shock that she'd interpreted his going as rejection. She must be fearful that her supposed parentage would make a difference to the way he thought of her. He walked back.

'There's no way you can be certain,' he insisted. 'You could just as easily be the daughter of Joe Bloggs. The English are a mongrel race and not everyone is an English rose. There are plenty with a skin that matches yours.'

She shook her head in denial and he tried to keep the exasperation from his voice. 'That's an inconvenient fact, isn't it? It doesn't fit the fantasy you've weaved around yourself. It's easier than accepting you'll never know your father. And what difference would it make to you if you found a name lurking deep in Sikaner? What would that tell you about your mother? That she had an affair, conceived you and died two years later. Her history would remain the same.'

'Now you're just being brutal.'

He could see the tears ready to spill. She pushed past him and marched through the door and out onto the veranda. In a few seconds, he'd followed. It was probably the wrong thing to do, but he couldn't leave her this unhappy.

'I'm sorry you're upset,' he began, 'but I'm trying to make you see the truth of the situation.'

She took a few deep breaths and then turned to him. 'Just for once, Grayson, I want to make you see *my* truth. It's not as simple as you suggest. But let's call my father Joe Bloggs. If I found Mr Bloggs, I might also discover where my mother met him, what kind of relationship they had, how they parted, why he never tried to claim me after her death.'

She stood looking straight ahead, absorbing, it seemed, the cool peace of the garden, but her body was unnaturally stiff and her hands locked tightly together. When she spoke again, there was real anguish in her voice. 'Can't you see that I want to know why nobody ever wanted me?'

He was swiftly beside her and took hold of the rigid knuckles, smoothing her hands soft. 'I do see. Really I do. But walking into danger alongside me isn't going to help you get answers.'

She shrugged away from him. 'What's the difference? I'll be walking into danger if I stay here.'

'I don't think so, not any more. I'm pretty sure the Suris won't bother you again – as long as you keep clear of them.'

'It's not just the Suris,' she said in a low voice.

He was instantly suspicious, his antennae bristling sharply. What else had she been up to? She was beginning to be a liability, and not for the first time on this trip he wished he'd left her safely in Brighton. He waited with some trepidation.

‘I found Parvati’s lover.’

‘What!’

‘Mr Bahndari. But don’t worry, he is a charming man. He didn’t at all mind talking to me. He was the one who told me Karan Rana’s real name.’

‘So that’s where you got your information. No wonder you didn’t explain.’

‘Yes. But it was afterwards...’ Her voice trailed off. ‘In the bazaar. I tried to find out where the Verghese family came from.’

‘Apparently you were successful.’

‘Only after I paid a man to tell me. He must have needed the money badly because he was thoroughly scared. As soon as he’d got his rupees, he melted away. There was a gang after him, you see. They didn’t get him but–’

‘But they got you? Threatened you?’

‘Yes.’

What felt very like fury coursed through him. It was almost as if she had some kind of death wish, pig-headedly walking into the most threatening of situations. It was worse even than that. Out of nowhere she’d created those situations herself, and was still creating them, even when she recognised how much she was putting herself in danger. He tried to keep his voice measured, though the more he thought of it, the more angry he grew.

‘If anything bad does happen to you while I’m away, it will be entirely your fault. You knew I had to leave and yet you laid yourself open to reprisals from whoever is behind this gang. It’s unfair of you, Daisy. I don’t need this additional worry.’

For a moment she seemed abashed, but not for long. ‘I don’t expect you to worry. I don’t want you to worry. You're not my keeper. You're not even my lover any more.'

'Is this what these stupid alarms are all about?'

She gaped at him and he wished he hadn't said that. Since coming to India they had more or less managed to put to one side the touchy subject of their relationship, but now he had opened the proverbial can of worms.

'No,' she said, her voice steely. 'It's not about you, it's not about us. It's about me. It's about me wanting to know more than anything in the world where I fit. And neither you nor anybody else is going to stop me.'

Over the past few minutes their voices had become loud without their realising it, until Mike stumbled through the door and onto the veranda. 'What on earth's going on here? You woke me up.' He gave what Grayson thought was a stagey yawn.

'Sorry. A slight disagreement, that's all.'

Mike looked from one to the other and Grayson knew he would have to admit at least some of the problem. 'Daisy thinks she may have found what she's been looking for. It's in Sikaner and she wants to come with me.'

Mike wrapped his pyjama jacket close to his body as though raising a shield. 'Why are you talking about Sikaner? It's a complete nonentity of a state. Not to say miles away, and with a hugely difficult journey.'

'I haven't had the chance to tell you, but it's where I believe Javinder was travelling, and where I've decided to head for.'

'Did you pull Sikaner out of a hat?' His colleague seemed fixated on the name.

'It might seem like that but Doc Lane put me on to it.'

'And you believed him. Come on, Grayson, he's an old man. Doddering, I hear.'

'Not that doddering and I think he's right. I'm setting off for there early tomorrow, but without Daisy.'

'I should think so – if you must go.'

Daisy had so far remained silent, but at this she decided to make her presence felt. Grayson had to step back as she carved a path between the two friends. 'You can do as you wish, but then so can I. If you won't let me travel with you, I'll follow. I'm quite able to hire a driver. Let's hope you're the professional you say you are, then I shouldn't get lost.'

'That's ridiculous,' Mike turned to him. 'You can't go, not like this. You'll be putting yourself in more danger with a woman trailing after you. She needs to stay in Jasirapur. She'll be safe enough here.'

Grayson was unsure how much to disclose. 'You won't know, but there have been threats made to Daisy. I won't go into them except to say that they're serious.'

'Threats she's brought on herself, I don't doubt. I'm beginning to understand how she operates.'

'However they've occurred, they're still threats.'

Mike walked over to him and grasped his arm. 'I'm here,' he said with emphasis. 'Daisy will be safe with me. I promise I'll look after her.'

Grayson felt conflicted. The last thing he wanted was to take Daisy with him. And it would have to be with him. He couldn't have her trailing behind in whatever vehicle she managed to commandeer. Not only would it make the two of them look foolish, it would increase their mutual danger. And ruin any plans he'd made to travel quietly and arrive without warning.

But he needed no distraction on this journey and travelling with Daisy would provide it in spades. They would be thrown together in the most intimate way, close companions not just for minutes but for hours on end. Apart from their dinner together, he'd kept their encounters brief and with Mike never far from sight. But that evening at the Paradise was warning enough. He'd found himself unable to keep his eyes from her, had crumbled at the feel of her hand and the sweet smell of her hair. At the moment, he was angry but if past experience were a guide, his anger wouldn't last. He'd never been able to withstand her charm for long.

He was hugely reluctant to have her alongside, but just as reluctant to leave her behind. He wasn't at all sure that she would be safe in Jasirapur, even under Mike's protection. His friend was no longer as strong or as capable as he'd once been and had no idea what Daisy had been up to. Grayson suddenly became conscious of the ominous silence that had fallen while he'd been preoccupied. Mike and Daisy, he saw, were at opposite ends of the room and glaring stonily at one another. He couldn't imagine how they'd fare if they were left together.

'She'll have to come with me,' he said in a burst of decisiveness. He saw Daisy's face clear and an almost beatific smile appear on her face. This trip meant everything to her.

But not to Mike. 'So what it comes down to is that you don't trust me. I'm too old, too infirm, is that it? I'm in India for the donkey work, to plough endlessly through papers and be at the end of a phone if you chance to call. But I'm not good enough for anything else.'

'Mike, please–' He put out a detaining hand but his friend had turned on his heel and marched back into the bedroom. The door shut with a loud slap.

Daisy's face was lit with an anticipation he couldn't share. He felt his lips compress into a thin, hard line– 'This had better work,' he said.

CHAPTER 12

It was barely dawn when they set off. The air was blissfully cool with a mist that hung low over the earth's tapestry of browns and ochres. Broad expanses of barley, wheat and gram stretched on either side of the road, the landscape as flat as a man's hand and running to a horizon so distant it could be the edge of the world. Until the last straggle of houses was left behind, the jeep managed little more than a crawl. The vehicle itself was old and crotchety, but even travelling slowly, it was not the most comfortable of rides, the road bumping and bucking every which way. Daisy was not about to complain. She'd fought hard to come on this journey and, whatever the outcome, she was convinced it would be worth the discomfort. If its only result was the death of her dream, she would at least know there was nothing more to find. She would relinquish her search. Grayson refused to believe it, but she'd promised and she would keep the promise.

He sat still and stiff beside her, his eyes fixed resolutely ahead. He had given her barely a glance since they left Jasirapur. Instead, his whole concentration was on navigating his way round and through wandering livestock and lumbering wagons, and on guiding the vehicle over the worst of the road's craters. She imagined the danger of an early puncture was uppermost in his mind. They passed through small village after small village, thatched clay huts speckling the roadside and beyond. The women were already up tending fires, fetching water for washing, churning buttermilk for breakfast. The smell of burning dung drifted towards them as they bumped their way through the small settlements. You could be nowhere else but India, she thought.

They had been travelling nearly an hour before he broke his silence. 'The road is getting rougher with each mile and at this rate, we won't get to Sikaner by nightfall.' He spoke without expression. 'We'll have to camp overnight.'

She didn't find the prospect enticing. 'How far away are we?'

'Far enough – around three hundred and fifty miles. But I don't want to be driving after dark and if the road is as bad as this all the way, we're looking at a day and a half for the journey. Unless something delays us further.'

He continued to speak in a voice devoid of colour, and she knew herself unforgiven. But at least he was talking. Three hundred and fifty miles was a long way to sit in angry silence.

'Did you manage to find out much about Sikaner before we left?' she ventured.

He seemed to weigh up whether he wanted to answer or preferred to stay mute, but then he said, 'There wasn't much to find. It's a small princely state and quite typical – bigger than a cow pasture but not much more than twenty square miles.'

Her brows drew together in surprise. 'That *is* small. I've always thought of Indian princes as being immensely wealthy.'

'You mustn't confuse size with wealth. States vary hugely in both. There are kingdoms ruled by some of the richest men in the world with populations as large as European countries. They're the ones you'll have heard of. But there are princes who may own little land but still enjoy great wealth and wield considerable influence.'

He seemed to be talking more easily now and she worked to keep the conversation going. 'Is that the case now though? The influence, I mean.'

'Princely power has waned enormously, it's true. Ever since the Viceroy managed to corral most of the states into joining the Indian union. And that can only be a good thing. Some of the rulers were progressive but most often they were anything but. Generally, the system was rotten.'

'They must be finding it difficult, though, to fit into the new India.'

'There's a role for them if they want it. The country needs efficient administrators, people who are used to handling the affairs of state. But not all of them are eager to contribute and there are still some hotheads around. That's what concerned Mountbatten most, I think – that they'd try to retain their privileges by launching the odd adventure. That would have left their towns looking like charnel houses.'

'And Sikaner?'

'Apparently it has a ruler who is holding out. Democracy isn't to his liking, which is hardly surprising. But it's what he's doing about it that's the worrying thing.'

'You think he's launching one of those adventures?'

'I think he may be planning to and in the meantime fomenting trouble. In fact, I'm almost sure of it. In the wake of Partition, it's too easy for him. Tension between Hindus and Moslems is high. It's existed for centuries, of course, but the recent appalling slaughter has made things so much worse.'

'You've never really talked about that.'

'It's too sickening to speak of. There's no official tally of the numbers killed or raped or maimed. Some have said it was over a million and that wouldn't surprise me. All I know is that it has to be one of the vilest moments in Indian history.'

She had known about the atrocities, of course. The papers and radio bulletins had been full of the news, but from the safety of London it had seemed short-lived – a quick flurry of violence and then peace. She could see now how naïve that view was.

'Could the police do nothing?' But even as she asked the question, she knew the answer. She remembered the riot in Jasirapur and how the military had had to be called in. This must have been a thousand times worse.

'They were overwhelmed. Completely. And so much of the violence was clandestine, they had no chance of winning the battle. It was wanton, senseless murder. Maybe a man wearing a Sikh turban would be attacked or a Moslem with a beard. Death in a flash, and before you could say "knife", a body would be dying in the street and the perpetrator melting away into a maze of alleys, with every door shut and no one in sight.'

She felt her stomach churn slightly. She knew that feeling. Of being a victim, of being alone, the door shut in her face. She had been lucky though. These poor souls had not.

'And you think that's happening in Sikaner?'

'The picture doesn't look good. There's a pattern to the violence. It's not random and senseless this time. Instead, individuals from certain groups have been picked out and hunted down. The killing and rape is systematic, the work of a group who possesses a command structure. The planning appears methodical and, since the number of deaths is growing, it's evidently an ambitious plan. Maybe there's worse to come. But the killers have to be paid for their services and it's the person who is paying that I need to find.'

'And Javinder...'

'Javinder too. Once I find who is behind the unrest, I'm sure I'll find him. He was almost certainly on to something and, in some way, he's been stopped.'

She didn't want to think in what way that might

be and relapsed into silence. The sun that had been a mere glow filtering through mist was now shining in earnest and when Grayson suggested they stop in the village they were passing, she happily agreed. They could buy water there and fresh fruit for lunch.

'Stay in the car,' he ordered when he'd parked the jeep. His voice had regained its chill. 'I won't be long and I don't want any trouble.'

She agreed meekly enough. She'd no wish to jeopardise the rest of the trip by quarrelling with him over something so trivial. It was clear she was most definitely on probation. But she wished she could have gone with him. It was almost lunchtime and they could have found somewhere to eat the picnic that Ahmed had made for them. Grayson had been adamant, though, that she stay in the car, remain inconspicuous, and she was left wondering why that was important.

For a time she remained where she was, while the air in the stationary vehicle grew slowly more stifling. He seemed to be taking an uncommonly long time to buy a bag of mangoes. She fidgeted on the hot cracked leather trying to find a cooler part of the seat, then stuck her head out of the window in the hope of a passing breeze. But an undiluted wave of heat was her only reward. She peered through the windscreen at the street ahead, then into the driving mirror at the road behind. Not a sign of Grayson. After ten minutes, she'd had enough, probation or no probation. She slid from her seat.

She wandered slowly along the road in the direction he'd taken. The village was larger than most and there were plenty of stalls to interest her. Even better, they were sheltered from the sun, now directly overhead, by wide, bleached canopies. She moved from one patch of shade to another, still uncomfortably hot, but her skin no longer raw. Most of the stalls she passed were filled to brimming with an array of fruit and vegetables, so why had Grayson not stopped at one of these? Several stalls displayed what seemed like a hundred different spices and one shop, in particular, she found fascinating. It was filled with bright dyes, Day-Glo colours – yellow, red, cerise, purple, turquoise – that fought each other in a clash for supremacy. The stunning rainbow of colour took all her attention and she walked further and further into the shop. She made sure, though, that every so often she glanced towards the entrance, on the lookout for Grayson's tall figure returning to the jeep. But the next time she raised her eyes, her breath caught painfully in her throat.

She shrunk back, trying to melt into the very fabric of the shop. The form she'd seen had not been Grayson's, but that of another man. A man she was beginning to know well. Dalip Suri. Her mind raced. What could he be doing in this anonymous village? The place was nowhere near Megaur, in fact in quite the opposite direction. And neither was it on the road to any larger town that he might be headed for. So why here of all places – unless he was after her? Less than two days ago, he'd tried to run her down and not succeeded, so had he been following her ever since in the hope of making another attempt? For a moment, her mind went blank and she had no idea how to react. Then a chaotic whirr began. Should she rush from the shop and make for the safety of the jeep? If she did, he might turn his head at any moment and see her. Or should she keep hidden and hope to grab Grayson on his return? She wasn't sure how successful that would be.

Several seconds passed before she made any move. Then she began slowly to inch her way towards the front of the shop. She would crouch down behind the shelter of the canvas awning. If she moved with caution, she would have a vantage point from where to check the street. But she was only halfway towards the entrance when a shadow fell across the front of the shop. It was Suri, and he seemed poised to come in. Hastily, she retreated and bumped into the shopkeeper busy unpacking a new box of dyes.

'Sorry,' she gasped out, 'is there anywhere...' She looked frantically towards the small door at the rear. It boasted the English word 'Private'.

'You are sick, memsahib?'

'Yes, sick, very sick.'

It wasn't an exaggeration. Her stomach was twisting horribly and she felt water beading her forehead. The shopkeeper looked alarmed and immediately ushered her through the door to his private quarters. She turned into a rudimentary bathroom and fastened the lock. Leaning back against the cool wood, she breathed long and deep. The brown spotted mirror on the wall opposite showed her face a ghastly shade of grey. No wonder the shopkeeper had been swift to act. But how was she to get out of this? Suri might not after all come into the shop, but without leaving her sanctuary, she couldn't know. And she couldn't stay here long or the shop owner would become concerned and set up a fuss. She looked around. Beneath the mirror was a cracked basin and to one side, a hole in the ground which served as the toilet. Other than that, nothing. Then she saw the stool, half hidden behind the door. If she dragged it to the window, already open to allow what fresh air there was to circulate the room, could she escape that way? The aperture was small and once she'd clambered onto the stool she could see there was no possibility of getting through the narrow space. But from this angle, she could also see that the larger side window had a catch that could be reached. It was stuck from being unused for so long and she had to tug and tug before she felt any movement. The stool began to rock from side to side, threatening to overbalance on the uneven floor. It was not going to stop her though. She was gradually prising the window open.

'Memsahib, are you all right?'

'Yes,' she called back, trying not to sound as breathless as she felt. 'Much better, thank you. I'll be out in just a minute.'

'Please to take your time, lady.'

In several more minutes, she thought, the poor man would be breaking down the door. A final tug with one hand and a push with the other and the window opened an inch, then another inch, and then just sufficiently for her slim form to slide through. She hadn't thought what she would find on the other side but luck was with her. It was a small fall to the ground and she made it without mishap.

She was in a narrow lane which ran parallel to the main street and was bisected by several even narrower lanes. Several of the shops had rear entrances and almost at the same time as she noticed this, a man came out of one of the doors further along the road and propped himself against it. He appeared to present no immediate threat but instinctively she flattened herself against the wall. He was talking to someone inside the building, smoking a cigarette and waving it this way and that as he made a forceful point. She edged away from him and when he ducked his head inside the shop again, presumably to berate his companion, she ran at an angle towards one of the cramped passages on her right. An archway stood guardian and she passed through it into deep shadow. When she looked back, two figures had appeared at the rear of the shop. The second man was doing the arguing now and in response, the shopkeeper threw his cigarette away into the gutter. A gesture of anger, or was it disgust? She didn't wait to find out, for the second man was Dalip Suri.

She hurried along the passageway of shuttered houses, avoiding the inches-deep rubbish and sidestepping several stray dogs. A child ran out from what appeared to be a slit in one wall and contemplated her solemnly. His mother's voice sounded in the distance and he gave her one last long stare and ran off. Daisy walked on. She knew she must find a way back to the jeep. She'd been lost before in Jasirapur's maze of small streets and alleys, and the memory of how that had ended was still with her. There was nothing hostile here though, just silence and the hot, heavy air. She consciously relaxed into a slower walk. As long as she was travelling away from Suri, she thought. She was unsure why she felt such fear of him. He'd tried to run her down, that was reason enough she supposed, but it had happened because she'd been asking awkward questions. She was asking them no longer, so why hunt her down? It made no sense. There had to be something more and she had a strong suspicion that Grayson knew what it was. He'd said nothing directly, but she was certain he believed the Suris were involved in Javinder Joshi's disappearance. It seemed most unlikely, but then she wasn't an agent in secret intelligence. Whatever the trouble, though, she was now well and truly caught in it, and, if Suri saw her, she wouldn't like to bet on her chances of disappearing alongside Javinder.

The passage had come to an end at a junction and she was faced with turning either to the right or the left. Where was she in relation to the main street? Right, she thought, I need to take the right fork. She looked at her watch. The minutes were racing by and she should be back at the jeep. She'd been gone nearly half an hour and Grayson was bound to be concerned, debating where on earth she'd got to. She scurried along this new passageway, the high buildings on either side offering her much needed shade, but at the same time trapping the suffocating air between their empty faces. She stopped to wipe her hands with her one clean handkerchief, then hurried on as quickly as possible. The narrow thoroughfare seemed far too long and she thought she must have taken the wrong route, but at last the end came into sight.

Except that it wasn't the end, for another junction had appeared. A choice this time between two passages, which branched at different angles, but, as far as she could tell, were both travelling in more or less the same direction. She must get back to the car, she must choose quickly. Could Grayson even now be deciding to drive away and leave her? Or would he be sitting sweltering in the jeep, counting the minutes as they ticked by, and in a towering temper? That was more likely. He could be setting out to look for her. If so, he would almost certainly start with the shops, and then just as certainly he would meet Suri. No, she thought, she couldn't let that happen. She must get to him and warn him. But which way to go?

As she stood irresolute, her body tense, her mind strained, there was a sound in her ear. Almost a low growl. She jumped, quite literally. The thin thread of control that had so far kept her going snapped and she nearly fled back the way she'd come. But she told herself not to be so foolish and stood her ground. She'd stopped outside a house a little more prosperous than the rest. There was a window at shoulder level and on its sill sat a large, glossy black cat. It was his rich purr of welcome that she'd heard. She reached out her hand and stroked the soft coat and in return he rubbed his head against her. Then he jumped lightly down from the sill and tangled himself around her ankles. She bent down and stroked him again.

'Which way shall I go?' she asked him.

He looked at her with wide green eyes and

bumped his head against her leg. Then he set off along one of the passages and for some reason she followed him. The passage began a snake-like progress, twisting and turning every few yards. All along its length, a multitude of alleyways branched off in different directions, making her head swim with the effort of trying to work out where she was. But the cat continued to pad forward and she continued to follow. She must be quite mad, she thought. The heat, the danger, had turned her mind, that was the only explanation. To be following a cat in the hope of ending up in the right place. She seemed again to walk for an age but in reality it could have been no more than five minutes before she saw a second archway come into view. The animal stopped in his tracks and jumped sideways up on to a small wall. He was going no further it seemed. She gave him a farewell stroke and walked towards the arch, peering cautiously around its ancient brickwork. It was astonishing, a miracle. She was back in the main street. The beautiful black cat had performed a miracle.

She glanced up the road. From here, she could just make out the jeep parked some way away but was unable to see if Grayson was at the wheel. She turned her head to look to the left and her heart was sent skittering again. Suri was still there, still in sight. She hadn't shaken him off. He must have visited every shop in the village, though why he'd done so was a puzzle. He was lingering now outside a *chai* stall, some way down from the dye shop, but at that very moment, she saw Grayson rounding the corner at the top of the street. Her first thought was to wonder where he'd been, the second was far more desperate. *Go in, go in,* her inner voice was shouting at the loitering man. She held her breath while the two figures drew ever closer, and at what seemed the final moment before they met, Suri ducked into the *chai* shop while Grayson walked past its door, oblivious of the threat.

She waited until he drew near, then walked out from under the arch and across his path. 'I'm here, Grayson.' He'd been deep in thought and at the sound of her voice his head jerked up and he looked dazedly in her direction.

'Don't scold,' she pre-empted him. 'I had to get out of the jeep. I was being roasted alive and you were so long.'

He looked guilty. 'I'm sorry. It took a little longer than I thought.'

'Buying mangoes?'

He didn't pick up her challenge but dangled a bag in front of her, bursting with fruit. 'These should last us several days. They were picked this very morning. Do you want one?'

'Not now,' she said nervously. 'We should go.'

'What's the sudden hurry?' He stopped dead, his gaze searching and ready for trouble. 'What have you been doing?'

'What do you think? Wandering around the stalls to pass the time.' She would save the details for later. 'But I saw something, someone who shouldn't be here.'

'Stop talking in riddles.' He sounded hot and irritated.

'I'm not. There's no riddle. I recognised him immediately. It was Dalip Suri.'

'Suri? Here? You must be mistaken.'

She shook her head. 'He is here. You can go into the *chai* shop to check. But please don't. He can't mean any good to either of us. Let's get out of here.'

Without another word, Grayson pushed her into the jeep's roasting interior and, in a second, had regained the driver's seat and hammered the engine into life amid a cloud of dust.

CHAPTER 13

When they were well clear of the village, he said, 'You are absolutely sure you saw him?'

'I couldn't be more certain. But what does it mean?'

'I don't know. It could be chance that he was there but it's unlikely. And if it's not chance, he's either following us or going where we're going. It's a mystery, that's for sure. He didn't see you, I suppose?'

'No, but it was a close call. I escaped through the back of one of the shops, then found my way round to the main street again.' If she didn't mention the cat, it sounded quite respectable.

'You're turning into a spook, Daisy. When we get back to London, perhaps you should rethink your career. I may take you on.'

He was smiling and she knew the frost between them was melted. She smiled back. She hadn't realised how much their renewed friendship meant to her, until it was no longer there.

'You were a long time buying fruit,' she hazarded.

'Mmm.'

'Which means?'

'I suppose it won't harm you to know. Javinder had an informant in the village. I went to see him.'

Somehow she'd expected something like that. 'Did he know anything about Javinder's disappearance?'

'He had a few interesting theories about what might have happened, but nothing concrete. Two months ago, he had an appointment to meet Javinder in Sikaner. He was told his help was needed and it was urgent. But Javinder never turned up at the meeting place. The man skulked around town trying to get information but rumours were all he heard. Then he was strong-armed by some of the Rajah's less civilised minions and was lucky to escape with his life. He made for the village we've just left. Nobody knew him there and he's been holed up ever since.'

'What does he think happened to Javinder?'

'It's looking grim. The men who pursued this chap meant business. He thinks Javinder must have been killed.'

She thought about this a while before she said, 'How did you know about the informant? How did you know how to find him?'

'I saw his name in a notebook Javinder left and then made my own enquiries.'

'Then Mike did find something?' she said surprised.

'No. I did.'

His tone suggested it might be better not to pursue this, so instead she asked the question that was burning tracks through her brain. 'Do you think that was why Dalip Suri was in the village – to find this informant rather than us?'

'Could be.'

'Then the Rajah's men must have traced him from Sikaner. So Suri and Sikaner are connected in some way,' she said excitedly.

'Almost certainly, though how is a mystery.'

'And your informant? Will he be safe now?'

'Let's hope so. I gave him money to move on – I imagine he's already on the road.'

Grayson knew more than he was saying, she was certain, but she would have to be content with what he'd told her. She could see he was struggling to untangle a puzzle where the links were tantalisingly there but where, for the moment, he could see no connection. The mystery was far wider it seemed than Javinder's disappearance, and the threat correspondingly greater. Yet since her experience in the village this morning, she'd begun to feel less fearful. It had been frightening, true enough, but just knowing that she'd been right about Suri had made her feel better. And knowing he'd been left behind was immensely reassuring. In a happier frame of mind, she settled herself to the long drive ahead.

They were several hours distant from the village, when she asked, 'When can we stop again?' Her stomach was beginning to feel very empty.

'Feeling tired?'

'Feeling hungry.'

'Once we're on the mountain road–' he

indicated the forbidding shape that loomed ahead '–we'll park up and have some lunch. A very late lunch.'

It would take at least an hour to get there, she calculated, and resigned herself to more discomfort. Hunger as well as heat. Over the last few miles, the jeep had managed to pick up speed and a slipstream of air was at least keeping her forehead cool, even though every other part of her was slowly baking. Like a nicely turned chicken, she thought. She saw runnels of perspiration streaking Grayson's face. But he seemed not to notice, his entire concentration on the difficult road ahead.

They were soon at the foothills of the mountain and began on the long haul to its summit. As the road climbed, it began imperceptibly to narrow and after a while, they appeared to be travelling on a single bare strip of gravel which wound its way ever upwards. On one side, the rough walls of the mountain leaned towards them and on the other, a few sparse bushes alone marked the road's edge. She was foolish enough to look down as they swung around a sharp double bend and wished she hadn't. The drop was vertical and far below the flat plain looked a toytown landscape. It felt as though the jeep's wheels were riding on thin air and at any moment the vehicle could plunge to its destruction.

'Close your eyes,' Grayson advised.

She must be looking an odd colour, she thought, but took his advice.

They swung around the answering bend and suddenly the tyres gave a high-pitched screech and they slammed to a halt. She felt her heart stall along with the car. Unwillingly, she opened her eyes. There was a man. He was seated in the middle of the road. And but for Grayson's swift action, he would have disappeared beneath their wheels.

She gripped her seat until the knuckles showed white. Their front tyres had stopped within inches of the man's crossed legs. Grayson was forced to reverse the car, the overhanging mountain on one side and a yawning void on the other. She stared determinedly ahead, refusing to see anything but the blotched windscreen. If she was about to topple to her death, she didn't want to know, but she was very aware of Grayson's tense figure beside her. From the jeep's new position on the road, he had somehow to swerve the vehicle around the unmoving form. Wholly unconcerned, the man continued to sit motionless, staring unblinkingly into space. His bare chest and forehead were streaked with ashes, his hair uncut and tumbling in matted black strands to his shoulders.

They trundled slowly forward, missing the seated figure by inches and edging themselves around the next bend. Grayson let out a long breath as though he'd been hugging it to himself. And why not? Her legs were jelly and she wasn't the one behind the wheel.

'Why the ashes?' she asked, in the hope of distracting herself from their narrow escape.

'I'm told they're a symbol of the body's transience.'

She digested this. 'But what is he doing halfway up a mountain?'

'Where better to meditate?' Grayson, it seemed,

had recovered his poise.

'He had nothing with him. No food, no drink. Don't you think that's strange?'

'Not entirely, if his life is one of renunciation. He's allowed only a stave, a skin to sit on and a water gourd, and I saw the gourd so he won't die of thirst.'

'*We* could have died though. He could easily have killed us.'

Grayson simply nodded. He appeared to think it quite normal to be brought to a halt by a man meditating on a precipitous road. This was India, after all. But the incident had been life threatening and coming so soon after her encounter with Dalip Suri, it didn't appear at all normal to Daisy. It was too much of a coincidence. She would like to have said as much, but her companion was concentrating on manoeuvring the vehicle round bend after bend and she felt nervous of distracting him. The terrors of the mountain track were very real and kept her silent for long periods, but eventually hunger got the better of her. It was hours since they'd had a very small breakfast.

'Are we renouncing life too?' she said at last. Grayson glanced across at her. 'I'm starving, and I know for a fact that Ahmed has packed some very good sandwiches.'

'I'm sorry, I should have stopped before we got this far, but I didn't realise the road would get this narrow. You'll have to eat as we go along, I'm afraid. There's nowhere I can pull off and I daren't risk parking on the road itself. We haven't met a single vehicle but that doesn't mean we won't.'

She was too busy reaching for the haversack to

shudder at the thought. Her stomach felt as though it had been put through several kinds of wringer. First the threat of Dalip Suri and now this terrifying drive. And the holy man's sudden appearance hadn't exactly helped. Ahmed's delicate sandwiches would put her right and she set about making sure. She'd munched her way through several of them before Grayson held out a hand for his share.

'I thought you'd become superhuman,' she said, handing him one of the largest.

'I'm just about to. It will be superhuman to drive this road and eat at the same time, but I'm willing to try. Not the mangoes though, definitely not the mangoes.'

She tried to match his cheerfulness but it was difficult. The bad feelings she'd had since her scramble from the dye shop had returned, and intensified with time passing. Between mouthfuls, she said, 'If Suri was in the village because of us, do you think he's still following?'

'It doesn't look like it. But on this road, how would you know?'

'So he might be?'

'We need to think he might. We need to be careful about where we hole up for the night. If Suri *is* on the road, I don't want to hang out a welcome flag.'

'I can't see anywhere that we can possibly get off the road.'

'Neither can I, and certainly nowhere that's reasonably well hidden. I'd hoped we might make the summit before we stopped. If we could get to where the road flattens out, there'll be more shelter. We can't be too far off but the sun's already sinking.'

It was hard to believe but he was right. The day had vanished like summer mist. They'd been held up in the village, of course, but the road was the real culprit. The road and the jeep itself. The journey had proved far more difficult than either of them could have imagined. They drove on, slowly upwards, ever upwards, winding around and around the mountain, the route potholed and in places barely surfaced. Another hour passed and Daisy felt her vision had narrowed to one small point above her head, to a summit that never came. She was used to the Rajasthan plain and this was completely new territory. Dangerous territory. On either side of the narrow track, the earth had been washed away by monsoon rain and months of erosion, and every so often the vehicle would round a bend and simply hang in the air. Dangerous territory indeed.

Light was fading and the jeep labouring badly. A grinding sound came menacingly from below, the noise increasing in volume as the road grew steeper with each mile they covered. At every bend the vehicle seemed ready to collapse as though it were an overworked donkey. She shot a glance at Grayson's profile. He was no doubt thinking as she was, that they would be lucky to finish this journey. It could only have been two or three miles before the ground began to open up on either side of them, but it felt like an eternity. At last, when her nerves had feathered to small pieces, she saw they were approaching a wide, spreading plateau. The road ahead ran straight for some miles; they had reached the summit. She felt the constriction in her chest ease. The tyres still jolted across lengthy cracks and gaping holes, and the jeep still slid and skittered on loose gravel, but the troublesome noise had abated. Somehow they limped across the plateau for a mile or so before Grayson pulled on the handbrake and brought them to an abrupt halt.

On their right was an apron of grass fronting an area of dense bushes and small trees. The space was small and hardly promising, but he got out to look more closely and then began to slide his way between the greenery. She expected him to give up at any moment but he kept on walking, right through the bushes. For a few seconds, he disappeared entirely behind what at first sight had appeared an impenetrable barrier. Then he was out again, wearing a satisfied smile.

He jumped back into the vehicle. 'This will do. Hold tight.'

The jeep was swung across the road and onto the grass. They nosed their way purposefully ahead, breaking several branches of the gnarled and stunted trees as they did, and trampling the knee-high grass to a pulp. Once through the barrier of bushes, they reached another patch of grass, a small circle just sufficient in which to park a car and pitch a tent.

As soon as the jeep was securely parked, Grayson jumped down and strode back to the entrance of the enclosure, gathering the broken branches up as he went. These he laid to one side and then very carefully rearranged the battered bushes to cover the gap they'd made. Anyone driving past, eyes necessarily glued to the road, would have no idea that anything lay beyond.

'That was clever.'

'Thank you, memsahib.' He gave a mock bow.

'And for your next trick ... how about pitching the tent? I don't think I'll be much use.'

'What tent would that be?'

'We're camping, aren't we? You camp in a tent.'

'We would if we had one, but we don't. We do have sleeping bags, or more precisely, one sleeping bag. But I'm feeling generous – you can have it.'

She met the news of their sleeping arrangements in silence, then said, 'And food? How much is left?'

'Chocolate, the fruit I bought, a few of Ahmed's rolls. Oh, and some dry biscuits but we'd better keep them for breakfast.'

It was hardly appetising, but neither was staying on the road during the night's darkness. Or trying to stay on it. In the distance, she'd glimpsed the descent. If anything, the track seemed even narrower as it wound its tortuous path downwards. No, she wouldn't want to be driving any longer that day, dry biscuits or not.

'I'll get the gear out and hopefully we can manage some kind of meal.'

She didn't have time to think how much of a meal chocolate and stale rolls would make before the 'gear', consisting of a pre-war primus stove, a battered aluminium saucepan and two canisters of water – one for cooking and one for washing, Grayson told her – were unloaded. Old the stove might be, but it took flame immediately he put a match to it and the water was soon boiling for *chai.*

Daisy unpacked what was left of Ahmed's picnic and then set about peeling several of the ripe mangoes. 'I suppose the holy man was really what he seemed.' She hadn't been able to forget her earlier worries.

'Maybe, maybe not.'

'But he couldn't have any connection to Dalip Suri, could he?' she persisted. She was hoping for reassurance. 'We left him behind in the village. He wouldn't have had time to plan an ambush.'

'Suri won't be our only conspirator,' Grayson said gently. 'Let's forget him for tonight.'

When they'd eaten their way through the meagre repast, he got to his feet, stretching cramped limbs, and then walked over to the jeep. It was almost dark and he fumbled around for a while before he located one of the torches and by its light, broke a bar of chocolate in two.

'Here. The *chai* will be even better with a chaser.'

Between sips of tea, she savoured the taste of the chocolate. It was smooth and rich and mingled in her senses with the heady scent of evening. She was overcome by a strange feeling of completeness. And that was decidedly odd. They were in the middle of nowhere and unnamed dangers waited ahead. But at this moment, it didn't seem to matter. The world was at peace and so was she. Around them the trees stood still and silent. Above, a shower of stars, pinpricks in the sky's dark void, as though thrown there by a wayward hand, and a half-moon hanging lazily overhead, edging the jeep, the grass, the bushes – and themselves – in a silver sheen.

She looked across at Grayson and laughed. 'In the moonlight we look as grand as Indian gods in a temple.'

He smiled back. 'But gods that need to sleep, I think.' He doused the primus and pulled from the rear of the jeep a ground sheet and a sleeping bag.

'Here you are, fit for a princess. I found it in the storeroom back at base. I can't guarantee nobody has ever slept in it before but it looks pretty clean.'

She took a closer look. By torchlight at least, it appeared presentable.

'It seems fine, but why only one?'

'I was coming on this journey alone, remember?'

She did remember and it made her feel awkward. 'So what will you do?'

'Let Mother Earth take me to her bosom.'

Daisy giggled. 'I wonder if you'll feel quite so poetic in a few hours' time.' She opened the sleeping bag and spread it on the ground sheet. 'Why don't we both share this? It looks big enough.'

'I doubt we'd both fit in there.'

'I was thinking we could sleep on top.' She could feel herself beginning to flush. 'It's a warm night and I think I saw an old blanket behind my seat. We could wrap that around us.'

When they were lying side by side, she said, 'I haven't dared to ask, but how's the wrist? The drive must have given you pain.'

'A little,' he admitted, 'but nothing that will stop me driving tomorrow. We need to get to Sikaner as soon as we can.'

'Because of what happened back there in the village?'

'Partly.'

She propped herself up on her elbow and looked down at him, a deepening frown on her face. 'I don't understand why Dalip still sees me as a threat. I've stopped asking questions about his family, but that seems not to matter. Somehow, I've acquired an enemy without any good reason.'

'There's sure to be a reason. And we have acquired an enemy,' he corrected. 'We're battling the same people, or so it seems.' He reached up and swept a stray curl from her face, his hand lingering in her hair. A small gesture but it made her breath catch. She lay down quickly, bunching herself into the smallest of spaces.

'That sounds crazy.'

'Maybe, but it's too much of a coincidence that we've ended up travelling to Sikaner together. The state is small and unimportant so why do we both need to visit? It's the unanswered questions that are sending us there. And probably sending Suri, too. Something is rotten in the state of Sikaner, to misquote *Hamlet,* and that's what I need to find out.'

For the moment, finding out didn't seem that urgent. She lay still and quiet, looking up at the sky. There was a majesty in this nightly unfurling of beauty that made their journey seem inconsequential. His body was warm beside her and she knew a deep happiness.

'I wish you hadn't come,' he said, breaking the silence at last. 'I'm fearful I may be leading you into the lions' den.'

'I asked to come.'

'"Ask" isn't the word I'd use. You insisted.'

'I had to. You were sounding as though I was ten years old and in need of a guardian.'

'I was concerned for you. Is that so wrong?'

'I was concerned for *you,* but that wasn't going to alter your decision, was it? I know you don't want me here, but now that I am, we have to be equal partners.'

She felt him turn towards her, his body moulding itself to hers. 'Haven't I been waiting for that for years?'

'That's not what I mean.' She knew her face had grown pink and was glad of the almost complete darkness.

'Sad but true.' He let out a heavy breath. 'There was a time when I believed we had a future together. But I guess that's the way love goes. People fall out of love as quickly as they fall into it.'

'I didn't fall in love quickly – not with you.' She was remembering her instant infatuation with Gerald. Her feelings for Grayson had been quite different. Were quite different. 'And I haven't fallen out of love.'

He turned his head towards her, but in the faint light his expression was impossible to read. 'You found reasons not to meet though, didn't you? You pushed me away. What was that about? I didn't understand you and I still don't.'

'I know,' she said unhappily. 'You're not able to put yourself in my shoes.'

'I've tried, really I have. I've tried to understand how wretched you must have felt. But that whole miserable business with Gerald was ten years ago.'

He reached across and slowly stroked her cheek.

She badly wanted to clutch hold of his hand and pull him close, but mastered the feeling and said as composedly as she could, 'I know it's way in the past, but it lives with me still. It lives with me every day. It makes me feel the world can fall to pieces at any time. That life is insecure, that my life is insecure.'

He sat up quickly and threw aside the blanket. 'You must know you'd be safe with me.'

'Rationally, I suppose.' She joined him sitting, her back arrow straight. She was ready to argue her case. It was important that she make him see the damage the past had caused. 'But fear isn't rational, is it? Of course, I know that you would never deliberately harm me, but I can't allow myself to be that vulnerable again. I've worked hard. I've a profession now, and that means I've a sure future. If I had to give that up–'

'Why would you give it up? Why does there have to be a choice? I would never ask you to leave nursing. Surely you must know that?'

'You wouldn't ask, but the world would expect it. There may not be an official ban on being married but it's definitely frowned on. How can you be a good nurse and look after a husband at the same time, that's what people would say. Matrons in particular. Most of them are single and reluctant to employ married women. That's especially true in a teaching hospital, and that's where I'm heading. I've tried the alternative and I don't like it.'

He stared straight ahead, his shoulders stiff. The line of trees rustled slightly from a puff of breeze. 'What you're saying is that your prospects at work are more important than any feelings you might have for me.'

'You make it sound cold and calculating. It's not. For me, it's a matter of survival. Try to understand.'

When he didn't respond, she leaned across and gripped his forearm. 'I don't want to be dependent, Grayson. Not ever again. I don't want to feel powerless and at someone else's mercy, no matter how good and kind they are.'

He ignored her hand and looked away. 'That's a skewed way of thinking. If you're true partners, then neither of you should wield ultimate power. Which is what you're doing. You're letting your bad experience distort your whole life – and mine.'

'It wasn't just bad, it was catastrophic. I trusted Gerald. For the first time in my life, I trusted another human being and look what happened. I lost my baby, I lost my peace of mind. I nearly lost my life.'

She couldn't keep the misery from her voice and it made him turn back to her. 'I know it's been foul. I know it will be difficult. But you *can* learn to trust again.' He seemed to struggle with himself for a minute and then his arms went round her and she could sense his lips close. 'We were lovers once and you must have trusted then,' he said quietly. 'Surely the prize is worth trying for again? I'm not talking about me, though I hope I feature somewhere in there. But a family of your own. It's what you've always wanted. It's what this mad journey of yours is all about, isn't it?'

'It's about a family I never had. And, as for a new

family, I can't think about that. Not after what happened. Maybe when this is over, things will be different. I need to know the people who brought me into the world; in some twisted fashion they're tied up with what happened here in India with Gerald, with Anish. I don't know how, I just know it. And I can't think of anything else until I'm sure there's nothing more to discover. Then I'll let the past go.'

'If only that were true...' He pulled her down once more onto their makeshift bedding, his arms still encircling her. It felt natural to nestle against him.

'I promise it is.'

CHAPTER 14

He was awake before dawn and lay relaxed, watching the sun slowly gilding every corner of the small clearing. Beside him, Daisy was still deep in dreams. He looked across at the sleeping girl and hesitated to bring her back to reality. He hadn't wanted her on this journey, had feared for her safety, but once she'd made dangerous enemies in Jasirapur, he'd had no other option. By playing detective, she'd become a threat to them both and he could see his plans being blown sky-high. No wonder he'd reacted furiously – but he could never stay angry with her for long. They'd been through thick and thin together and it felt good to have her near. To talk with her, laugh with her. To lie beside her, feeling her breath on his cheek, her soft contours against his body. Last night she'd cuddled close as though nothing bad had happened between them. But it had, and he only half believed her promise that if she found nothing in Sikaner, she would give up all thoughts of uncovering the past. She'd offered the faintest hope that things could come right between them and like a fool, he'd wanted to believe her even while he knew in his heart that she was still as far away from him as ever. His best bet would be to forget the old dreams and concentrate on doing his job.

Throughout the war he'd clung to the idea of a settled life, with Daisy at its centre, once the enemy was routed and England safe. But when the day came and he'd asked her to marry him, she'd prevaricated, finding first one reason and then another to avoid commitment. At first he'd been bewildered, then frustrated, and finally filled with resentment. The job in Brighton had been the last straw. It was a promotion, she'd said, yet she could have found that easily enough in a suburban hospital, in London itself, if she'd chosen. But she hadn't. He'd had to acknowledge then that she'd chosen Brighton to get away from him. That she would never want what he wanted. When his mother heard the news, she'd suggested in the most delicate manner that in some way Daisy must be 'damaged' and he would be best to cut his losses. After that, he'd allowed himself to drift, trying to keep her far from his mind. But the minute he'd known he was embarking on a hazardous assignment, he'd also known he had to see her again. To say goodbye. Except that it hadn't been goodbye and she was here with him, sharing the dangers as she had so often in the past.

He wondered what alarms this day would bring. Sliding carefully from under the blanket, he walked to the rear of the jeep to look for water. Its cold splash stung his face. Shivering, he fired up the primus and put the kettle on to boil, then rummaged in the haversack for something to eat. There was little left of Ahmed's feast and breakfast would be a poor thing. He laid out the two remaining bread rolls, now woefully stale, a handful of dried biscuits and the one last bar of chocolate. Once they were down from the mountain, they would need to stop at the first village they came to in order to buy food. The kettle hummed in anticipation, but there was time to check on the road. He pushed past the blockade of bushes and stepped out onto the grass verge, and for some minutes stood there, quiet and unmoving. Not a sight, not a sound.

Ranged all around in a majestic circle, the mountain's rocky promontories were turning rosy with the sun's warmth, while its hidden crevices and gullies wore a patchwork of black and grey. He shaded his eyes and craned his neck forward as far as he could, following the road across the flat plateau, then seeing it fall out of sight to re-emerge twisting its way downwards in a seemingly endless loop to the plain beneath. He was trying to calculate the likely time it would take to drive when he heard the kettle's muted shriek.

Daisy had heard it too and he found her kneeling up on the blanket, still a little dazed, and wondering, he imagined, how she'd managed to land on the top of a mountain and in the most uncomfortable of circumstances. She blinked owlishly at him, trying to shake off the last remnants of sleep, then scrambled to her feet and shook out her badly creased dress.

'I hope I don't have to meet the Rajah in this. He'll think I've come from scaring the crows.'

'He'll think you charming – the heat will soon put the dress to rights. Here, have this.' He handed her a steaming mug, then proffered one of the sad rolls. 'I can't offer much in the way of food, I'm afraid.'

She shook her head and began to drink the tea. 'This will do, thanks.'

'I'm afraid you're right.' He bundled the bread from sight. 'But a few more squares of chocolate might help. And there's water for washing, though it will test your stamina – it's super cold. I'm going to reconnoitre again.'

Daisy had finished her tea and chocolate when he returned.

'We're fine to go,' he said, throwing the sleeping bag and blanket into the back of the jeep. 'And it's downhill all the way.'

'And the bends?'

'What goes up has to come down,' he warned.

She grimaced, but then seemed to shrug the thought away. 'My stomach survived yesterday's pounding, so why not today's?'

The engine fired first time and they nosed out on to the empty road. Already the sun's rays were shooting experimental sparks from off the metal of the bonnet. Despite the morning cool, it would be another scorching day. The first few miles of their descent were very steep and the road became rougher and more damaged as they progressed. His foot hovered constantly over the brake as they toiled slowly downwards. At times, he was forced almost to a stop as loose shale crunched and slithered alarmingly beneath the tyres.

Daisy's face had lost its early pink. 'I take back what I said. These bends are even worse than yesterday's.'

'And your stomach?'

'Wretched,' she said succinctly.

'Once we're down, there'll be a village and we'll stop.'

But they were to stop much sooner than that. Guiding the car around the most contorted bend yet, he had suddenly and violently to slam on the brakes. For several sickening seconds, the car skidded and then slid to a halt. A rockfall covered the centre of the road and there was no going forward.

'And just as we were doing so well.' He grasped his wrist as he spoke. The hasty stop had given him pain. 'We'll have to clear it,' he muttered, and went to get out of the jeep. But, as he did so, the vehicle rocked to one side and he felt the far rear wheel slip. He sensed her snatch a look at him, and knew she was terrified. The wheel was floating, he was certain. It had lost all contact with the surface beneath and hung crazily against the skyline.

'Don't panic. Breathe normally. We seem to be in a bit of spot.' It was the understatement of his life.

'Okay, I'm breathing normally,' she said through a clenched jaw. 'Now what do we do?'

'I'm heavier than you.' He tried to keep his own voice calm. 'If I try to get out, the jeep will tilt your way.'

'And that will be ... goodbye Daisy? Is that what you're saying?'

'That's about the size of it. So it's you that needs to get out. If you can manage to wedge some large stones beneath the back wheel, I should be able to follow and finish the job.'

'And just how am I supposed to get out? There can't be six inches between the door and the edge of the cliff.' Terror had given way to indignation.

'With great care.'

'Grayson!' She exploded at what she saw as his flippancy.

'I mean it. But you're going to have to try. It's our only hope.'

She felt her stomach, her lungs, her heart, jumping together in a crazy rhythm. He was asking her to step out into fresh air. But if she didn't, they would stay where they were. That's if they were lucky. One false move and they would both end messily.

'Can't we wait for someone to come along?' she pleaded.

'Is that a serious question? You've seen how isolated this road is. Now take a deep breath.'

'Another one?'

'Yes, another one. Then very carefully nudge your door open. See how much room you have to manoeuvre.'

She took more than one breath while Grayson sat patiently beside her. Then, gathering what was left of her courage, she began to creak the door open. The jeep had some advantages. The body of the vehicle was high off the ground but at least it meant its doors were small and relatively easy to swing back. Five minutes of gentle pushing got the door fully open, but its hanging weight made the vehicle list even more frighteningly. She peered down and saw the narrowest strip of earth, a strip which separated her from this world and the next.

'How much room have you got?' His casual tone suggested they were parking in the forecourt of the Paradise Hotel.

Keep the breathing going, she told herself. Aloud she said, 'Six inches, maybe nine.'

'Good.'

'Good!'

'You've small feet. You should be able to stand with your back to the vehicle. Then edge along its side until you can slip around the rear and on to the road.'

'Why didn't I think of that? Simple really – if you work in a circus.'

He ignored her, remaining quite still and looking directly ahead of him. She hoped he knew what he was asking of her.

'I'll say goodbye then.' Was it goodbye? Quite possibly. He reached across very carefully for her hand and squeezed it hard, but all the time he continued to sit rigidly upright. She swung her legs out from the well of the car and dangled her feet just above the ground, then very carefully placed one foot at a time on firm soil. Her hands were on the sticky leather of the seat and slowly she pressed down and levered herself into a standing position.

'Don't look down,' he said. 'Feel your way round to the rear.'

She couldn't hear her heart beating any more. Perhaps it had stopped. Her whole body was filled with noise, though, the noise of sickening, churning fear.

Her left hand stretched out and felt nothing. Nothing. My God, where was the jeep? Where was its comforting metal?

'Flatten your arm more.' His voice calmed her and she did as he suggested. Pulling her arm back she felt the strip of metal, then the rim of glass of the rear window. All she had to do was move, but she couldn't. Her legs would no longer function.

'I can't do it.'

'You can, Daisy, you can. Shuffle your left foot to the side. Find the ground, then follow with your right foot. Keep your arm on the car to guide you.'

She tried to do as he said, moving like a crab along the narrow space. Inch by inch, shuffle by shuffle, until her hand touched the corner strut of the jeep and she knew she was almost there. Don't hurry, she told herself. Keep doing this slow shuffle and you'll turn the corner. And she did.

She stepped clear of the vehicle and was immediately very sick. Grayson was watching her in the wing mirror. 'You probably won't want to buy food after all.' He allowed himself a smile.

She tottered up to his door. 'I've a good mind to leave you here.'

'And where will you go without me, pretty maid? Talking of which, we should be off soon.

Look.' He pointed to the circle of golden heat that had sliced its way through the peach clouds of early morning and was climbing the sky to sit serenely overhead. 'You better get cracking.'

'You might at least thank me for risking my life.'

'I might but perhaps I'll wait until I'm safe. Are you willing to try?' He didn't wait for an answer but went on, 'Take the largest stones you can carry from that jumble ahead and push them hard against the back wheel.'

She walked to the avalanche and considered the pile of rocks flooding the road. Grayson was too optimistic if he thought she could carry any of them. Something about the arrangement of the boulders and stones made her pause, but he was still in danger and she had no time to work out what it was. It needed all her strength to push and pull several large rocks the few yards to the back of the jeep. With a massive heave, she rammed several into place. The effort took its toll and she fell back with a thud on to the roadside. She lay there temporarily winded.

But instead of stabilising the vehicle, the rocks had caused it to slide further towards the abyss which yawned below. She sat staring, unable to believe what she was seeing, then let out a tormented wail. 'Why is this happening?'

'The rock is behind the wrong wheel,' Grayson yelled, for the first time abandoning his infuriating calm. 'Move it to the other side. Now, or I'm gone.'

In her disoriented state, she had misjudged the angle at which the jeep was lying. But her body was wrung. Her limbs shaking. Every muscle had been pushed beyond endurance in the effort to manoeuvre the enormous granite rocks into place. All she wanted was to lie by the side of the road, eyes closed, and drift into a state of oblivion. But she couldn't. Grayson was depending on her and she had to try again. Somehow she got back on her feet and staggered to the rear of the jeep. Pulling the rocks from under the wheel was harder even than pushing them into place. Muscles screaming, legs and arms beyond full stretch, she tugged. Over and over again. The first rock slid to one side and she stood upright for a moment, breathing so heavily that it seemed the whole mountain rang with the noise. Her ears buzzed loudly and her head felt ready to explode. Back to the second and then the third and largest rock. Would she ever be able to move it, let alone in time? But if she didn't, Grayson was going to die. The phrase danced before her eyes and hammered through her head. Slowly, very slowly, her grasp on the rock tightened and the boulder started to move. Her eyes were staring, her cheeks gaunt with effort. Grayson sat behind the wheel staring ahead and not daring to move as much as a finger. Once she extricated the rock from beneath the wheel, she was able to exert greater pressure and slowly use her whole body to get behind it. At last it was free and, with one last enormous surge, she pushed it across the few feet to the other axle and under the far wheel. She breathed for a moment, dizzy and sick. Then pushed the two smaller boulders into place and kept pushing until she was certain none of them would move.

She looked up to see that the jeep had stopped listing. Grayson turned his head very slightly in her direction. 'Looks like you've done it.'

'I think so.' Her voice was rough with fatigue but inside she was jubilant.

'Who says five-footers are weaklings?'

'I say, or rather my muscles are saying it. They're torn to pieces.'

'But you're still whole. And so am I, which has to be the best news of the day.'

'So are you going to try to get out?'

'Watch me. And wish me luck.'

Very carefully, he opened his door and took a step onto the road. The vehicle remained stable. Then sliding from behind the steering wheel, he eased himself out of the seat and walked clear. Her stomach kicked. He was safe, at least for the moment.

He came over to her, wrapping his arms around her and hugging her close. 'You've done it again, you know, Daisy.' She stayed muffled in his embrace for some minutes unable to speak. She felt like shouting for joy and crying at the same time.

'You've saved my life,' he said into her ear. 'Again. You're so good at it, I think I should keep you with me always.'

All she could manage was a shake of her head. At length, he said. 'Come on, you must sit down and rest. I'm going to move some more hardcore, then I'll have a go at driving the jeep into the centre of the road.'

More terror, she thought, as she slumped down on a patch of bare earth. *I can't watch this.* And she didn't. She closed her eyes but she couldn't close her ears. Rocks being pushed in behind those she'd moved, one, two, three. Then the door of the jeep opening and the gear stick being thrust forward. The rev of the engine sounded like the day of doom itself. She squeezed her eyes tight. There was a massive crunching of gravel and then a loud jolt. She squeezed them even tighter. The engine revved again, the gravel crunched, crackled, spat out beneath the wheels, but then miraculously the engine roar decreased and finally stopped. She dared to open one eye, half expecting to see the jeep and Grayson vanished over the rim of the ravine. But instead, there he was, leaning out of the window and beckoning her to get in.

'That was an exciting interlude,' he remarked once she'd regained her seat, a half-smile on his lips. He always seemed able to turn terror into the most mundane happening. But she wasn't to be deflected so easily. Now that they were both safe, her mind was thinking rapidly. After a while, she said, 'Did you notice anything strange about those stones?'

'Apart from the fact they were sitting dead centre of the road?' He was still in teasing mood.

'That's the point, isn't it? They were dead centre and piled high. A natural rockfall would have splayed out, some stones falling at a distance, others perhaps tumbled into the ravine. But these made an almost symmetrical shape.'

'I wondered if you'd noticed.'

'So you did think it was odd? You didn't say anything.'

'I didn't want to worry you any more than you already were. You had enough to deal with.'

'It means it was deliberate.'

'Yes, it does. And it wasn't only the trajectory of the fall that was odd. The rocks didn't quite match with the cliff they'd supposedly fallen from.'

She felt slightly annoyed. 'I didn't notice that,' she was forced to confess.

'Ah, but you're not a special intelligence agent.'

'No, I'm just someone who goes around saving the lives of special intelligence agents.'

'Touché.'

She took a deep breath. 'If the holy man was a ploy ... someone is trying very hard to stop us from reaching Sikaner.' She hadn't truly believed it before.

'That's the sensible conclusion. Unless, of course, we've been unlucky enough to meet a bunch of murderous psychopaths who want us dead for no particular reason.'

'But you still intend to go on?' She didn't know why she was bothering to ask.

'I have to. It's my job. But it isn't yours. There should be a village after we leave the mountain road – Kamghar – or it may be just before the road ends. The map isn't too clear but when we get there, I'll arrange transport back to Jasirapur for you.'

She glanced sideways at him and saw that he was serious. 'You're not getting rid of me that easily.'

'It won't be easy,' he said. 'Far from it in this out-of-the-way place. But it will be a lot safer for you.'

She shook her head vehemently. 'I'm coming with you.'

He lifted his hands from the steering wheel in a gesture of surrender and she wished he wouldn't, not at least until they'd waved goodbye to the petrifying bends. As they descended, though, the road became less steep and the bends less convoluted and spaced further apart. She felt she could begin to breathe again, though the road still snaked its way round and around in dizzying fashion. But they were making much better progress now and in less than an hour they drove into the promised village.

'We'll have to stop here for petrol. If the gauge is to be believed, we've used a lot more than I bargained for. It must be the rough driving.'

'And some food?' she said hopefully, her sickness forgotten.

'And some food. We've just passed a mobile shop at the top of the road. Did you see it? He'll almost certainly sell hot snacks and he'll probably have water too. I'll park up and you can choose a picnic.'

They locked the jeep and walked as quickly as the mid-day sun would allow, back to where Grayson had spotted the van. There were several people already there waiting to be served, but as they joined the queue, the men in front began to shuffle uneasily, shooting covert glances at them over their shoulders. Then one by one, they melted away.

CHAPTER 15

'We're evidently bringers of the plague,' Grayson said, half joking, but she noticed that he cast a searching eye around the nearby streets. 'We'll grab the food and go.'

'Choose for me,' she urged. 'It will be quicker.'

It seemed important to be away as soon as possible. In a few minutes, the street had completely emptied. It was as though someone had turned the page of a picture book, banishing the brightly coloured illustrations from sight and staring instead at a blank page. She had seen that blankness before; her recent walk through the Jasirapur bazaar was ingrained in her memory. Did the ruler of Sikaner hold sway here too? It would seem so.

Grayson made his choice: spinach pakoras, spicy crackers, potato skins and banana puris. The man behind the counter hardly raised his head and almost threw the items into brown paper bags. He thrust two large bottles of water at them then held out his hand for money. His eyes remained averted during the entire transaction.

'Not too friendly a lot are they?' Grayson remarked, as he scooped up the bags and led the way back to the jeep, 'Definitely time to go.'

But, as they approached the vehicle, he came to an abrupt halt. 'Now that's a little unfortunate.'

Daisy followed his eyes and saw immediately

what he was staring at. A line of something damp had trickled from beneath the jeep and was marking the dust of the road. He handed her the food and bent down to get a closer look. 'That explains the petrol gauge. The fuel tank is leaking. We must have caught it on the rockfall and we've been losing fuel ever since.'

'Can we drive like that?' To her inexperienced eye, the trickle was beginning to look more like a flood.

'It should just about get us to the nearest garage, that's if they'll serve us. Jump in and we'll do a quick recce.'

He drove as slowly as he could, trying to conserve what fuel was left, while Daisy kept a lookout for any kind of garage. If they didn't find one, she thought, she wouldn't take bets on any of the townspeople helping, not even to hire them a donkey. The ruptured fuel tank might be an accident but the rockfall certainly wasn't. The jeep limped along the main road, then turned into one of the side streets.

A child of about ten was playing with a battered football, kicking it in and out of the gutter. 'Hey,' Grayson shouted in Hindi, 'is there a garage near here?'

At the sound of his voice, a woman came rushing out of a nearby house and dragged her son back indoors, but not before the boy had said, 'In the next road.'

'The next street,' Grayson confirmed.

The child was right, though the garage was no more than a collection of tin huts with one forlorn petrol pump standing on the cracked concrete of what passed for a forecourt.

'This is where money could be useful.' He jumped down from the jeep and walked into the smallest of the huts, its door standing open to the world. She imagined the owners hadn't yet heard there were strangers in the village.

After some minutes, Grayson reappeared bringing with him a highly reluctant mechanic. The man bent down to look at the damage and shook his head. She was sure Grayson had already bribed him to come out of his hut but now he proffered several more notes.

The man spoke in Hindi. 'He says it will take at least two hours to mend the fuel tank,' Grayson translated.

'But will he do it?'

'I think so, though he wants me to drive around to the back, out of sight of the road. We can wait in one of the huts, he says. Let's take the food with us. We might as well eat while we wait.'

The hut had been constructed from sheets of corrugated iron, lashed together with copious amounts of rope. Beneath a throbbing sun, it was almost hotter inside than out. Daisy slid onto one of the wooden benches that lined the small space and wondered how long it would be before she blacked out. Within minutes, her hair was damp from the roots and sweat was trickling freely down her face. When Grayson came in from speaking to the mechanic, his shirt clung to him as though it were a second skin. He sat down beside her and opened the brown paper bags. Neither of them could summon much enthusiasm, but knowing they were unlikely to eat for some time, they dutifully ploughed through several of the pakoras and puris and drank the entire contents of one of the large bottles of water.

'I'd like to throw the rest over me,' he confessed, 'but we're bound to need it. That business on the mountain has delayed us badly and now this. We'll be lucky to make Sikaner by nightfall.'

In fact, they were to face a full three hours in a crucible of heat. Daisy was sure that sooner or later she would simply melt and all that would be left would be a puddle on the mud floor.

'He seems to be taking a very long time,' she said at one point.

'His tools are pretty primitive and the tank isn't easy to get to.'

'I thought he might be working deliberately slowly.'

'It's possible but at least he's mending the tank. I'll make sure to check it as best I can before we leave.'

The mechanic was finished at last. He came into the hut, wiping greasy hands on overalls that were already more grease than cloth.

'Ready,' he said abruptly in English. More notes passed hands and Grayson went to inspect the man's handiwork.

'I'm not sure which is worse,' Daisy remarked as she clambered back into the vehicle, 'the hut or the jeep.'

'At least the jeep moves. Let's get out of this place.'

They regained the main street and were forced to drive its entire length before they could escape into the countryside again. It was an unpleasant experience. Not one face had been raised to welcome them to the village, and now not one watched them go. If that was the treatment they could expect in Sikaner, she couldn't see how it was possible for either of them to find what they'd come for.

'How much further do you think we have to go?' she asked, once they'd been driving for a while.

'Far enough to make things difficult.'

'In what way?'

'It's nearly dusk. After that rockfall, the last thing I want is to be driving on a lethal road with only the dimmest of headlights to guide us.'

'Are you saying we have to camp again?' For hours she'd been looking forward to sleeping in a comfortable bed.

'I'm afraid we will. But look on the bright side. We'll be driving into Sikaner first thing in the morning, before most people are up.'

'And that's good for some reason?'

'It's far better than getting there at dusk. We can get a sense of the place before we fetch up at the palace.'

Once out of the village, the road had continued to snake downwards, looping its way around wide swinging bends. She'd hoped they had finished with mountain driving but Grayson had to keep his foot on the brake almost the entire time. The terrain, though, was growing noticeably less steep and he was able to push the complaining jeep a little harder. Despite the growing gloom, the view was magnificent. The plain stretched below them and now she could see distinctly the ditches and fields, animals and vegetation that made the world below. The blobs dotted rash-like across the plain's surface she took to be small huts and houses. Around them the night air was bisected by wisps of smoke as fires were built to cook the evening meal. Every so often, the road widened and grassy spaces appeared on the near side. It was almost dark now and she wasn't surprised when Grayson slowed the jeep and swung it to one side. The enclave he'd chosen was open to the road but wide and deep. One corner was overhung by trees.

'We won't be as well hidden as last night but at least we should hear anyone who intends us mischief.'

'Do you think they'll keep trying?'

'I'm hoping they've fired their last shot. But who knows? They've already managed to delay us hugely.'

She felt a rush of tiredness. It had been an exhausting day, in many ways a terrifying day, and reaction was setting in. She slid down from the jeep and went to help him set up camp, but he stopped her.

'You look bushed. Take the sleeping bag and lie down. Unless you fancy some *chai?* I can get the primus going in no time.'

'We should probably keep what tea we have for the morning.'

Their supplies were at rock bottom and it was fortunate they'd eaten in the village, though in the crushing heat every mouthful had been torture.

She lay down on the sleeping bag and pulled the rug to her chin, while she watched him unpack what was left in the jeep and lock it for the night.

He came over to where she lay and kicked his shoes off. Then settled down beside her.

They lay on their backs, gazing up at the spangled sky. 'Do you think Javinder discovered something big?' she murmured.

'It looks likely. But if he did, he wasn't able to tell anyone.'

'You must have an idea what it was.'

'Yes,' he said guardedly, 'but until we get to Sikaner, it's all guesswork.'

'I only hope we do – get to Sikaner, I mean. After today, I'm not so sure.'

'Whoever has been messing with us must be running out of ideas by now.'

'Unless he or they come out of hiding and attack us directly.' After today, it was more than possible, she thought. 'They seem to be getting more dangerous.'

'Or more desperate.' He reached out for her hand. 'Try not to worry. We've come through so far and we'll get there – in one piece.'

She was silent for a while, her eyes closed with fatigue, but her mind too busy to sleep. 'But when we do, it won't be easy. If Kamghar is anything to go by, people will be hostile. How do we begin to ask questions? How do I begin to ask the Rajah about his dead son?'

'I'll leave that to you. My time will be taken up sounding out others.'

'Who exactly?'

'The palace servants to begin with. Then the townspeople.'

'And that won't be easy.'

'No, it won't, but then I never expected it to be.'

She felt herself rebuked and said nothing more. But then he leaned towards her and touched her cheek with the crook of his finger. 'You could always cut and run, you know, even at this late stage. I did warn you it wouldn't be worth your coming.'

She roused herself to answer. 'If I hadn't, you'd be at the bottom of this mountain right now.'

'True but–'

'No buts, Grayson. I'm here, and this is where I'm staying.'

'Now how did I know that's what you'd say?'

His finger uncurled and she felt its warmth travelling down the side of her cheek. He tipped her chin upwards and placed a gentle kiss on her lips. 'Sleep well, sweet Daisy.'

She drew the tenderness of his touch into herself and raised her lips to his, kissing him gently back. His lips found hers again and this time the kiss demanded more.

She should stop now, she thought, before they sowed the seeds of another disaster between them, but his lips were lingering on hers, his tongue gradually teasing her mouth open. She felt the pressure of his body lying half across her, his leg straddling hers. His mouth hardened, his body hardened, and here was the familiar slow melt as she accommodated her form to his.

'I guess we shouldn't be doing this,' he whispered, while his hands fumbled with the buttons of her dress.

'I guess we shouldn't,' she said, slipping the light cotton over her head.

His fingers traced the curve of her bosom, then

cupped one soft breast after another, lifting each to his mouth and kissing her slowly into a state of the deepest pleasure. His breath was a little ragged but he still had sufficient control to ask, 'Are you sure about this?'

It was madness, she realised, but to feel him again, to feel his lips, his hands, the solidity of his body, was a kind of liberation. She ought not to go on, but she knew she would. 'I'm sure,' she said, and in that moment she was.

It took a second for her to unbutton his shirt and reach out to stroke the firm, warm flesh. A few seconds more and their clothes lay abandoned by their side. 'Naked to the world,' she murmured.

'Not while I'm here. Let me cover you.'

And he did. A tumbling of emotion, the satisfying of a passion that for so many months had gone unsatisfied.

For most of the night he hardly slept, falling into a deep slumber an hour before dawn. The loud call of two grey francolins engaged in their morning duet woke him. He was startled and for a moment utterly confused. He knew where he was and he knew where he was going, but the girl who lay naked in his arms was unexpected. Then memory flooded back and he felt suffused with a heat that defeated the temporary coolness of the day. For some while he lay listening to her quiet breathing, aware of the fine dark hair tickling his chest, and aware, too, of the smallness of her body, its softness, its vulnerability. He loved her. What was new about that? He'd loved her from the first moment he'd seen her and through the years had continued to love her despite ... despite her turning away from him, despite the hurt she'd inflicted. He understood the damage life had done to her. In a way he wished he didn't. He might not feel so bereft then each time she dealt a blow to his heart. If only she could learn to trust him, not just for a day, for a week, for a month, but for a lifetime together. He would do well by her. If he could only make her see that. Last night, she'd allowed him to trample the barrier she'd erected, but how long would it be before she rebuilt it?

She was lying against his left arm, blocking the sight of his watch. He looked around, trying to estimate the time. The sky was swaddled in bands of grey and gold, peach and deepest pink, which spread skywards from a horizon where the faintest outline of a rising sun wavered into view. He wanted to be in Sikaner as early as possible and the sooner they were up and away, the better. Gently, he extricated himself from her embrace and shrugged on his clothes. The sun was still little more than a golden blur and would make for comfortable travelling.

He fired up the primus for a last time, then a final rummage in the depths of the haversack. The promised biscuits came into view. Not quite up to the standard of the Ritz, he thought wryly, but then their night at that hotel hadn't been the luxury they might have expected. The Blitz had seen to that, and now the rigours of rough travel were doing the same. If relationships thrived on shared discomfort, theirs must be doing extraordinarily well.

He bent down to kiss her forehead, smoothing

her hair back from her face as he did so. 'Breakfast is served, memsahib.'

She opened her eyes instantly but he could see from her unfocused gaze that she was as puzzled as he had been. She sat bolt upright, then realising her nakedness, grasped the folds of the blanket and clutched it against her breasts. He made a neat pile of her clothes and left them beside her, turning back to the jeep and spreading the map wide. He would give her sufficient time to collect herself.

When she joined him, her face was rosy in the dawn light. She looked rested. She looked satisfied, and he dared to think that he had had a part in that. 'It's another cold water sloosh, I'm afraid.'

'I can cope.' She was smiling a little shyly. 'The *chai* will be hot.'

'It will. It is,' he said, handing her a plastic beaker of steaming liquid. 'But what can I say about the biscuits?'

She laughed and the sound was happy and free. He hadn't heard her laugh like that for a very long time. 'The less the better, I think.' She chewed down on one of the digestives but refused a second.

'When you're ready, we should go.'

The primus was extinguished and the rest of their scanty equipment loaded. Within a quarter of an hour, they were on the road again. Their route stretched ahead, still looping in and around the mountainside but descending now at a far gentler rate. Judged against its usual performance, the jeep was fairly bowling along, and he thought they should reach Sikaner before the sun was riding too high. Neither of them spoke but it didn't seem to matter. They were at peace, he thought, at peace with themselves and with each other. He wished it would last.

It was a wish that wasn't to be granted and he wondered how many more times he could be wrong; it was getting to be a bad habit. As they rounded the last long, wide bend, the vehicle's engine spluttered and died. Their speed dwindled to nothing and they came to a halt at the apex of the bend.

'Whatever's happened?' Her face was creased with worry, as well it might be. They couldn't have broken down in a worse place.

'No idea. Until now, the engine has been going great guns.' He reached forward to the dashboard and tapped one of the dials. 'This isn't too reliable, but it should show plenty of fuel.' Together they peered at the small glass circle. The petrol gauge showed empty.

'There we have it. No fuel.'

'But you filled the tank.' Alarm had crept into her voice.

'I did. I filled it to the maximum before we left that inferno at Kamghar.'

'So how–? Has someone siphoned off the petrol?'

'I don't think so. We would have heard any visitors in the night. And they wouldn't just have robbed us of fuel. They would surely have found a way to finish us off for good this time.'

'So how has it disappeared?'

'I imagine we have our greasy garage owner to thank.'

‘But he mended the tank. You saw it.’

‘I saw as much of it as I could. But it’s always possible that he deliberately left a hairline fracture unrepaired. I wouldn’t have seen that. We’ve got this far after all, and the petrol must have been leaking since we left the village.’

She sat staring blindly through the windscreen. They had come to a stop in full sunlight and he could feel the heat crashing through the glass, but she hardly seemed aware of it.

‘After all that effort,’ she said in a crushed voice. ‘After the lucky escapes we’ve had. All for nothing. We’re stranded in the middle of nowhere.’

‘Not necessarily,’ he threw over his shoulder, jumping down and unrolling the canvas cover at the rear of the jeep. ‘I just happen to have–’ he delved into the vehicle and tore up a section of the floor ‘–two very large jerry cans full of petrol.’

‘You hid them,’ she said almost accusingly.

‘Just as well, wouldn’t you say?’

He poured the precious fuel into the tank, then carefully stowed the empty cans back in their secret compartment. ‘This should get us to Sikaner, leak or no leak. By my reckoning we’ve only another twenty miles or so to travel.’

‘Did you have the jeep specially adapted?’ She sounded intrigued and he imagined this was the kind of thing she expected special intelligence to excel at.

‘Heath Robinson,’ he replied enigmatically. ‘I did it myself – needs must.’

‘What other conjuring tricks are you hiding?’

‘Only the trick of getting there as swiftly as we can.’

CHAPTER 16

Within an hour and before the sun had had time to burn the world to a crisp, they'd arrived at the outskirts of the town. A signpost, buckled at the edges from contact with a passing truck, announced they'd reached Sikaner.

Daisy craned her head, scanning first right, then left. 'The town is bigger than I expected.'

'That's because it makes up most of the state of Sikaner – the map shows precious little beyond its boundaries.'

They drove slowly down the wide main street, avoiding small children, stray dogs and several donkey carts. On one side of the road, an odd cluster of shops was set two feet above the ground.

'Just look over there.' She nodded in their direction. 'They look for all the world like cages on stilts.'

'I imagine that's to protect the goods from sudden flooding. This place is surrounded by mountains. During the monsoon, the streets must be deluged.'

'The town looks reasonably prosperous though.'

At first sight, it did. A number of jewellers' shops lined the main thoroughfare, their trays of gold bangles flashing in the bright sun; a flower seller sat behind a mountain of roses and garlands of jasmine, piled high and strung like beads on a string; several merchants displayed a range of teas from jet black to olive green. But if you looked closely, he thought, that sense of settled prosperity proved deceptive. A stallholder here, one there, wore an apathetic face. Most sat huddled over their wares in garments that appeared poorly made. Many of the buildings, when you studied them, were undermined by walls that were deeply cracked and roofs that sported a scattering of holes. One or two of the shutters hung lopsided from a broken hinge. It could have been a theatre set, bright and convincing on the surface, but with an emptiness beyond.

He'd been aware for some time of eyes swivelling in their direction and hoped that Daisy hadn't noticed. But she had.

'We're being watched.' She sounded apprehensive.

Small knots of women and children in the maze of mean alleys that radiated left and right from the main street had stopped their work or play to gape at them.

'Perhaps they've never seen a European before,' he suggested, making light of the situation. 'Or maybe they've never seen a jeep.'

'I don't know, but whatever the reason, it's making me feel uncomfortable.' She slunk back into her seat, seeking what cover she could find.

'We may have to put up with being the local freak show. Sikaner seems a pretty enclosed community.'

That was one way of putting it. The town had certainly been difficult enough to reach and, now they were here, he felt as much as Daisy the wall of blank indifference that rose to meet them. It was the same passivity they'd encountered in Kamghar, but more aggressive if that were possible, and so more worrying.

'I can understand why Karan Rana had to escape.' Daisy's voice sounded a trifle hollow. 'This place seems completely cut off – not just from the rest of India but from the rest of Rajasthan. It must have been so isolating to grow up here.'

'It wasn't much of a getaway though. He escaped, but to what? To fight and then die.'

'At least for a while he could feel part of a wider world. This town is creepy.'

The long main road had come to an end at last and, when they turned the corner, it was to be met by an immensity of stone wall rearing up in front of them, broken only by a pair of equally immense iron gates. The wall appeared to spread for miles on either side and the gates were guarded by two uniformed soldiers, weapons at their waist.

Grayson brought the car to a halt. 'The Rajah's palace, I presume. We'd better go and introduce ourselves.'

He sprang out of the jeep and spoke a few words into the nearest guard's ear. As if by magic, the gates were flung open and they were able to drive forward into a large courtyard. Here, a group of armed men were loitering in what shade there was. One of their number hastened to a second set of gates that barred the way. His face red with effort, he cranked the handle of an enormous wooden wheel and the twenty-foot high barrier creaked opened. Ahead, they could see a ribbon of road winding its way far into the distance.

'What did you say to him? The man on the

gate.' Daisy jerked her head back towards the way they had come.

'I gave my name. It seems that we're expected.'

'Should we be?'

'I wouldn't have thought so,' he said carefully, 'but perhaps the Rajah will enlighten us when we meet him.'

'I can't say I'm looking forward to it.' She waved her hand at the vast expanse of land sliding past the vehicle on either side. 'This must all belong to him.'

Grayson grimaced. 'He goes for the impressive, doesn't he? The palace is just coming into view.'

A forbidding oblong blotted the horizon. The palace was built on top of a large rock formation; indeed it appeared to have risen unstoppably from the rock itself. The walls were dark grey, hard granite, and rose steeply from a base three or four storeys high. The surface of the walls was flat and uncompromising: no curved dome, no delicate tracery, no ornamented arch. Instead, an unyielding, almost blind face, interrupted only by rows of small windows. The sun beamed an invitation for them to open, but their closed panes flashed back a warning. A crenellated roof completed the image; beauty wasn't this building's speech but fortification, as though the palace itself might be preparing for war.

'We keep calling him a rajah, but is he? The ruler, I mean.'

'He is. I made a point of checking before we left. Always a good idea to get the title right. Princes can be touchy about these things. His first name is Talin, which doesn't inspire confidence.'

'How is that?'

'It's one of many names that mean Lord Shiva – the destroyer of the world.'

'Let's hope he's not true to his name then.' She'd said it lightly but he knew they were both thinking otherwise.

He slowed the jeep as they neared what he hoped was the final barrier. There were no guards here, but their progress must have been watched because, as they approached, the gates swung wide. Through the gates, across another bare, open space and through another thick granite archway. They had reached the inner courtyard at last and it was grander than anything they'd seen before. In an instant, the forbidding exterior of the palace was forgotten. Here the walls were no longer rough hewn but cloaked in a shining marble which had been meticulously carved into the most intricate of designs. Lush green trees lined every wall and large containers of floating flowers filled the corners, each with a brigade of green parrots perched on their rim. A fountain splashed somewhere to their right.

'We seem to have arrived.' He switched off the ignition.

Immediately, a servant, dressed head to toe in purple and gold livery, emerged from some concealed enclave and began to unload their few pieces of luggage before either of them had climbed from the jeep. The man stood to one side politely waiting, his eyes downcast, then marched towards the palace entrance, a bag in each hand. Obediently, they followed him up the stone staircase, past the line of traditional metal pots, one for each step, to the wood-panelled door. At their approach, it swung effortlessly open. He might have felt pampered, Grayson thought, if it hadn't all been so pat.

Daisy felt the merciless sun beat down on her bare neck as she climbed the stairs to the palace entrance, but once she'd stepped across its threshold, the building was cool. So cool, she thought, that you could bathe in the air and feel refreshed. A second liveried servant was waiting a few feet inside the door and gestured for them to follow him. They walked in single file along a wide corridor. Its walls were hung with damask and its floor covered in a rich carpet of thickly woven red silk. The Rajah evidently possessed riches beyond counting. But though she might gasp at such opulence, her spirit was tempered by the poverty of an East End childhood, and any admiration was tinged with a splinter of contempt. She hadn't forgotten what lay outside this magnificence.

Their bags had vanished and she wondered if they would ever see them again. The building appeared labyrinthine. Anish's description of Indian palaces came back to her: *They are built around endless courtyards with arch after arch of carved stone and each small piece of decoration inlaid with coloured gems. Then there are huge audience halls, every wall mirrored, with silk carpets on the floor and tons of crystal hanging above. And outside, broad terraces where you can walk and view the sweep of the mountains or the curve of the Ganga itself.*

They had been riding, she remembered, riding to the river and had stopped for a rest by its waters. It had been a wonderful day, a day when Anish had talked to her as a true friend. Or so she'd thought. But it was also the day that she'd come close to tragedy because someone had deliberately tampered with her saddle. She hadn't known then, couldn't have guessed, that it was Anish himself. He'd wanted her away from the bungalow and staged increasingly desperate accidents to ensure that she left. But she'd refused and instead had discovered the building's darkest secret. Accidents were no longer enough. She had to die. Not that Anish would have killed her himself – she still believed that in some twisted way he'd cared for her – but he had left her to perish at the hands of his henchmen. And that amounted to the same thing.

She pushed the terrible memory away, as she had so often in the past. She didn't think she would be seeing the Ganges today, but this building was certainly as large and as ornate as Anish had predicted. It seemed that they walked for miles, along corridors that stretched for ever. Corridors that were dotted with shuttered doors, hushed and secret spaces lying behind their closed grilles. On and on, until finally they were ushered through a pair of massive wooden doors and found themselves in a huge and empty space. It had to be an audience chamber, she thought, and again the contrast with what they had seen of Sikaner town was remarkable. Red and gold divans lined the walls. Rustling silk curtains hung from floor-length windows and, in the centre of the room, a carved and gilded chair imposed its presence on everything around it. The servant indicated that they should take a seat on one of the divans. They had hardly done so when another retainer appeared noiselessly at their side, bowing low and offering them the familiar tray of cold drinks.

Daisy gulped hers down. 'It would be good if there was something to eat,' she whispered.

'Ingrate. When I gave you the last of my biscuits.'

She smiled at him and their glances met. They hadn't spoken of the previous night, hadn't felt each other's touch since then, yet all day she had sensed his soul walking with hers. She hoped she wasn't being fanciful, but whatever the outcome of this journey together, she had new and happier memories to hold fast to.

Grayson took a second glass from the tray and spoke directly to the manservant. 'I imagine you're kept busy in this weather.' The young man smiled vacantly.

'You must have a fair number of visitors,' he pursued. 'And every one of them desperate for a cold drink.'

The smile grew more vacant still. Grayson switched to Hindi but, as far as Daisy could tell, it made little difference. There was a long pause and he seemed to be getting ready to throw out yet another question when the servant found his tongue at last. 'Excuse, please,' he said in a reedy voice, and backed hastily out of the room.

'That went well,' Grayson said laconically.

'Do you think he understood you?'

'He understood all right. There's nothing much wrong with my Hindi. He didn't *want* to understand, that's the truth.'

Before they could say more, there was a bustle outside and a noise came barrelling down the corridor towards them. They stopped talking and looked expectantly at the doorway. A small, round man sprang into the room and bounced towards them. He wore European dress, his feet in shoes so highly polished they reflected in faithful detail the chandeliers above. He had thin hair slicked back from an unlined face and the slightest hint of a moustache on his upper lip, as though it hadn't quite had the courage of its convictions.

'Miss Driscoll, Mr Harte, how good to see you safely arrived,' he oozed. His English was only slightly accented, Daisy noticed. 'I am Mr Acharya, secretary to His Royal Highness. Allow me to welcome you to Sikaner on my ruler's behalf. The Rajah is most anxious that you are comfortable. He is delighted to be entertaining such honoured guests.' Mr Acharya snatched up the gold pocket watch that dangled from his shiny waistcoat and shook it energetically. The action did nothing to stem his flow of words. 'In a very few minutes, dear guests, you will be shown to your quarters. A most delightful suite. I am sure you will be happy there. But first, of course, you must meet His Royal Highness. This is most important. His Highness begs your indulgence. A few minutes only. He will be with you presently–'

'Thank you, you are most kind.' Grayson waded across the river of eloquence. 'We must apologise for arriving out of the blue. I'm sorry we weren't able to give you warning. I take it you had no warning?'

The man gave an uneasy smirk, then rushed

once more into speech. 'But of course you must know that once you reached our town, the news travelled fast. You know Indian ways, Mr Harte,' and he wagged a stubby finger at Grayson. 'One cannot keep a secret here.'

'No, indeed,' Grayson interrupted. 'And I imagine you must often provide for travellers. From what I've seen of the town, there seems little accommodation. So we must thank you again for your hospitality.'

'We do our best,' the secretary said guardedly. 'But Sikaner is a long way from anywhere and we have very few visitors.'

'Are we your first this year then?'

The smile faded very slightly. 'I am almost sure you are, Mr Harte, but I am a busy man – as you are too, of course – and it is sometimes difficult to remember.'

'Difficult to remember who has met His Highness? You're his secretary, aren't you?'

'Indeed yes. But you have reminded me. I must be getting back to work. Please forgive.'

And Mr Acharya began walking backwards at an astonishingly quick rate, his eyes never leaving theirs, before he whisked himself out into the corridor like a startled rabbit regaining its burrow.

Daisy didn't know whether to laugh or cry.

'A comic turn,' Grayson remarked. 'But not one without use.'

'You got nothing from him.'

'And that told me everything I wanted to know. Quite clearly, he has entertained other visitors – maybe Javinder was among them. And just as clearly, he's giving nothing away.'

'Neither did the servant earlier.'

'No, he didn't, did he? It looks as though the entire household has taken a vow of *omerta.* I'll have to look elsewhere, though I haven't quite given up on the palace. Perhaps the Rajah himself will volunteer a nugget or two.'

'I take it that's a joke?'

'You never know. Stranger things have happened.' He shook himself free from the embrace of a mound of soft cushions. 'The building is beautifully cool, but somehow I've still managed to stick to this divan. A shower is what I need. I wonder how long the old boy will be?'

'You'd better sound more respectful than that.'

Respectful or not, it was a long time before 'the old boy' made an appearance. The secretary had said his employer would be with them in a matter of minutes but the time dragged on and they'd almost given up the idea of seeing him or even being escorted to the promised suite, when they heard a soft, whispering sound travelling up the corridor and in through the door.

'Listen.' Daisy held up her hand. 'Who's speaking and what are they saying?'

'The Rajah.'

'What?'

'That's what they're saying, the servants. *The Rajah, the Rajah,* over and over again. I think our host may be about to grace us with his presence.'

Grayson was right. Several minutes later, a man walked through the door into the audience chamber. Not walked, Daisy thought, but stalked. When she looked at his face she could see he was old, very old, but his carriage was still that of a young man and the white and gold robes he wore, almost stark in their simplicity, only reinforced that impression. The room was filled with a powerful authority and instinctively they rose to their feet. The Rajah moved unhurriedly towards them. He held his hand out first to her, and then to Grayson. His every action was performed with deliberation.

While he was enquiring of Grayson how their journey had gone, she had time to study him. She was trying to see a resemblance with his grandson but at first could find none. This man's complexion was weathered, his nose sharp and aquiline, his face one of stern strength. Anish had been a beautiful man, she remembered, yet when she brought his image into clearer focus, she recalled a handsome face that masked the same uncompromising force she saw in his grandfather. Anish had been prepared to sacrifice everything – his career, his life, her life – for the cause in which he believed. And this man would do the same, she was sure. His grandson would feel he'd died for independence, an independence that India now possessed. But there was an irony here perhaps. Was it the very same cause, turned upside down, for which his grandfather was willing to die?

'So your journey went smoothly?' he was saying.

He could simply be making small talk or his question could mask something infinitely darker. If he'd been behind the trials they'd encountered, their arrival must have disconcerted him. At best, they were not meant to have reached the palace but instead returned to Jasirapur, their commission a failure. At worst, they were not meant to have survived at all. If what they suspected of this man were true, he must be wondering just how they had come through the dangers he'd instigated.

'The mountain road was a trifle rough, but we took it slowly and it gave us no great problem.' Grayson was poker-faced.

'Excellent. We are delighted you were able to find us. You see, we are so out of the way here, that visitors are scarce and therefore very welcome. I hope you have no pressing need to return to Jasirapur and will stay a while.' The Rajah was courtesy itself.

'That is most kind of you, Your Highness, but I regret we can stay only a few days.'

'All this way for a few days? Mr Harte, what are you thinking? To be dragging this young lady over hill and dale for a mere two days. If you have come to see our country, you must stay a while. This part of Rajasthan has a wild beauty and is worth seeing.'

'I'm sure it is and being a tourist would certainly be enjoyable. But I am in Jasirapur to do a job of work and will need to get back there as soon as I can.'

'And you, Miss Driscoll. Are you in India to do a job of work too? Surely you will stay longer with us.'

'I'm afraid not.' She felt discomfited. There was one reason alone for her being here and now was not the time to declare it. It was a crazy reason, too, according to Grayson, and she was sure the Rajah would agree with him.

'Dear me.' The old man sighed and sipped from the glass he'd been carrying. 'That is a shame. We have so few visitors.' There seemed a need to emphasise the fact. It certainly fitted the sense they'd had, as they'd driven through the town, of a people cut off from the outside world. 'But for the few days you are here,' he continued, 'we must make sure you enjoy yourself to the full.'

Grayson smiled politely. 'I fear I'm unlikely to have the time. I've come to Sikaner on business, Your Highness.'

'And what might that be?' The man's black eyes were suddenly sharply appraising and the aquiline nose jutted aggressively.

'I have been asked by His Majesty's Government to come to India to find a missing employee. It appears that he travelled to Sikaner.' Grayson had evidently decided on the direct approach. It was probably the best way with a man this slippery.

'My goodness, Britain must have money to waste – and after the costly war she has just fought. To send you all the way from London to find a missing coolie.'

The words were utterly disparaging and she felt Grayson stiffen beside her. 'Javinder Joshi is a most respected officer in the civil service.'

'I am sure.' The Rajah waved his hand languidly. 'But all the way from London ... you have Indian colleagues, I imagine, who could go looking for him?'

'I have colleagues,' Grayson said evenly, 'but I consider this to be *my* job.'

'Then I am afraid you have had a wasted journey, Mr Harte. Sikaner is very small, too small for the British government to concern itself with, and your colleague is unlikely to have visited us.

You will leave disappointed.' There was a distinct edge to the old man's words.

'Sikaner may be small but it holds a strategic position. I am sure it assumes far greater importance in the mind of government than you realise.' Daisy could see that Grayson was deliberately flattering the man in an attempt, no doubt, to get him to talk.

'Once it was important. And if honesty and justice had prevailed, it would still be important. But Sikaner has become a force from the past, a princely state that has had its day.'

The old man hunched his shoulders in annoyance and strode towards one of the many long windows. On the way, he jettisoned his glass on a small table, casting it carelessly aside and causing it to slide perilously close to the edge and hang suspended there. He glared through the window for some minutes, then turned and walked back towards them.

'But you will know about that, who better? Mountbatten and his gentlemen are lauded in London, I believe. Lauded for an act of betrayal.' He swaddled his robes tightly against his body.

'Your words are harsh, Your Highness.'

'They are true words, young man. I have lived long enough to know truth from falsehood and no matter how the situation is glossed, the destruction of the princely states is a betrayal on the grandest scale. We have been handed to the enemies of those we thought our friends.'

It was as Grayson had said. The Rajah's disaffection was clear. And his anger no doubt behind the violence that had marred an otherwise peaceful Rajasthan. 'I take it then, that you have not joined the Indian Union, sir?' Grayson asked guilelessly.

'No, we have not joined. Not Sikaner.' The voice was quiet but entirely steel.

'And you don't intend to?'

'You are right, Mr Harte. Sikaner does not intend to join. If you know your Indian history, you will be aware that many years ago we surrendered our powers to the British Crown. That Crown no longer holds sway in India, and therefore those powers should revert to us. Anything less is a violation of the treaty we signed.'

'That is certainly one way of looking at it.'

'It is the only way.'

The words seem to provoke painful thoughts in him and for some time he stood gazing into the empty distance, his guests seemingly forgotten. At length, he roused himself to bring the audience to an abrupt end. 'But you must be tired. Hakim will show you to your quarters. We eat at six.'

'Your Highness.' Grayson bowed over the thin hand and Daisy wondered if she should curtsy. She was saved the embarrassment of deciding by Hakim, who appeared at her elbow and began very gently to shepherd her towards the doorway.

CHAPTER 17

Instead of retracing their steps to the inner courtyard, the servant opened one of the many doors they'd passed on their way to the audience chamber. Rather than the closeted space that Daisy had imagined, a spiral staircase of white marble was revealed, the curling black ironwork of its bannister swirling upwards three or four floors high.

'His Highness thought you would like a panoramic view,' Hakim remarked as they climbed. 'He asked for the blue suite to be prepared. You will see the whole of Sikaner from there.'

She exchanged a look with Grayson but neither of them spoke. In Hakim's wake, they climbed three flights of stairs until they emerged into a large open space, a marble-floored square, with glass running the length of one wall. Carved marble window frames looked out over the vast expanse of land through which they had driven. In the distance, a spread of dwellings marked the limits of the town.

'Here, please.' Hakim was opening a door on the other side of the square.

'Could you wait a moment?'

On impulse, Daisy darted across to the far wall. She'd glimpsed a large glass case filled with photographs. Even from a distance, she had seen they were very old and marked some kind of celebration. Might they give her the clue she sought?

It was a foolish notion, she knew, for how could pictures of a local festival tell her anything? Her mother had never visited India, yet Daisy knew there was a connection. The image of another old photograph coalesced with those in the case. The image of Lily Driscoll in nursing uniform and wearing a brooch that could only be Indian, a celebration of the goddess Nandni Mata, the daughter. How did it all add up? It didn't, that was the answer, and she scolded herself for her desperation, even as she was drawn to the display.

All the pictures recorded the same event and, by the look of it, it had been a magnificent affair. Elephants paraded through the streets of the town, draped with elaborately woven blankets of flowers, their foreheads studded with jewels and gold. The beast leading the convoy, by far the strongest it seemed, carried the Rajah's throne, a massive pedestal draped in gold brocaded velvet. She peered closely at the figure sitting atop, but he was in shadow. A string of elephants followed in the Rajah's wake, the two immediately behind decorated almost as splendidly as his, but bearing empty *howdahs.* That was interesting but hardly significant. She was clutching at straws.

'There's no one riding in them,' she said hopefully.

'There won't be. They're empty because they contain the spirits of the Rajah's forebears.'

Grayson had punctured whatever bubble had been brewing. She was trying to make something out of nothing and she must stop. She walked back to join Hakim waiting patiently for them, a large brass key in his hand. He gave a small bow and flung open the double doors to the most sumptuous apartment she had ever seen. A huge sitting room decorated in blue and gold, two similarly lavish bedrooms, a marble tiled bathroom for each of them and what she imagined was a sizeable balcony, hidden for the moment by the bamboo blinds that reached to the floor. The few clothes they'd brought had already been unpacked. She wandered into one of the bathrooms and saw her modest toiletries arranged neatly on a marble shelf.

'There's nothing for me to do,' she remarked, walking back into the sitting room.

'The way to live. I could get used to it.' Grayson had thrown himself down on one of the long silk-covered divans and kicked off his shoes.

'It may be, but the Rajah doesn't seem too happy with his life.'

'He doesn't, does he? In fact, I would say he is one angry man. And he didn't try to hide it.'

'It was the talk of independence that upset him most.'

Before Grayson could respond, there was a knock at the door and Hakim appeared on the threshold, towing behind him two fellow retainers and a wheeled trolley.

Daisy's eyes opened wide. Food. Thank goodness. There was a limit to how long a dry biscuit could keep you going. The servants unpacked the trolley with care, arranging the plates and bowls in a circle on the low table that stood between the two divans. To Daisy, each dish looked better than the one before, and she itched for the men to leave.

The door had barely closed, before both she and Grayson dived into the feast. For some while, they were too busy to talk.

'I can see the Rajah feels bad about independence, but why is he so very angry?' she asked eventually, munching her way through a second stuffed *vada.*

'Because he feels coerced into becoming part of an India that he doesn't recognise. His ancestors signed a treaty with Britain and that treaty is now defunct, so he argues that the powers his family gave up should return to him.'

'I think he has a point.'

Grayson pursed his lips. 'A small point perhaps,' he conceded, 'but the world has moved on since those treaties were signed. Britain's conquest of India was haphazard, that's always been the problem. Any rulers who welcomed the invaders or proved a worthy foe were allowed to remain on their throne, provided they acknowledged Britain as the paramount power. So there's always been two Indias – one administered by the government in Delhi and a separate India of the princes.'

'But he's not alone, is he? You said there were other states that have refused to join the union.'

'A few, but Mountbatten managed to persuade most of them to sign up. To be fair, they didn't have much choice. Some of the big boys are still holding out – places like Hyderabad and Kashmir – but the very small states gave in months ago.'

'But not Sikaner. So the Rajah is out on a limb. I wonder what he hopes to achieve.'

'That's what I'm wondering too. Perhaps he thinks Britain will relent and agree princely independence for the most stubborn. I know that some of the more bolshie states have lobbied for it, but since they've never been formal British territory, it's impossible. In any case Britain couldn't be seen to support rulers against their subjects. That would undermine any notion of democracy. Or maybe–'

'Maybe he hopes to make enough trouble that India won't want his state in the union?'

'Something like that. Here you've missed these pakoras.' He pushed the bowl towards her.

'I can't eat another thing. What a spread. But the trouble you spoke of doesn't seem to be happening here. The people we've seen don't appear fearsome and they don't look as if they've suffered violence either. The town might not have a good feeling, but it's more like apathy than anything else.'

'We saw only a small part of the town,' he warned, 'then we were whisked into this privileged enclave. What it's like out in the villages, in the fields, could be very different. That's what Javinder would have wanted to find out.'

Daisy lay back on the divan, replete. 'The Rajah was pretty certain Javinder hadn't come this way.'

'A little too certain,' said Grayson sombrely. 'It's too late to do anything today, but I'll be up at first light before Verghese or his household get wind of my intentions.'

'And they are?'

'To ask a lot of questions of a lot of people. But first I'll phone Mike – the police station should have a phone I can use. He needs to know we've made it here and, by some miracle, he may have turned up something useful by now.'

Daisy couldn't quite keep a yawn from escaping. She was feeling cool and rested and she'd barely slept last night.

He looked across at her. 'We still have dinner to get through. You better snatch some sleep while you can. I promise not to wake you – unless there's an emergency. Sorting out my bow tie, for instance,' he teased.

Dinner was not something she wanted to contemplate, but sleep most definitely was. She stumbled into her room and saw that the bed was large enough to fill almost one wall. Its sheets were freshly ironed and its pillows plumped. It looked so inviting, and she was so tired. She fell asleep almost instantly.

Daisy had barely shut her bedroom door, when a knock sounded from the corridor. Not Hakim this time but a young boy, bare-headed and wearing a simple white tunic.

He hovered on the threshold, pointing mutely to the dishes on the table. He had no English, it seemed, and Grayson spoke to him in Hindi. 'You've come to clear what's left? It was a very good meal. Thank you.'

The boy smiled shyly and began rather awkwardly to pile dishes on to the large tray he'd brought.

'Here, let me help. That tray is almost as big as you.'

'Thank you, sir, but no. It is not fitting.'

'Who's going to see? I take it you're new here? What's your name?'

'I am Chintu. I am training to wait at table. Soon I will have my uniform,' the boy said proudly, balancing one dish on another in a precarious fashion. 'This task is the very first I have been given to do alone. Hakim is busy below.'

'Then we must be sure that you make a good job of it.' And despite the boy's protests, Grayson continued to load crockery neatly on to the tray.

'Was it difficult to find work here?' he asked conversationally.

'It was not easy, sir. Life is hard.' The boy's expression had changed subtly.

'Hard in Sikaner?'

'Yes, sir. Very. My mother and father are poor and I have many brothers and sisters.'

'So working here is quite a promotion for you?'

The faintest shadow passed across the boy's face, but he said nothing.

'It must be good, though, to find yourself a place of safety in these difficult times,' Grayson pursued. Chintu's eyes met his, but his face remained blank. 'I heard there had been problems, you see. An outbreak of violence, but no doubt it's been exaggerated. You know how tales start.'

'It was not exaggerated,' the boy said. 'It has been bad.'

Grayson sat down and rested his hands casually on his knees. 'Tell me about it. Don't worry, there's no one to hear you other than me and I'm always interested in the places I visit.'

Chintu let go of the tray. 'Things had settled down after the troubles, you see.'

'The troubles that followed Partition?'

'Yes indeed. But it was never so bad in Rajasthan. We are mainly Hindu, as you know, sir. We heard the most terrible things were happening elsewhere. In Bengal, for instance. People trying to escape and the trains becoming rolling coffins.'

'Calcutta, yes, I know. I read that it was very dreadful.'

The boy's eyes had grown large and, without thinking, he sat down on the divan opposite Grayson. 'Many, many people died. Do you know they took Moslems to the Hooghly River and decapitated them on the bridge there? They say that vultures were feeding off the bodies as they floated downstream.'

'It doesn't bear thinking of. But that didn't happen here, surely?'

'There were some problems.' Chintu paused briefly as he thought back to the previous year, but then hastened to assure Grayson, 'Some problems, but nowhere near as bad. And after Partition, things were quiet. The Moslems who stayed were happy enough. There was no enmity.'

Grayson nodded understandingly. 'But...'

'But then it started. A Moslem girl was attacked–' Chintu looked embarrassed '–you understand?' Grayson nodded again. 'Then a Hindu was murdered. For revenge. Then another Moslem and so on.'

'Random attacks?'

'Yes, I suppose so,' the boy said uncertainly. 'Each time there was a rumour. No one knew who started it, but the rumour was believed, a tale about some person in the town and then they would be killed. But there was unhappiness and several people spoke out against what was happening. They were murdered too.'

'So not so random. And is it still happening?'

'I don't know, sir. We hear nothing in the palace. But do not fear, you will be safe.'

'I'm not worried for my own safety, but I have a young lady accompanying me.'

Chintu looked concerned. 'Then perhaps it would be wise to go soon. I think there will be more trouble.'

'Yes?'

'This time, big trouble. My uncle...'

'What about your uncle?'

'I must not say.'

'Come, Chintu. You can tell me. I'm a stranger and know no one here. Is your uncle dead?' The boy shifted uneasily on the divan, but Grayson needed more. 'Did he die because of another rumour?'

'No, not this time. My uncle knew something bad was to happen. He told people. He told me, don't go to work in the palace. There is evil there.'

'But you didn't believe him. You still came to work here.'

'I had no choice,' the boy said simply. 'My parents are very poor and now that my uncle is gone, there is less money still.'

'Then, of course, you must do your duty.'

Chintu seemed suddenly to realise where he was and started up from his seat. He collected the tray of china, but for a moment stood irresolute. 'You will not say we have spoken, sir?'

'I will say nothing, you have my promise. But before you go, tell me – did you have a visitor to the palace a few months ago? A young man who had travelled from Jasirapur. You would remember him, I'm sure.'

'No, nobody, sir. I must go now. Hakim will be angry.'

The boy had clammed up. He had been unwilling enough to speak of his family but would say nothing of what was going on in the palace. Not that he would know a great deal, but Grayson would have bet his life that he knew about Javinder. *Omerta* ruled once more and he had no choice but to let Chintu go.

When the boy had shuffled out into the corridor, the tray tilting dangerous to one side, Grayson lay down on the divan and thought. Things were getting decidedly murky. There had been violence here – he knew that from reading Javinder's early reports – but Chintu had suggested there was worse to come, far worse. And Daisy was sleeping in the room next door. He didn't like the situation one little bit.

He wondered at Hakim sending the boy alone to the room. Perhaps he'd had no other option, but it was a risk. Still, Chintu was desperate for the work and had probably been drilled into silence. It was only the fact that Grayson knew Hindi that enabled them to talk, and Hakim might have been told that the visitors spoke only English. If so, the Rajah's spy network had let him down. He would take heed of Chintu's warning that trouble was about to engulf Sikaner, but Javinder had to be his goal and there he'd learned nothing. If the boy hadn't suddenly remembered his vow of silence, he would have asked him about Dalip Suri too. There had been neither sound nor sight of their enemy from Megaur. Perhaps they had been wrong about him. Perhaps it had been coincidence that he was in the first village they'd stopped at.

There were too many unanswered questions. All he could do was follow his plan and slip into town early the next morning, before the household woke and discovered him missing. He would have a couple of hours, no more, to make the call to Mike and then to ask around for the answers he needed. After that, he'd be forced to make a swift return to the palace. If only he could find one reliable source in those few hours, someone who would know Javinder's likely whereabouts or, God forbid, give him news of his death. Once he knew the score, he could act. The army was on standby and he'd have no hesitation in bringing the soldiers in.

But speed was of the essence. If Chintu was right and the trouble he talked of imminent, then Daisy needed to be got to safety. The Rajah had already attempted several times to rid the world of both of them, and failed. But he wouldn't fail again, not on home turf. Grayson didn't want to worry the girl he loved, but he did need to warn her. The last thing he wanted was her to blunder into matters that could be incendiary, not with a man who was already burning bright with anger. She was never going to find what she sought, not in this guarded and repressive place. He could see that, but could he make her see it? He must persuade her she would find nothing within the palace walls. Persuade her to act as naturally as possible. Above all, persuade her to stay silent. It wouldn't allay suspicions entirely but it might keep her safe.

A hand on her shoulder woke Daisy some hours later. Grayson's voice came to her from what seemed a long way away.

'Time to get ready for our second audience. Before you do, though, come and look at this.'

She forced her eyes open and stumbled out of bed. Back in the sitting room, the blinds had been raised and she saw they'd been covering a wall of floor-length windows that overlooked a new stretch of land. This expanse must lie at the rear of the palace. Grayson opened one of the windows wide and the warm air of evening poured into the room, sweet and spicy. The scent of the last magnolias. It travelled around the walls, then weaved a path over carpets and between chairs and tables and divans.

Together they walked out onto the balcony. He stepped back against the balustrade and faced the building. 'See.' She joined him and looked to right and left, then craned her neck upwards. Every window and every crenellation of the roof was outlined by a thousand light bulbs. Their radiance dazzled the surrounding darkness.

'We look like an ocean liner,' he joked, 'except for the fact that we're landlocked.'

Daisy's eyes widened as she took in the sight. 'Amazing. And to afford such a display. Think how much wealth there must be in this place.'

'And that's where the Rajah intends to keep it. Come on, we'd better do our duty. You've got ten minutes to throw on a frock.'

She did it in less. Her one spare dress was pulled from the hanging rail and the pair of red-heeled sandals, which matched its flower print, fished from under the bed. By some miracle, both shoes and dress were presentable. A dab of powder, a slick of lipstick and a brush pulled through curls tangled by sleep, and she was ready. Although not, she felt, for dinner. She had eaten only a few hours previously and thought it unlikely she could do justice to the meal. But when they reached the dining room, escorted by the faithful Hakim, the aroma that reached her was so enticing that she decided she might manage a few dishes after all. It was as well since the Rajah was looking even sterner tonight, and a great deal more magnificent. A bejewelled turban sat astride his head and an imposing array of decorations hung from a beaded tunic. She stole a swift glance around the table; it was so long it might almost be an ocean liner in itself. She and Grayson were sitting opposite each other, with the Rajah at the head of the table, stiff and upright in another vast gold and red chair. Several of his advisers – at least she imagined they were advisers – were arranged around the far end.

The dining room was smaller than the vast audience chamber of this afternoon, but what it lacked in size, it made up for in the splendour of its fittings. Every wall was draped in swathes of embossed silk, and crystal chandeliers, four or five tiers high, hung from a carved wooden ceiling. A sequence of jewel-encrusted arches sitting atop highly decorated pillars travelled along one complete side of the room, their architecture echoed by the row of ornately carved window arches opposite. Behind the Rajah's imposing chair was a wall of glass cases and, from where she sat, Daisy could see that each boasted a richer display than the next. The most fabulous collection of jewellery glinted from their depths: emerald rings, diamond brooches, necklaces made from layers of rubies the size of pigeon eggs. As the precious gems caught the light, shards of colour were thrown across the room. She tried not to stare but it was a mesmerising spectacle.

A line of servants, dressed in purple and gold uniforms, brought dish after dish. She ate well, not realising that these were merely the appetisers, and when bowls and plates had been cleared, she saw with dismay that another enormous spread had found its way to the table. With every succeeding course, she had to force herself to take at least a little of the food that was offered. It was unlikely she would need to eat for a month, she thought, once they'd left Sikaner. A retainer poured wine for her and for Grayson, but she noticed that neither the Rajah nor his advisers partook. She sipped sparingly. She would need her wits about her. Grayson had his job to do, but she had set herself her own quest and she was determined to fulfil it.

The Rajah had remained silent for most of the meal. Now he stopped eating and looked across at her. 'You enjoy Indian food I see, Miss Driscoll.'

'I do.'

'And is this an acquired taste?'

The question seemed odd. 'I'm sorry, I'm not sure I understand you,' she said.

'It is simple enough. Have you always eaten Indian food? Somehow I imagine not. English people are so very conservative. They alone could have brought the execrable Windsor soup to my homeland. So you have acquired a taste for our food it seems. You have been in India before.'

The same uncomfortable prickle started its dance up and down her spine; here was someone else who'd taken the trouble to discover her history.

CHAPTER 18

'I have, Your Highness. There's no secret to it.' She sounded a little too bold, she knew, and felt Grayson's gaze intent on her across the table.

'No secret indeed. From what I hear, quite the opposite. But perhaps we should not talk of it. I understand your stay with us ended badly. I must apologise on behalf of my countrymen.'

She was beginning to feel flustered. 'It's really not necessary. Whatever happened took place years ago and quite some way away.'

'Ah yes. In Jasirapur. Where you have returned to.'

She said nothing and he fixed her with a sardonic eye. 'A curious decision, I feel.'

'I don't consider it so,' she said, now in battle mode. 'I was offered an opportunity to return to a beautiful country and I wanted very much to take it. Why would I not?'

'At the moment, Miss Driscoll, I am unsure.'

'There's no mystery, Your Highness.' She tried

to sound casual. 'I loved India on my first visit and when I had the chance to accompany Mr Harte, I took it.'

'How delightfully positive. Though Jasirapur is hardly a magnet for visitors.' A slyness had entered his voice and it reminded her very much of Ramesh Suri.

'I agree that Jasirapur is a modest town but it was where I lived.'

'And almost died, so I hear. Tell me why you returned.'

She could sense rather than see Grayson flash a warning, but she was feeling decidedly ruffled and very slightly angry. What right had this man to speak so dismissively to her, to interrogate, to question her integrity, for that was what he was doing. No right whatsoever. In that moment, she made a decision. Grayson might caution as much as he liked but she wouldn't be silenced. She would abandon pretence right now and go straight for her quarry.

'I knew happy times in Jasirapur as well as bad, Your Highness, and it's been a pleasure to return. I made a very good friend when I lived there. A friend I still carry in my heart. Your grandson.'

Your grandson but my good companion, she thought, someone who had taught her to ride and to revel in the beauty of the Indian countryside. Who, for a short while, had helped her discover the joy of friendship.

There was no reaction. The old man's face was an empty canvas. 'Anish,' she prompted, wondering if, like Suri, he would deny his relatives, deny that he had ever had a son or a grandson.

'I know the name,' the Rajah conceded. 'But if you were his friend, you will know his story. You will know that his father left Sikaner many years before the boy was born. I am unlikely to have any interest in him. And unlikely ever to wish to talk of him.'

'How very sad. I wonder – did you never once wish to see your grandson?'

The advisers moved uneasily at the end of the table. It was evidently a subject that was not to be broached.

'Never, Miss Driscoll. Did you think I had? I'm sorry to disappoint you.' There was a spiteful smile on his face. 'My only son was killed fighting for the British. Did you know that too?'

She nodded.

'Then you will also know that after his death, his wife wished to keep the boy. I really had not the energy to fight the woman. He could have come to me if he had chosen. But he did not.'

That seemed to be the end of the conversation, though his body language spoke something quite different. He was hunched forward almost leaning into the various dishes scattered on the table and fixing both Daisy and Grayson with a malignant gaze.

'Karan Verghese fought for the British and died for them,' he said forbiddingly. 'Died a thousand miles from home for a country that has now abandoned us. We princes have been the British Crown's staunchest allies. We have feasted their dignitaries and paid homage to their king. We have been loyal and lavish. And much more.'

No one spoke and the Rajah muttered, 'Much,

much more. At our own expense, we have raised forces for Britain's wars and fought in them bravely. Our blood has watered foreign fields in their cause. And with what reward? What have we reaped? Gratitude? Honour? No, nothing like. Betrayal, that is what we have reaped.'

The advisers shifted even more uneasily and it was only the return of the battalion of servants that broke the tension. Expertly, they delivered several trays of desserts and sweetmeats alongside finger bowls of water and, by the time they had left the room, the conversation had returned to the mundane. Daisy was forced to accept defeat. Talin Verghese was implacable and she knew he would not lift a finger to help her.

But minutes before the meal came to a final end, he unexpectedly broke through the trivial chatter to fling a comment that stirred her interest. 'I have another son, you know, Miss Driscoll. Adopted, of course, but what can one do when one is given five daughters and a single boy?'

'Is he here in the palace?' She wondered why they had not yet encountered him.

'You will meet him tomorrow. Adeep is travelling with a friend, but I have every expectation of seeing him in the morning. You will like him, I'm sure. He is a good boy and he is my future. His name means "light" and that is what he is to me. A light that I thought never to have. When I am gone, he will rule Sikaner.'

The same implacable note had returned and it made Daisy feel very tired. The difficult journey, the sleepless night, the strain of maintaining a facade against a formidable adversary were taking their toll. She wanted to escape this laden table, this opulent room, and escape quickly. Grayson helped her out.

'It is has been a delightful dinner, Your Highness. May I thank you on behalf of myself and Miss Driscoll for your generous hospitality.'

Daisy had never heard him sound so formal. The old man simply bent his head, but she thought she could discern a guileful smile on his face when he murmured, 'Our former rulers are always welcome, Mr Harte.'

He clapped his hands and one of the servants lingering in the doorway came forward and bowed to them. Hakim had disappeared it seemed, and this man was to escort them to their suite. They might have been hard put to find their way, but there was something oppressive in not being allowed to walk alone.

They were halfway back to the apartment, when a large dog, hair flying, came racing at full stretch along the corridor and cannoned into them. Grayson had to grab her arm to prevent her being knocked to the floor. Brought up sharply by several unexpected legs, the dog promptly turned tail and rushed frantically back the way he'd come, only to crash heavily into a servant coming from the opposite direction, a loaded tray in his hands. The tray flew outwards and with it the contents. Dishes of sticky sweetmeats tumbled to the floor. Their escort grabbed the dog and, signalling to them to stay where they were, dashed off towards the small staircase she'd noticed earlier. It ran down one side of the building, down to the servants' quarters, she imagined, where the hound would no doubt face imprisonment. The servant who had been carrying the tray began hastily to clear the carpet of its unwanted covering.

'We're to stay here?'

'Presumably,' Grayson replied. 'I don't want to upset the apple cart just yet by stepping out of line. You've done enough of that for one evening. And it's odds on we'd lose our way if we tried to get back ourselves.'

She looked along the passage. There were rooms aplenty, but every door was closed except the one nearest her, and this showed only the smallest chink of light. While the servant had his head down sweeping the floor clean, she pushed the door gently ajar and glanced in. It was a study or office and immediately she felt herself grow tight with expectation.

At the far end of the room, beneath the slatted window, was an enormous desk with a tantalising array of drawers and, across its top, a scatter of papers which looked as though they had been abandoned in a hurry. On every wall, bookcases reached for the ceiling, for the most part filled with old and decaying books but here and there they housed the odd dusty photograph, the odd sheaf of paper filed horizontally. The room gave her food for thought, food for exploration. She felt Grayson watching her and affected indifference, bringing her gaze back to the servant who had finished his cleaning and was now bowing his way past. Their escort appeared around the corner at that moment and motioned them to follow. The servants in this palace seemed to appear and disappear like wraiths, she thought. Within five minutes they were back in their suite.

'What was that about?' Grayson asked. He shut the door smartly behind them.

'What?' She tried to sound innocent.

'Your interest in the room back there.'

'It was just another door,' she answered airily. 'There are so many in this place and most of them closed. I thought I'd like for once to see what was lurking on the other side. As it turned out, not a lot.'

He strode over to her and took hold of both her forearms. 'We need to tread softly, Daisy. No more confrontations.' His grip and his voice were firm.

'Which means...?'

'What I say. We'll only ever find out what we need to by stealth. No more confronting the Rajah or his minions directly. Not the way you did at dinner. The lower the key, the more we'll discover.'

'The more *you'll* discover,' she retorted.

She wandered out on to the balcony for a last look at the town. Here and there a few lights still glimmered, a few fires still burned.

Grayson soon joined her. 'I'm serious about keeping a low profile. If you haven't realised it yet, we're surrounded in this place by danger.'

She had realised it, but she couldn't let go. She'd set out for Sikaner without any real idea of what she would face. It was clear now that there would be no gentle conversation with the Rajah, clear that she would have to dig for the information she wanted. But she did still want it. Yet Grayson was warning her off as strongly as he could, and she felt herself bridling at what she thought an ambush.

He was watching her closely and when he spoke, his tone was conciliatory. 'The room below might be disappointing but I do have something interesting to tell you.' She could see he wanted to brush their disagreement to one side. 'While you were asleep, I managed to get one of the servants to talk a little. He's only a young boy and not working here willingly. I got enough from him to confirm what I thought – that the violence in this region has been emanating from the palace. Unfortunately, though, I didn't get enough to know where Javinder might be. The boy clammed up immediately I mentioned him.'

'That suggests Javinder was definitely here, doesn't it?'

'In the district, at least. I'll need to slip away tomorrow before anyone stirs. Asking questions in the town won't be easy, but if someone lets just one thing slip, it might be sufficient.'

'We could have asked questions today, before we knocked at the palace gates.'

'I don't think so. Did you notice the car that was shadowing us?'

She turned a shocked face to him. 'No.'

'It was there all right. A large black saloon. An expensive saloon, and it joined us a few miles before we got to the town. If I'd stopped, it would have stopped too. I doubt I'd have managed a sentence before some heavyweight was at my side.'

The danger he'd talked of suddenly became very real. A cold hand clawed at her stomach and she turned to walk back through the open windows without a glance at the view that minutes earlier had entranced her.

'Are you okay?' He'd followed her back into the sitting room.

'I'm sorry to be feeble,' she apologised, 'but it's unnerving to think that someone has been following us from the moment we got here.'

'It may be unnerving, but on the other hand, it tells us that our Rajah has most definitely got something to hide. And quite possibly that something is Javinder's whereabouts.'

If Talin Verghese was indeed complicit in Javinder's disappearance, he was as malign as her mind had been painting. It would explain the tension she'd felt since they rolled through the first set of iron gates, explain her discomfort when the Rajah's eyes rested on them. As though he knew exactly who they were and why they were here. A sinister puppet master. It was her experience at Amrita all over again, but more menacing still. She prayed hard that tomorrow Grayson would manage to elude the heavyweights, as he called them, and return to the palace before anyone realised he'd gone. If he didn't, if he were caught, she would be alone in this place and a hostage. And that was an even more discomfiting notion.

'We should get some sleep.' Grayson had come close and brushed his finger down one side of her cheek. She'd been staring into space, she realised, while her mind lost itself in a web of distrust.

She padded into the bathroom, allowing her one decent dress to fall into a heap. She was too abstracted to pick it up and walked into the shower in a daze. She cranked the handle and nothing happened. In the next-door bathroom she heard the water bouncing merrily against the tiled walls. Grayson was having no problems. She tried again, wrenching the handle first one way, then another, but without success. She began to shiver. The days might be burningly hot but the palace at night seemed to have its own refrigeration unit.

'Grayson,' she called out. 'Can you hear me?'

There was no answer and she called louder. The water came to a halt. 'What's up?'

'I can't get this damn shower to work.'

'Tut, tut, Daisy. And you a lady. I've never heard you swear before.'

'I'm so tired, I think I'll drop. What am I doing wrong?'

'Probably nothing.'

She jumped. Grayson's voice was right behind her. He stood in the doorway, a towel wrapped around his waist. And she was utterly naked with nowhere to hide. He seemed not to notice, but strode up to the shower and gave the handle an almighty thump. Water cascaded down, the torrent almost knocking the breath from her body.

He stood and laughed. 'You wanted water and there it is.'

'Not this much,' she spluttered.

'You are never satisfied, Miss Driscoll.' He came back into the cubicle and gradually eased the flow.

'Are you?' he said in her ear. 'Satisfied, I mean.' He nibbled at the other ear.

She felt his hands come round her waist and allowed herself to be pulled hard against his body. His fingers reached up and traced the outline of her breasts and his lips planted a kiss on the nape of her neck.

'Come on,' he said in a low voice. 'We're far too wet.' He wrapped her in a large towel and before she could protest, had lifted her off her feet and carried her to the bed. 'This is where we should be.'

They landed in a heap, rumpling the sheets and sending the bedcover tumbling to the floor. She didn't protest. Tiredness was forgotten and it seemed exactly where they should be. He put his arms around her again and drew her close. Her hair was still damp and spiralling wildly, but, with long, slow strokes, he smoothed the curls back from her face. She lay for some time, enjoying his touch, enjoying his warmth, but wanting more. Then his hands were on her body and she was tingling from the tips of her toes to the smallest hairs on her head. She put her arms around his neck and brought his mouth down on hers. There was the slightest taste of the sweet wine they had drunk. He kissed her open mouth, deeper and deeper, while her body softened beneath him. She reached out for him, but his lips weren't yet satisfied. His mouth moved slowly downwards, caressing soft skin with small, moist kisses. Every last piece of her seemed marked by his mouth, his hands, his kisses And it seemed the most natural thing in the world, to be loving him again.

She'd discounted the night they had spent on the mountain as simply an interlude, an aberration from the neutral friendship they'd agreed upon. But it seemed that it hadn't been such an aberration. They had fallen back in love, she thought with amazement. Or maybe they had never stopped loving each other. They'd given up too easily. She'd given up. It had been too difficult and she'd taken the easy way out. She'd run and locked herself away in solitude. But not any longer. The unexpected had happened. She hadn't wanted it but it was here: she was being loved and she was loving it.

'Why *did* you leave me?' he asked drowsily, as some time later they lay side by side, their hands clasped, their faces turned to each other. 'What was the real reason?'

'You know why. I was scared.'

'Scared of loving me?'

'Scared of taking the next step.'

'And I didn't help, did I?' he said ruefully. 'I tried to badger you into marriage.'

She nuzzled his cheek, wanting to reassure him. 'It was reasonable for you to expect I'd say yes.'

'And now? Is it still reasonable?'

She took a little time to answer. 'I think so.'

'Then I'd better hope that "think" turns into a definite "yes".' He kissed her hair, then closed his eyes.

She hoped it would too, but she knew that in her mind, in her heart, it was difficult for her to make the commitment Grayson wanted. She wished she understood why she felt this way. It had to do with discovering her true identity, that was clear. But what was keeping her chained to a solitary life was more than this. The hurdle she couldn't jump was higher, tougher. It had to do with India itself, with what had happened here ten years ago. It had to do with Anish and losing him, though why she couldn't imagine. He had plotted against her and been willing to see her die at the hands of his confederates, yet since his end in the mud and water of the monsoon, she had felt incomplete. If her world were a jigsaw, the pieces were at odds, jumbled and misshapen, and she was missing the most important, the piece that was key, the one at the very centre of the picture. She should rejoice that Anish had met his comeuppance, but she couldn't, no matter how often she took herself to task for romanticising his memory.

She looked across at Grayson. He was still lying stretched out beside her but had fallen into a deep sleep. She snuggled into him, ready to follow suit, wondering what the servants would make of finding that only one bed had been slept in. But she was too happy to be worried by the likely gossip. No doubt it would be duly reported to the Rajah, and no doubt confirm his every bad opinion of his former masters.

She must have slept for several hours and woke only because Grayson had flung himself horizontally across the bed, and was pinning her arm beneath the weight of his body. Pins and needles raced up and down her trapped limb. Very carefully, she slid herself free. The light from an enormous moon flooded through the room, touching their faces, etching their profiles. She lay for some time looking at him, not quite believing that at last it might be coming right for them. He was a good-looking man, she thought. He always had been. Even when she was married to Gerald, she'd been unable to stop herself from being attracted. But if a handsome face and figure were his sum total, she wouldn't be lying here. He was far more: interesting, courageous, loving. Above all, an honest man in his loving. Another woman would have delighted in his constancy. Instead, she had distanced herself from him; the more he'd wished to spend his life with her, the more distant she had grown. It was perverse.

Yet it had a kind of logic. A logic that held, even if she were able to put aside her confusion over Anish. How could she be a good wife when she carried with her the miseries of a wretched marriage? How be a good mother, when she'd known only rejection as a child? She'd all but come to terms with her disastrous marriage, but her abandonment as an infant was something quite different. She could not forget that. She would never forget. Her mother had done what she could for her small daughter, Daisy was sure, but what did it amount to? A single woman with a fatherless baby was an outcast in society. And sure enough, Lily Driscoll had been cast out – to a pauper's grave. And, all the time, in the background, there must have been a man, the man who was her father. Why had he not done the decent thing and married Lily? Where had he been when her mother died? Far away was the answer, no doubt in body as well as in spirit. But he could have returned to save his daughter from the wretchedness of an orphan's life. He could have, but he hadn't. If he was still in this world, she had to confront him. If he was in India, she had to meet him. She had to know why he'd abandoned her.

Grayson flung himself to the other side of the

bed. He was having an energetic dream. She smiled to herself, wondering a little wickedly just what that might entail. She lay looking up at the carved ceiling, an intricate pattern of interlocking geometric shapes, and the image of another room floated into her mind. The room below. The office she'd seen when the dog had sent the tray of sweetmeats flying. It had tempted her then, but there had been no opportunity to explore. Was it possible she might find something there? The jumble of books and papers and photographs had suggested it was a private space, not an administrative office for palace business. If the room were used by the Rajah, there was the possibility that she might find something personal, something that had belonged to his son. If Karan Verghese had left notes, letters, a diary perhaps, there was the smallest glimmer of hope that he might have mentioned her mother in one or other of them. Said aloud, it sounded hopeless, but it was all she had. Mr Bahndari had mentioned that Parvati refused to accept any of her errant husband's possessions when news of his death arrived, so where would they have gone but to his estranged father? The Rajah might simply have burned them, as Ramesh Suri had done his sister's, but she didn't think so. Even though Karan had proved a sad disappointment, the old man must have retained some feeling for him. He hankered for a son, else why the adopted boy, Adeep? She was almost certain he would have kept Karan's few belongings but locked them away, not wishing to remember. So why not lock them away in a private room?

CHAPTER 19

That decided her. Grayson had been adamant she must say nothing that could precipitate the danger he feared. But she wouldn't be saying anything. She wouldn't be involved in any confrontation. In the strictest sense, she wouldn't be going against his wishes. If she crept to the room while the palace slept, no one need ever know. She could make a brief search and return before anyone was awake.

She slipped noiselessly out of bed and dressed in the clothes she'd worn the previous day. Grayson was still sleeping soundly when she let herself out of the suite and tiptoed into the corridor. Despite the brave words to herself, her fingers were tightly crossed that she could find her way back to the study and without meeting a fellow night wanderer. It turned out to be a more difficult journey than she'd anticipated. On several occasions, she turned in the wrong direction and found herself looking at a blank wall or down an unfamiliar corridor, and all the time her heart was in her mouth at every creak of a wooden door or sigh of the palace walls. But eventually she stood outside the room she sought. Its door was no longer ajar and that halted her. She could have no idea what, or even who, was behind its blank facade. She breathed deep and gathered her courage. She needed all of it to turn the door handle.

There was nobody. For a moment, she was overwhelmed with relief and had to grasp the back of the nearest chair to steady herself. She waited until her breathing had settled before she gave the room a swift scan. She must be quick, she couldn't afford to linger. Grayson would be awake in less than an hour and ready to leave on his own adventure. She made for the desk. It was the most obvious place to look, but a cursory glance at the papers strewn across its surface, made plain there was little to interest her here. She bent down to the drawers on one side of the desk, methodically flicking through their contents and making sure she replaced everything as she found it. One side completed, but again nothing of interest. On to the drawers on the far side. She found them locked and her pulse beat a little quicker. This could be it. Inside could be the letters she sought, the diary, the journal, anything that Karan had written in his time in Brighton. She tugged at each of the three compartments in turn, hoping the locks were too old to withstand an assault, and forgetting in her furious concentration that she'd intended to leave no trace of her visit. The drawers remained obstinately shut. Frustration made her careless and she shuffled the papers here and there on the desktop, looking for anything that might be strong enough to break the locks. A tray of pens, a sheaf of blotting paper and a paper knife, were all she found. Nothing she could use.

But perhaps, after all, it wasn't the desk she should focus on. The bookcases that lined every wall might hold what she wanted. She walked slowly from one set of shelves to another, searching first the lower tiers and making sure she felt behind each row of books, then when that proved unsuccessful, dragging a chair to each bookcase in turn and clambering to the very top shelves. Still nothing.

It had to be the desk. She bounced back across the room. There was a madness in her now; the more frustrated she became, the more she believed there was something in this room, something locked in this desk, something that Talin Verghese did not want to be seen. If so, it had to concern his dead son, and she had to get those drawers open. She went back to the desk and picked up the paper knife. It looked a feeble tool, but it was the only thing possible. She bent over the top drawer and had begun prodding and poking the lock with the knife, when a voice from the doorway made her heart jump in fright.

'Are you quite mad?'

It was Grayson. Thank heaven for that at least. 'I have to get these last three drawers open,' was her sole explanation.

'What are you thinking of? This is a private office, and if I'm not mistaken the Rajah's personal domain. And you're burgling it?'

'It looks bad, I know.'

'Looks bad!' Grayson's expression was explosive. 'It looks bloody lethal – for us. Now come back to the room, for God's sake.'

'I can't. I have to open these drawers.' Her whole life, it seemed, depended on opening them. It was stupid, but if she had been drowning and the drawers were weighing her to the ocean floor, she would have clung to them still.

Grayson took only an instant to decide. He strode over to the desk and took the paper knife from her hand. In three swift clicks, he'd opened three drawers.

She gaped at him.

'What did you expect?' His anger hadn't abated. 'That I couldn't open locked drawers? Now get on with it.'

She scrambled through their contents as quickly as she could, but finished desolate. 'There's nothing.'

'How surprising. Now let's get the hell out of this place.'

'Excuse, sahib, memsahib.' A servant had slipped from behind one of the pillars lining the corridor and was watching them from the open door.

Grayson slammed the drawers shut, his face the picture of chagrin. 'We couldn't sleep,' he lied blatantly, 'and decided to explore a little and then became lost.'

'Of course, sahib. Please to come with me. I will escort you to your suite.'

In single file, they trooped back to the apartment, their feet as heavy as their hearts. As soon as the door had closed on their escort, Grayson turned to her in a fury. 'You realise what you've done, don't you? Compromised the whole expedition. How could you?'

Despite his anger, she stood her ground. 'I had to get into that room and this was my only chance. I can't speak to Verghese. I can't speak to his advisers or his servants. You've laid the law down on that. So how else can I get to what I need?'

'What *I* need,' he mimicked. 'It's always what *you* need, isn't it? Everyone and everything else can go to hell.'

'That's not true. How can you, of all people, say that?' She turned away from him and walked to the closed windows, her arms folded across her chest as though to keep the hurt she felt enclosed within.

'I owe you my life, Daisy. Don't you think I don't remember that every single day? You're brave, you're determined, you're loyal – up to a point. But if push comes to shove, it's what *you* want that will count. And with this obsession of yours, push does come to shove fairly frequently, doesn't it? And this time, we're talking a matter of life and death.'

'It's not like that,' she said desperately. 'You don't understand.'

'I never do, according to you. But what I do understand is that you're prepared to act as selfishly as you choose. So selfishly that you'll endanger not just your own life but others' too.'

She had never seen him so furious. His jaw was rigid and in the muted light his blue eyes were the darkest of navy, glinting and angry. She was forced to concede then that she had done a very stupid thing and the fight went out of her.

'I'm sorry. I'm truly sorry. I was so sure that I would find something.'

She must have been in the grip of madness, she thought, to think she could rifle the Rajah's sanctuary and not be discovered. Even to think she could uncover any kind of clue.

'But you didn't find anything, did you? And just

suppose you had.' His voice was quiet but brittle. 'Is that more important than finding Javinder, than saving Javinder?'

'No,' she mumbled miserably.

'That's what it amounts to, doesn't it? You've put your own concerns before a young man's safety and, to add insult to injury, you found nothing.'

She *had* found nothing and her heart ached for it.

'I'm going back to bed.' He began untying the robe he'd worn. 'There's little point in doing much else. Whatever plan I had is in tatters. From now on, they'll be watching us every minute of the day and night.'

And without as much as a glance at her, he stalked into the adjoining room, leaving her staring at the closed door. The servants wouldn't be gossiping after all, she thought forlornly. She was filled with sorrow, her legs weak, her feet shuffling into the bedroom they'd shared just an hour ago. The outline of his body was still there in the sheets, the pillows that had nursed his head still dented. The most abject misery gripped her. It was as though the ribbon of her life had unspooled and, in that instant, been wiped blank. The quest, the obsession – and Grayson was right, the need to discover her history had become an obsession – had died an abrupt death. Why had she thought it so very important?

At eight o'clock the next morning, their escort was back, this time to deliver them to the top storey of the palace where it seemed they were expected to take breakfast. They were ushered into a room far less ornate than last night's arched and bejewelled chamber, but still airy and spacious, with a wall of glass doors leading out onto the palace roof. From this height the panorama of houses and fields and distant mountains was stunning. Or would have been stunning if either of them had had the desire to look. Grayson had barely spoken to her since he'd walked into the sitting room five minutes before the servant knocked. He'd been tight-lipped and anxious to be on his way. Their love-making had faded from sight; it seemed to have happened in another life, a life before his plans had been destroyed. She felt sick inside. He blamed her entirely for the catastrophe and he was right. She had been utterly selfish in pursuit of her goal, infected last night by a kind of lunacy that had blotted from view every rational strand of thought. How could she have behaved that foolishly? She had let him down so badly that it was difficult to imagine they would ever find their way back to each other.

Talin Verghese was already seated at the long, wooden table, his carved chair this morning only a little less throne-like. He did not rise to greet them.

'Good morning, Miss Driscoll, Mr Harte. You find us already at breakfast.'

His expression was impenetrable, giving no sign that he was aware of the night's events. She knew, of course, that he must be. A young man was seated at his right hand. Dark hair and eyes were set off by a robe of pure white, the only splash of colour being the long waistcoat he wore, embroidered in blue and silver thread. He came forward to shake their hands.

'You must meet my son, Adeep.' From the table, the Rajah waved a languid hand towards the trio.

The boy flashed a smile that encompassed them both, then offered his hand to Grayson. 'I am most honoured to meet you, Mr Harte. I trust you slept well?' His expression was friendly, that of a host eager for his guests' comfort.

'Very well, thank you,' Grayson replied gravely. Neither of them would give a thing away, Daisy thought. Unlike her. Secret intelligence was a poker game and she had never been good at cards.

'And this is your delightful companion, I believe,' the boy was saying. 'Miss Driscoll, may I welcome you to Sikaner?'

'Thank you.' Her smile barely reached her lips.

He held out his hand to her and, as he did so, she saw the ring. She stared at the small circular object, hardly believing what she was looking at. A frantic urge engulfed her, an urge to take the hand and hug it close, as though in that way she would ensure she was seeing right. She stared again and was convinced, and the knowledge almost made her heart stop. The evidence she'd sought for so long was here. Not in Verghese's study, not at the Suris' house. But here, on this boy's finger. She clung to his hand for far too long, her gaze buried deep in the ring. There was a singing in her ears, a blur to her vision. Only gradually did she become aware of Adeep's quizzical expression and dropped his hand abruptly.

'I'm sorry.' She flushed a bright red. 'But the ring. It's truly beautiful.'

'I'm glad you like it. I believe it was actually made in England, which seems quite strange to me. But I understand the British are fascinated by Indian mythology, so perhaps it is not so strange. The ring is inexpensive, of course – a trinket only – but it means a great deal to me. It was my dear father who gave it, and I wear it all the time.'

'Then the ring is indeed valuable,' she managed, recovering herself a little.

'And for all kinds of reasons, Miss Driscoll. You see it belonged to my dead brother, Karan, a man I never knew.'

'I understand.'

And she did understand, quite clearly. The ring was valuable to the boy, not because he had known and liked Karan Verghese, nor because Karan was a supposed brother or half-brother, but because the humble ornament was a symbol of power. The ring had belonged to the heir to Sikaner and now Adeep wore it.

But the ring meant more to her, so much more. Her mind tossed and turned with the advent of this amazing discovery. Amazing indeed – and then the full implication of what she'd seen broke over her. She felt her chest contract so tightly that she could hardly breathe. It can't be true, her mind was saying, but it had to be. There was no other explanation. And it explained so much.

'Grayson.' She twitched at his shirt. Whether or not they were speaking, she had to tell him this most momentous of news. But he was not paying attention. Instead, he was looking over her head at the figure who had just entered the room.

'While we are busy with introductions, it is right

that you should meet Adeep's very dear friend,' the Rajah said smoothly. 'May I present Dalip Suri.'

Daisy stared incredulously at the man coming towards them. It *was* Dalip Suri. How could that be? She had last seen him in the village where they'd stopped to buy fruit, but there had been no further sighting of him and she'd assumed – they'd both assumed – that his appearance there had been coincidental after all, and that he must now be safely back in Jasirapur. They had been very wrong.

'Dalip has been travelling with my son,' the older Verghese drawled. 'They are very close, almost like brothers.' His smile was slyly satisfied. 'And he brings us news. But you will know much of what he has told me. I believe you have met before, in somewhat difficult circumstances.'

She felt Grayson stiffen beside her. 'We have, Your Highness,' he said curtly. 'But "difficult" is not the word I would use to describe our encounter. Murderous would be nearer the mark.'

'So I understand. You must allow me to apologise for the discomfort you were caused. And apologise, too, to your fair companion. Your little contretemps with Dalip was by way of being a misunderstanding, but you above all people, Mr Harte, will know that at times – what is the saying in English? – needs must.' He paused, looking slowly around the room, a sardonic smile lighting his face. 'As indeed, they must this morning.'

He nodded across their heads at the two men standing at either side of the door. It was only then that Daisy realised they were not the servants she had seen last night. They were large, very large, and the Rajah's livery had been exchanged for rough, workmanlike clothes. At their master's signal, they advanced into the room and grabbed Grayson and herself by the arms. In alarm, she glanced across at her companion, but his eyes were fixed straight ahead, never wavering from their host's face. The two younger men had retreated to stand together beside the Rajah's chair. Daisy saw them exchange a covert smirk.

'You would do well to accompany my men quietly,' Talin Verghese warned, his gaze locked with Grayson's. 'But do not fear you will go hungry. You will still enjoy breakfast, but you will enjoy it elsewhere.'

They had no alternative but to comply. Two more retainers, equally burly, were waiting for them outside the room and they were marched unceremoniously across the marble landing to the staircase she had seen earlier, a staircase that led down to the servants' quarters and beyond. The little troupe wound its way downwards, from floor to floor, until they reached what Daisy decided must be dungeon level. If so, the Rajah was keeping few prisoners for a deathly quiet filled the air, the only sound the echo of their footsteps on the cold, hard stone. A damp haze hung a few feet above the floor and even in the dim light she could see that the granite walls leaked water. They turned the corner into a narrow passage, flanked on either side by small cells, every one of them bolted and barred. One of the men produced a large iron key and opened the door at the far end of the passage. He pushed them none too gently ahead of him into the confined space.

She looked around aghast. Through the murk, she could make out the few pieces of furniture: two truckle beds, two hard chairs and a table, which leant drunkenly to one side. High above their heads, a narrow slit in the colossal stonework threw a fragile beam of light around the top section of the room, but had no chance of penetrating the gloom below. A liveried servant pushed past the heavyweights and dumped a tray on the earthen floor. Then the door of the cell clanged shut and the key ground in the lock. The men's retreating footsteps sounded loud on the flagstones beyond, but steadily grew more distant until at last there was silence. Except for the steady drip of water from somewhere on the outside walls.

They stood motionless, staring into space, paralysed by this calamitous change of fortune, and stayed there for what seemed an age. Then Grayson lifted the tray from the floor and placed it on the rickety table.

'It's a good job we ate well last night,' he said.

She had refused the unappetising bowl of what appeared to be grey porridge, and he couldn't blame her. He hoped the next meal would be an improvement or she would waste away. Against the massive walls hemming them around, she looked smaller than usual and even more delicate. She was responsible for their predicament, there was no getting away from it, but seeing her so dazed and hardly able to grasp what had happened, it was difficult to keep his anger hot. And really, what was the point? The deed was done and his chance to save Javinder was over. If he knew Daisy, she would have that on her conscience for a very long time to come. It was punishment enough.

'Here.' She was still standing in the middle of the room and he dragged one of the hard wooden chairs towards her. 'I've a feeling we'll be here a considerable time, so you'd better rest.'

She began to move towards it, then stopped in her tracks as though she felt her body folding beneath her. The shock was taking its toll. He saw her knuckles white as she reached out to grab the chair.

'Better drink this.' He fetched the jug and earthenware mugs that had been left by their jailers. 'After that little pantomime, I could knock back a double brandy, but I fear we'll have to make do with water.'

'I'm so sorry,' she whispered. 'This is all my fault.'

He wasn't going to dispute it but instead said in a bracing tone, 'Spilt milk. What we must do is to think our way out of this mess. We have to find a plan B.'

She looked around at the high bare walls, the small grille perched way above them and the barred and locked iron gate. 'There's no way out of here. It's impossible.'

'Nothing is impossible,' he insisted. 'We must put our mind to it. We may be too late to help Javinder, but if that wicked old man gets his way, there are other people's lives at stake. Many other people. There's a reason why those wretches upstairs have gathered at this time, and why we've been incarcerated. Something is about to happen,

I'm sure, and, when it does, I need you safely out of the way. Chintu – the boy I mentioned – talked to me of a big evil to come, an evil that was being plotted here. His uncle knew of it and was killed for his knowledge.'

There was a long silence while both of them considered the terrible possibilities. When at last Daisy spoke, it was clear she had turned away from the dreadful future and retreated to the past.

'Verghese must have tried to grab Anish when his father died,' she said jerkily, her voice hardly seeming her own, 'but he met with resistance. Parvati refused to relinquish her son. I bet the Rajah threatened her in some way – he's quite capable of it – but she must have held fast. In the end, he erased his daughter-in-law and grandson from his life and cut them off without a penny. It was only thanks to Mr Bahndari's generosity that the two of them survived.'

'And then he took this Adeep as a son and grandson combined. A practical man,' Grayson said dourly. 'I wonder where he found him?'

'Maybe Jasirapur. Maybe the Suris suggested it, if the two families were on speaking terms after Karan died. Ramesh Suri would do anything to serve his sister a bad turn. But what are the chances of Adeep making Dalip Suri a friend?'

'I doubt he is.'

'The Rajah said–'

'A lot of things and few of them true. I can't think Dalip is in Sikaner out of friendship.'

'He's been travelling with Adeep,' she reminded him.

'So his father says, but my guess is that Adeep was sent to Jasirapur to summon Dalip here.'

'So you think they were in that village together?'

'It's more than likely, even though you only saw one of them. No doubt they were checking with their informants to discover how far Verghese's great secret – whatever it is – might have leaked.'

'I still don't understand why Dalip was there. If he's not Adeep's friend, what has he to do with any of it?'

CHAPTER 20

She looked confused. She was no longer a naïve young girl, he thought, but her mind was still innocent. She'd believed the Rajah's tale of two friends. She believed in people, believed what they told her. That had always been her undoing. For a while, she'd had a total belief in Gerald Mortimer and the stories he'd spun.

He crouched down beside her chair and took her hands in his. 'There's some connection between the Suris and Verghese that goes beyond family. Almost certainly, it isn't friendship. Dalip Suri has been ordered here because of us. The Rajah will have his own communication channels, you can be sure, and my bet is that he got wind of the questions we were asking in Jasirapur and wanted to discover exactly what we knew.'

She looked down at him with a stricken expression. 'It's all my fault. Not only last night but earlier – in Jasirapur. If I hadn't gone to the Suri house none of this would have happened.'

'I don't think that's true. It's unlikely it has anything to do with the perfectly innocent questions you asked. The reason the Rajah became jittery and ordered Dalip Suri to report here was not because of you, but because of your associates. You were living with SIS officers and therefore suspect. But all you'd done was enquire about a dead woman. That might have ruffled the Suri feathers, but it shouldn't seriously have bothered Verghese once he knew the score. Remember, he spoke of a misunderstanding? He obviously considers Dalip's hit and run an overreaction. Particularly as there's a far greater prize at stake.'

He straightened up, but not before he'd given her hand a comforting squeeze. 'I think you'd find if you had stayed in Jasirapur, they would have lost interest in you. It's our arrival in Sikaner that's proved a complication. No doubt it's made the Rajah bring forward whatever horror he's put together. That would explain the gathering of the coven upstairs. Suri probably had instructions to stop us from getting here, Adeep too no doubt, but they failed. Having us as guests is highly inconvenient – the Rajah would much rather that we'd never made it here. Particularly when we've just confirmed every suspicion by poking about in his private domain.'

'You see, it *is* my fault.'

'It hasn't helped,' he admitted. 'But it was always going to be risky. Don't forget, I've been asking as many questions as you, first in Jasirapur and then here. Yesterday, I tried out several of the servants and you can be sure that was diligently reported. I'm pretty certain that if I had managed to escape into the town this morning, they would have found me before I got within a mile of Javinder.'

The soothing words left her unconvinced, he could see; her eyes were still wide with alarm and her face frozen. He tried again. 'You think Dalip Suri is here because you've been asking after his aunt? That he's come all this way to retrieve a postcard from the Brighton Pavilion?'

She smiled very slightly. 'It sounds silly, when you put it like that.'

'It is silly. They didn't appreciate your scrutiny, I'm sure, but it's me they're after. Think about it. I'm an SIS man come looking for my colleague, at a time when the last thing they want is the authorities to take notice of them.'

'But how exactly do the Suri family and the Rajah fit together?'

'At the moment, I've no idea. Maybe it's money. If Verghese is behind the violence, he has to have money to pay the thugs who do his bidding.'

'There's enough money in this place to equip two armies,' she protested.

'But it's not ready cash. It's money tied up in expensive tapestries, gold vases, precious jewels. Verghese may initially have had a safe full of rupees, but he must have been paying men to stir up violence for some time, and the more violence he creates, the more money he'll need. The bank is not an option. They would suspect where the money was going and report it to central government. Unless, of course, there's a private Sikaner bank. That's always a possibility. But my guess is that he's selling off the crown jewels.'

'And the Suris?'

'Someone has to sell the goods and who better than a slime like Suri.'

'And the families knew each other,' she said eagerly. 'Suri's sister married the Rajah's son. They must have kept in some kind of touch.'

'There were probably years when there was no contact. When Karan was killed, for instance, and Parvati driven from her family. But that doesn't mean communication couldn't be reinstated. If Verghese needed money, Suri might have been employed to sell on the black market. You said his house was stuffed with antiques. He'd have been more than happy to oblige his one-time relative. No doubt there was a tidy commission involved and if I'm right about a catastrophe looming, he must have been doing a fair amount of selling of late.'

He was sure that he'd guessed right but it didn't exactly help. They were prisoners and likely to remain so, unless the Rajah had ideas of getting rid of them entirely. That would be foolish of him since their disappearance would almost certainly bring retribution. If they didn't return, Mike would alert every branch of authority. But the man was half-mad. He had to be to contemplate the kind of massacre Grayson suspected was in the offing. Perhaps the old man calculated that once mayhem ruled, another two dead bodies would go unremarked. And the more he thought of it, the more certain he was that mayhem did threaten. Something far, far worse than the sporadic violence the region had seen up until now. Some last great push. That's how the Rajah would see it, he was sure. The man would go down fighting and hundreds, if not thousands, would perish with him.

He couldn't allow that to happen. He had to get out of here and get Daisy to safety. But she hadn't been far wrong when she'd said escape was impossible. He'd tried to rally her spirits but privately conceded her point. The only chance he could see lay with the guard who brought them meals. Presumably a man would arrive with food, if the Rajah wanted them to stay alive, and for the moment he must. They couldn't be expected to exist on two gelatinous bowls of porridge. So the food would arrive, he thought, and if there were just one guard – maybe even two, if he were quick – he might just manage it. The heavies who'd brought them down here had left him unbound, for which he was thankful. He suspected he'd gone unmolested because he was seen as an English gentleman. The kind of gentleman the Rajah knew well and despised equally. An Englishman who played by the rules, he thought wryly. Except that he didn't.

He pulled up the second chair and sat down beside Daisy. Neither of them spoke for a long time. The only sound to break the oppressive silence was the constant drip of water from the outer walls and an occasional scurry of small feet as the mice played hide and seek in an adjoining cell. Daisy didn't appear to hear them, but in any case, she was unlikely to panic. She had survived attempted murder, a ne'er-do-well husband and the rigours of the London Blitz. She would survive a few mice, he thought. Even a few rats.

She had fallen into a fitful doze where she sat, her feet and fingers occasionally twitching and then being deliberately stilled as she forced herself awake. There was something she was struggling to remember. Something beyond this cell, beyond last night's disaster, beyond even the search for Javinder. Something of the utmost importance. But what was it? Her mind jolted first in one direction, then another, a dizzying, random lurching, where nothing met, nothing connected, nothing made sense. And her eyelids were so very heavy and pulling her down into a blessed nothingness. To a place of peace. But she mustn't stay. She must make herself remember. Then it was there, floating in the spaces of her mind. The ring. The fulfilment of her quest, the end of a long, long journey. That moment when she'd first glimpsed the ring had disappeared beneath a torrent of guilt. Guilt and recrimination at pushing Grayson into this terrible predicament, at sentencing Javinder to almost certain death. But now it was once again before her eyes. The ring.

'Adeep's ring,' she said suddenly.

Grayson looked across at her.

'Did you notice his ring?' The question quivered with a suppressed excitement.

'I saw you were unable to take your eyes off it. Was it that fabulous?'

'It wasn't special, a simple trinket as Adeep said.' Her expression belied the downbeat words. 'It once belonged to Karan Verghese.'

'Which is why I imagine Adeep took such pride

in wearing it. The ring makes him the true successor.'

'Yes,' she said slowly, 'but there's something else.' She seemed to have difficulty continuing, and he waited. Then the words came tumbling out. 'It was fashioned around the same image as my mother's brooch. It was the emblem of the goddess Nandni Mata, the daughter.'

'That girl gets everywhere,' he said lightly, but she could see he'd begun to feel uncomfortable. He thought her disturbed or exhilarated, or both. Whatever it was, he didn't like where the conversation was going.

'But she doesn't, that's the point,' Daisy said earnestly. 'She doesn't get everywhere. In all the time I was in India, I saw her image only twice. Once at the temple you took me to, and once when I really looked at the photograph of my mother. And now I've seen it a third time, on a ring belonging to Karan Verghese who just happened to have been a patient at the Pavilion hospital at the same time as my mother was nursing there.'

'I don't see how that's significant.'

He was playing down her discovery, she thought, fearing no doubt that it would end in tears.

'They knew each other,' she said. 'Karan must have given her the brooch.'

'That's quite a jump to make. But what if he did? Perhaps she helped him in some way. Perhaps they were friends.'

'They were lovers,' she said flatly. 'They had to be. He gave my mother the brooch; she gave him the ring. A lovers' exchange. The ring would have been returned to India when he died on the battlefield. The Rajah wouldn't have known who gave his son the ring, and if he still had feelings for Karan, he might have kept it as a memento of a lost son.'

'Lovers! But that's a preposterous idea. A wild stab in the dark, even for you. You mustn't pursue such a crazy notion. If you were right, it would mean–'

She looked directly at him, her gaze unwavering. 'It would mean that Karan Verghese was my father.'

He stared back at her for several long minutes, his face a study of incredulity. 'That's impossible. More than impossible.' He had to dissuade her from such a lunatic idea.

'The dates fit,' she said stubbornly. 'Karan died at the Somme in July 1916, and I was born early the following year. Before he died, he wrote to Parvati telling her their marriage was over, that he wasn't coming back to India when the war ended. He'd met an Englishwoman and fallen in love. I know that's true. Anish told me that he read that letter from his father years later, and hated the man for what he'd planned to do. The Englishwoman was my mother, Grayson. She had to be.'

She took a large gulp of air, but it didn't prevent the tears from spilling down her face. 'Her lover died before I was born – he probably didn't even know my mother was pregnant. That's why nobody ever came for me.'

The best he could do was pat her hand ineffectually. He'd been thrown completely off balance by her fervent acceptance of what seemed to him romantic fantasy. It was clear, though, that the discovery of the ring had affected her profoundly, and he tried to be diplomatic. 'I suppose it might have happened as you say, but if so, it would be an extraordinary twist of fortune.'

She got up from the hard, wooden chair and for some minutes walked up and down, from one wall of the cramped cell to the other. 'I know it sounds far-fetched,' she conceded at last, 'but it explains so much.'

'Why you were consigned to the Cobb Street orphanage?'

'It explains being an unloved orphan, yes, but a lot more too. My skin colour, for instance. For a long time, I've suspected that my father was Indian. I told you as much. And that woman at the Officers' Club all those years ago, her words are ingrained in my memory. She looked at me and said, *Touch of the tar brush, I reckon.*'

He got up and walked over to her, stilling her restless pacing. 'Daisy, my love, I've no idea who this woman was, but your complexion is certainly no darker than many English skins. We're a mongrel race.'

'It's not an English skin, though, is it?' she insisted. 'And there's the fact that when I arrived in India for the first time, I immediately felt I'd come home. And I went on feeling that, even though bad things were happening to me.'

He hunched his shoulders, trying to quell his exasperation. This was getting out of hand. They were into impressions now, vague feelings of belonging and not belonging that his hard-headedness judged pointless. He might as well say that when he first walked through the hallowed doors of the Secret Intelligence Service and found work and colleagues that were congenial, he knew he'd been born to be an SIS officer.

She loosened her hands from his grip and resumed her slow walk to the far wall, then turned and paused. She wasn't giving up.

'And Anish,' she said.

'What about him?'

'You do realise that this makes him my half-brother? That's why I felt such closeness to him.'

'A half-brother who would have had you killed.' He couldn't resist the jibe. He needed to bring her down to earth.

'I loved him. I've grieved for him,' she went on. 'It's why I haven't been able to get over his death.'

And why, he thought, this obsession has grown too strong and too wild. But if there was just a chance that she was right – and he had to concede there was an outside chance – then Talin Verghese was her grandfather. The Rajah had imprisoned his granddaughter in one of his dungeons. It was a thought he didn't share, but it wouldn't be long before the realisation dawned on her. The realisation, too, that she had a grandfather who was willing to kill and maim to maintain his privileged existence.

He had to shut down the conversation before she got that far. If they were to have any chance of escape, he needed her calm and with a clear mind. 'It's a lot to take in and now is probably not the best time. You should sleep while you can. The bed hardly looks inviting but it's a good deal better than the flagstones.'

She seemed about to argue, but then drifted across to one of the narrow straw pallets. 'How long do you think they'll keep us here?'

'Until they've decided what to do with us.'

He saw her scared face and berated himself for his clumsiness. He hadn't meant to frighten her. 'I doubt they'll kill a British government agent and a visiting tourist.' He wasn't at all sure but there was no point in alarming her unnecessarily. 'And while they're deciding what to do, rescue will be on its way. I haven't been able to get through to Mike as I promised him.'

'How does that help?'

'He's expecting my call and when he doesn't get it and no other message reaches him, he'll know we're in trouble. He'll mobilise the army to come looking for us. I had words with the area commander before we left Jasirapur.'

All that was true, but it was the timing that was making him anxious. It would take several days for Mike to get worried enough to ask for help. Then his colleague would have to convince the army chiefs that the situation was dangerous and that they should intervene. And more time for the military to arrive. He wasn't sure just how many hours they had.

But his mention of Mike seemed to comfort her, because she settled herself on the hard truckle bed and closed her eyes. He lay down on the other pallet, his head teeming with one plan after another. Everything he considered seemed to have a crucial flaw and eventually he was forced back to his first idea, that the guard might in some way be distracted and then overpowered. He would have to wait and see what happened when their next meal arrived.

When it did, there were two guards. Not what he'd hoped for. One stood outside wielding the key, while the other carried a tray of food into the cell. It smelt marginally more appetising than the breakfast gruel, but fell a long way short of yesterday's feast. He stayed lying on the bunk while the guard put the tray on the table and backed out of the room, keeping the pair of them in sight the whole time.

If there were always to be two guards, how best to tackle them? His mind began its restless churn again. When he was certain he'd devised the best plan possible, he went over to where she was sleeping. Or wasn't sleeping, he thought. Her eyes were closed and her legs scrunched into a tight knot. She looked horribly vulnerable and he cursed himself for ever agreeing to bring her here. He knelt down at the bedside and stroked the part of her arm that was visible.

'They've brought some food, Daisy. Some rice and vegetables – pretty frugal, but it doesn't look too bad. You've got to eat something – you're going to need all your strength in a short while.'

And then he explained just what he wanted her to do.

Her stomach had started fluttering unpleasantly the minute Grayson told her his plan. It seemed risky, highly risky, but she understood there was no other choice if they were to have the smallest chance of escape. And he seemed intent on escape for there was no further talk of rescue. She was to play an important part in his plan, and that in itself was miraculous. She'd thought herself unforgiven, thought he'd never absolve her from destroying whatever hope he'd had of rescuing Javinder. Before their arrest, he'd hardly spoken a word. He'd seemed unable even to look at her. But once they'd been thrown into this wretched cell, he'd suppressed whatever anger he still felt and shown her only kindness. He'd even listened when she'd poured out what she believed was the truth of her identity, though to him it must seem nothing but wild speculation. He was a good man, a staunch friend, what Connie would have called 'a keeper'. He was a man she could trust with her life. She couldn't truly believe they would escape from this terrible place, but if ever they did, she would remember that.

The afternoon wore on, the light gradually fading from the small oblong grille above. She felt her shoulders tighten and her hands grow clammy. Any moment now the guards would bring supper, and they must make their break for freedom. She could see Grayson listening intently, and then his signal came. He'd told her she needed to stage the best performance of her life, and she retreated to the bed in readiness. As soon as she heard the first distant footsteps, she began moaning, pulling her legs up to her chin and rocking herself from side to side. Her hands clutched fretfully at the lumpy straw. She could only hope her acting would pass as realistic.

Meanwhile, Grayson had leapt to the iron door and was banging on its bars, making as much noise as he possibly could. 'Help,' he yelled, 'you men, help! I've been calling for hours.' That was a clever touch, she thought. They would never know it for a lie. The cell must be many feet underground and way below the servants' own quarters. The two men came up to the cell and peered in. They looked confused by the clamour.

'She's ill, damn you. Can't you see? What was it you put in those vegetables?'

The man carrying the tray shook his head vacantly. 'Nothing.'

'Something bad must have got into the food. She's been like this for an age–' Grayson flung his arm towards the bed '–and she's getting worse. I've called and called, and not one of you came. She needs a doctor.'

'We go to ask – later.' The heavyweight with the keys appeared unimpressed by Daisy's theatricals.

'Then ask, man, and do it now or her death will be on your hands.'

She glimpsed the other servant from the corner of her eye and saw that he was visibly shaken. He muttered a hurried, 'Yes, yes,' and put the tray down on the floor outside the cell. He was making off rapidly back down the corridor when his comrade shouted after him. 'Deliver the food, Manu. We can ask later.'

'No, no, urgent,' was all they heard.

The remaining guard stayed outside the door, the keys hanging from a belt on one side of his shirt. 'Back!' he barked at Grayson, who was still clutching the bars of the cell door. She hoped he was as stupid as he sounded.

'Okay, I'm going.' Grayson feinted a few steps and then said over his shoulder, 'Your friend has dropped his keys. I think you should know that.'

The man looked down on the floor for the non-existent keys and, before he realised that he was the only one to possess any, Grayson had leapt forward and shoved his arm through the narrow gap in the bars. His hand was on the man's throat. There was the most horrible rattle as the Indian fought for breath. Daisy hoped she would never hear such a noise again in her life and it seemed to go on for ever.

There was a thud as their jailor's body met the floor. Grayson bent down and put his fingers on the man's neck. 'Don't fret.' He looked up and grinned at her. 'He's still alive. Just. Out for the count but not for too long. We have to move quickly.'

He unhooked the ring of keys from the man's belt and flicked through them, choosing the largest. He was right. The door swung open. 'Sesame! Come on.' He was at her side, dragging her towards the door.

She was forced to step over the man's body and shuddered a little. 'Are you sure he's alive?'

'Unfortunately, quite alive. Come on – we can't waste time on him.' His voice had a new urgency.

He turned in the opposite direction from where the men had come. 'Not that way. It will lead back to the servants' staircase,' he said in her ear, 'and we don't want to meet Manu or his fellows.'

He strode forward and she followed in his wake, though unsure where the narrow, flagged passageway would lead. The sparsest of lights had been drilled into the rock above and, by their dim illumination, she could see there were dozens of cells on either side. She wondered dazedly what the Rajah did with them all. Surely he didn't have sufficient enemies to fill them, especially if he made a habit of killing his opponents. They walked on swiftly. Occasionally, the passage swooped around a corner, occasionally it changed direction, but they continued to follow where it led. And all the time she expected to hear footsteps in pursuit. If Grayson had been telling the truth and their jailor was still alive, he must have come round by now.

She wasn't at all certain that Grayson had been telling the truth but she couldn't let her mind wander in that direction. The floor of the passage was uneven and there was barely any light; she had to concentrate hard. Once or twice she stumbled on a raised flagstone and it was only Grayson's solid figure ahead that prevented her from falling. He was setting a cracking pace and after what must have been at least a mile, a painful stitch began to throb in her side. She tried to forget it, and when the path turned an abrupt corner and began to slope upwards, she forgot it entirely. This was a good sign, she thought, this forgotten passage was winding its way upwards to the ground floor.

'There's another set of stairs ahead.' He sounded exultant. 'Look, they've been cut into the stone. They must be very old and no longer used. We'll use them though.'

For the first time, she began to think they might escape. They were still a long way from freedom, but even a yard nearer was worth celebrating. She tried not to think what would happen if they were caught. They were within several feet of the ancient staircase when a noise sounded in their ears. It was coming from somewhere on their left, from the darkness that crouched in every corner. They stopped dead. Daisy felt herself petrified, turned into the stone that surrounded them. They were discovered. All the plans she had not even known her mind was making fell to pieces. She would never return to England, never have the chance to wipe clean the messy slate of her past, never live the life she should.

Grayson put his finger to his mouth, signalling they should stay silent. He crept towards the patch of deep darkness from where the noise seemed to emanate and she followed suit. The clamour grew louder. A chilling sound. A ghostly clanking and rattling. Then suddenly in front of them, swimming out of the darkness, was another cell, quite different from those they had passed. It was solitary and cut so far into the rock on which the palace stood that in the intense gloom you had to reach its very door before you knew it existed.

Grayson arrived at the cell an instant before she did. She heard his sharp intake of breath. Then she was there beside him. Facing Javinder Joshi.

CHAPTER 21

'Javinder?' Grayson peered through the gloom into the cell. 'My God, Javinder!'

Daisy hardly recognised the young man. It was ten years since they'd last met, but he had aged far beyond that. His face was gaunt, his skin stretched so tightly over his cheekbones that it seemed at any moment they might rupture its surface. She saw his eyes were hazed with weariness and his hands red raw and dreadfully bruised from the iron handcuffs he wore.

His vision must have cleared then, because he ceased the furious tugging at his restraints and peered back at them. For a minute, it seemed he could hardly believe what he saw. Then he peered again. 'Mr Harte?' His voice was the crackling of ancient paper.

'Yes, it's me, old chap. How long have you been in this wretched hole?'

His erstwhile protégé shook his head. 'A month, two months. I don't know.'

'It doesn't matter. What matters is to get you out of here.'

Javinder shook his head again, his eyes travelling down to his feet. Daisy's glance followed him. The young man's ankles had been cuffed, too, and fixed by a chain to a large iron circle melded into the wall.

'I've got keys. One of them is bound to fit.' Grayson spread the bunch he'd stolen. 'You'll be free in an instant.'

That was optimistic. They had to endure several false starts before he found the key that unlocked the cell door and then a frantic scurry through the remainder to find the one that would free Javinder's feet and hands. He tried one after another without success.

'It's got to be one of these,' he muttered. 'That thug was only carrying one set on his belt.'

Any minute now, she thought, that thug would be coming round from his induced faint, and here they were flipping through a bunch of keys over and over again. She wished she could emulate Grayson's calm.

'Give them to me,' she demanded, unable to stand helplessly by a minute longer. He looked up in surprise but handed her the keys.

'We're in need of a feminine touch,' she said, slipping past him and bending over the prone man.

'I don't see how,' he began, when a loud click echoed through the empty space.

'Just womanly finesse.' But she had the grace to smile.

Javinder remained motionless as she released first his feet, then his hands. He was staring at her, staring through her. 'Mrs Mortimer? Surely it cannot be you?'

'I'm afraid it is, though I'm plain Miss Driscoll now. But please call me Daisy.'

'Can we forget the introductions.' Grayson's voice was just this side of irascible. 'We're not at a tea dance, remember.' He lunged forward and grabbed the prisoner's arm, supporting him as Javinder clambered to his feet. The man rocked back and forth, his legs scrabbling to gain an uncertain purchase on the rough floor of the cell. 'You're going to have to try and walk, old man. We have to make a run for it.'

Javinder was hardly in running mode. Even in the intense gloom, she could see pain written across the poor man's face. But he was still as brave as she remembered and after a few muffled yelps, he followed Grayson out of the cell and back into the passage.

Just in time. A scuffling and swearing came winging its way to them on the empty air. There was the sound of a tray hitting the wall and plates being smashed against it. It seemed their guard had recovered.

'Quick, up these stairs.' Grayson pushed the injured man onto the first step, then gestured to Daisy to go in front of him. He was planning to fight off any attack from the rear, she thought.

'You found out what was going on then?' Grayson asked, as they began the long climb. 'I thought as much.'

Javinder paused to get back his breath. He was finding the stairway difficult. 'I did find out – they call it the project – but then I was caught, so it did no good.'

'On the contrary, it alerted headquarters that something very bad was up.'

'And they sent you, Mr Harte?' Javinder's expression as he looked down the stairs at them was almost comic.

'I'm sorry if you'd have preferred someone else, but it looks like you're stuck with me.'

'No, no, not at all.' He was too serious a young man to appreciate Grayson's kind of humour.

'But what *was* the project?' Daisy asked, as they resumed their climb.

'Arson. And rape. And murder.' Javinder's voice shook a little as he recounted what he'd learned. 'The Rajah intends to launch assaults all over Sikaner. He will set Hindus against Moslems, Moslems against Sikhs. He has recruited some evil men to do his bidding and he is paying them well.'

'But we know there's been violence before, so how is this different?'

'There have been incidents, Miss Driscoll,' Javinder admitted. 'But so far they have been on a small scale. Almost as though someone was testing the ground. But the project is far, far bigger. It will create widespread chaos and much bloodshed. Houses will be set alight, women raped, children murdered. It is too terrible to contemplate.'

'Did you find out who is behind it?' Grayson asked. 'The Rajah must be the prime mover, but the Suris?'

'They are the middlemen. I think they will make sure they are not implicated in whatever happens.'

'But they supply the money and the goods?'

'Ramesh Suri sells the Rajah's jewels for him. And antiques, precious tapestries, that sort of thing. He pays him in cash and asks no questions, but of course he takes a commission.'

'No wonder he lives in luxury,' Daisy put in.

'Oh yes,' Javinder said confidently, 'Mr Suri is living high. At first I wasn't sure he was involved. There were reports of trouble, but I didn't know names. The Rajah, I suspected, of course. It's well known that he hates Congress, and I knew that he'd tried to broker an agreement with neighbouring princes to declare independence together, and that it hadn't worked out.'

'That's when he must have decided on the project,' Grayson said.

'It was hard for me to believe a respected ruler could encourage such dreadful deeds,' Javinder went on. 'But I found that he could. It took longer to uncover the Suris' involvement and it didn't do much good when I managed to. The Rajah found me out almost immediately.'

They had almost reached the top of the winding staircase when an enraged roar from below told them that Javinder's escape had been discovered. Heads down, they sprang up the remaining stairs. Javinder was moving far better now, Daisy noted, and a real possibility that they might escape began to tantalise. When they reached the top step, though, it was to find a wooden door blocking their way. It had been cut into the rock and looked as though it had remained unopened for many years. Grayson edged past them and tried the catch. It stuck. He tried again without success and then put his shoulder to the wood with a thump. The noise made her cross her fingers painfully tight, hoping that no one was walking by on the other side. But his heave had worked and very cautiously he was able to push the door open an inch. He put his eye to the crack.

'We're on the ground floor, all right,' he said. 'But where in the palace, I haven't a clue.'

Which meant, Daisy thought, that they had no idea of where their exit might lie. They would have to search for a way out and risk detection in doing so. And, if they managed to reach the outside, what then? The spirits that had recently kept her buoyed sank from sight. They had no transport. Their jeep had a fuel leak and, in any case, had almost certainly been impounded. And, if they made it into the town on foot, who would help them? The townspeople must either be in the pocket of the Rajah or deadly afraid of him. There would be no aid from that quarter.

Grayson pushed the door fully open and slipped through, beckoning them to follow. They found themselves standing in one of the marble-floored open squares that dotted the palace, and from which a labyrinth of corridors and rooms radiated outwards.

'Any ideas?' he asked. A window filled most of the wall to the right of them and he walked across to it.

He gazed down on a section of the ornamental planting, his brow creased. 'Judging from what I can see of the garden, I think we must be somewhere in the middle of the palace.'

Whichever way they walked, she thought, they faced danger. There was no easy way out. As they stood there undecided, a low hum swooped over them. Voices. She clasped Grayson by the arm.

'We should hide.'

'No, we shouldn't.' His face was alert. 'The voices will help us find our way. I'm guessing they must be coming from one of the main reception rooms, the audience chamber if I'm not mistaken. The one we were taken to yesterday. If we find that, we'll find the way out.'

Every one of her nerve endings was telling her to hide, but she had to concede that Grayson was right. Yesterday, they'd walked along several very long corridors to reach the audience chamber. If they could get back to the room, they could get back to those corridors which would lead them directly to the front entrance. It was a bold plan, fraught with danger, but she didn't have a better one. She crept silently alongside her companions until the voices became loud enough to distinguish individual words. The men were speaking in Hindi and she didn't understand.

'They are discussing how best to deal with us,' Grayson said. 'One or two are arguing that once the project begins, we should be released. But others aren't quite so happy. It's a close-run thing. Javinder, do you know if the Suris supply this madman with his weapons?'

'They do, Mr Harte. The Rajah has a ready supply of knives and swords. But Suri purchases guns for him – at a distance. He stays in Jasirapur, far enough away to avoid suspicion. He is very careful about that. But I never discovered just how he organises the shipments or how the weapons get here. I was apprehended before I could.'

'You found out enough to be a great danger to them.'

'I found out the date they intend to strike. The twenty-fifth of April. That was it. That is when the killing will begin.'

'The twenty-fifth begins at midnight. And I'm pretty sure Verghese won't be late. We're going to have to move fast.'

'They will never let us live,' Daisy said, her voice dull with foreboding. 'We know far too much.'

'Then we'd better take leave of them right now, don't you think? The first corridor we want has to be around the next corner. It should lead us to the front entrance.'

'And when we get there, how are we to get past the servants?' she asked. 'Yesterday there were at least two of them guarding the door.'

'The same way as we got out of the cell. By distraction. Whatever happens, Javinder, one of us must reach the town. There are two courtyards you have to pass through – one is little more than a set of gates – before you get clear of the palace grounds. There may be ways around them both but if you have to cross them, you'll need to be clever. Choose your moment well. If you get through undetected, commandeer a vehicle, any kind of vehicle, and drive to a telephone. Make sure it's well out of town. Here–' and he fished a crumpled piece of paper from his pocket. 'This is the number you must ring. I know it by heart. It will get you through to the nearest army unit. They won't be surprised to hear from you – I put them on alert before I left Jasirapur. You'll need to use the code name – Rohira. It will ensure they'll mobilise immediately.'

Javinder's face brightened at the prospect.

'We have to get out of the palace first,' Daisy reminded them. It seemed to her that both men were in danger of being carried away by the sheer excitement of the adventure.

'You're right. Let's go. I don't need to remind you both to walk as silently as you can.'

Very slowly and very quietly, they crept along the corridor. There was not a sound except for the soft hush of their breathing and, in the distance, the same hum of voices. The passage they were in was a minor one, but when they turned the corner, they would be in one of the long corridors that ran from the front of the palace to the rear. The audience room, she thought, had been bang in the middle. They would be in the thick of things and servants were likely to appear at any moment. It was an almost impossible hope they could reach the huge, wooden door through which they'd walked twenty-four hours ago, unmolested.

They turned the fateful corner and waited, peering down the long red silk carpet which led to freedom. The audience room was on their right and its door was slightly ajar. The voices were much louder now and Daisy let the stream of Hindi flow over her. Then words that were clear and distinct and spoken in English.

'You must let them go the day after tomorrow.'

She was startled and looked towards Grayson. His expression was masklike and he made no response except to edge closer to the open door. But the voices had become muted once more and she doubted he could hear very much. The men must have moved to the far end of the room and were again speaking in a language she didn't understand.

Grayson turned to them both. 'I want you to walk as fast as you can to the front entrance,' he said softly. 'When you get there, take cover and watch for the moment when there's only one servant around. Then throw this,' and he handed Javinder a small chunk of rock he must have collected from their cell. She didn't like to think what use he'd imagined putting it to. 'When the man goes to investigate,' he continued, 'slip through the door and run. Keep to the parkland, definitely keep off the road. It may be easier than we think to get round the guards by sticking to the park. I'll follow you when I can. And, Javinder, remember the code.'

'Yes, of course, Mr Harte, but–'

'–but why aren't you coming?' she finished for him. She was gripped with fear.

'There's something I need to sort out first.'

She knew what it was and her heart turned over. 'You're deliberately walking back into danger. Please come with us.'

'I can't,' he said firmly, 'I haven't a choice.'

Grayson's plan worked better than she could have hoped. The walk along that endless red carpet was terrifying and she literally held her breath with every step. But their luck appeared to have turned and they met no one. When they got within a few yards of the front entrance, they hid themselves securely behind a marble pillar and, for some minutes, watched the comings and goings. Two servants were arranging a vast quantity of flowers, sharing them between several oversized ceramic vases. She recognised the men from yesterday. A third man, dressed in working overalls, rushed back and forth with armfuls of blooms. He seemed to be one of the garden staff and, as soon as he'd finished delivering his flowers, he was despatched smartly back to his domain. One of the house servants said something to his companion.

'He's gone to fetch more water for the vases,' Javinder said in her ear. 'This could be our chance.' The rock was in his hand, she noticed.

As soon as the man disappeared, Javinder waited only for the remaining servant to bend over the flowers and begin tweaking them this way and that, before he stepped out from his hiding place and hurled the piece of granite along the corridor that ran at angles to the main passageway. It narrowly missed an expensive-looking statue and fell with a crash almost out of sight. The startled servant left his flower arranging and rushed off to discover the source of the crash. Before he returned, they'd slipped through the door, ran down the stone steps, past the fountain and across the open space to the granite archway. Then turned sharp left, away from the road and into the bordering expanse of grass, now burnt to a crispy brown. A heavy planting of trees and bushes was scattered randomly through the park and, in the fading light, the cover they offered proved sufficient. By dint of moving from one shelter to the next, they managed to remain invisible to the one or two vehicles that passed them on the road.

Grayson had been right about the courtyards. The smaller, inner courtyard at least. By keeping to parkland, they were able to walk around its iron gates instead of through them. But that wouldn't work on the heavier ramparts of the outer courtyard. Apart from the guards on either side of the gate, she'd noticed yesterday that a small platoon of soldiers was being rigorously drilled in one corner of the fortified square. There was no way Javinder could fight his way through this miniature army. And to scale the great stone walls that enclosed the Rajah's estate was unthinkable. It was impossible, even for a fit man and she was sure that after weeks of imprisonment, Javinder was far from fit. The only alternative was again to distract the guards' attention. It had worked before, so why not again? And they had one advantage. Dusk was beginning to fall and, in the muted light, it might be easier to sow confusion.

They had been half walking and half running, and though the approaching night had cooled the air a good deal, it wasn't long before they were both feeling unpleasantly sticky. They paused for a moment beneath one of the largest trees, blotting their faces and trying to recover their breath.

'Do you think the Rajah knows of our escape by now?' she asked. 'If he does, every one of those soldiers ahead will have been put on alert.'

'I don't think so.' Javinder's response was heartening. 'The meeting the Rajah has convened is of the utmost importance. Our jailors won't want to interrupt it with news that will probably hang them. But, even so, we must move quickly.'

He strode ahead, eager to find a way of negotiating the outer courtyard, but Daisy remained where she was. Their escape had been frenetic and so far she'd had little time to think. Now she tried to clear her mind. Could they get through this last guarded outpost? Even if they did, how likely was it they'd alert the army speedily enough? They might succeed in reaching the town, in commandeering a vehicle, finding a telephone even, but in time? The army would arrive – eventually – but it would be too late to save Grayson. And he'd known that when he'd sent them on their way. They had left him facing overwhelming odds so what was she doing, walking away from him, leaving him to face death alone?

When Javinder realised she was no longer following him, he turned around and urged her to make haste.

'I can't go on,' she said. 'I have to go back.'

He gaped at her. 'If you go back, they will make you a prisoner again, or worse.'

'Then I'll be a prisoner or worse. I can't leave Grayson alone to face whatever's coming.'

'Miss Driscoll, please, think for a moment. Consider how very dangerous these men are. They will not exempt you because you are a woman.'

'I don't expect special treatment.'

'But Mr Harte would want you to escape,' Javinder pleaded. 'He was most insistent that you did.'

'Of course he was. He thinks he's a hero out of the *Boy's Own Paper,*' she said shakily. 'But he isn't. He's a decent, honest man who has been dreadfully deceived.'

Javinder looked at her and his eyes were filled with a deep sadness. 'I think I understand how Mr Harte must feel.'

She hadn't time to ask him what he meant, though she could guess well enough. Instead, she spurred him on. 'You must go, and raise the alarm. And I must go back.'

She clasped him by the hand and gave him a brief kiss on the cheek. Then turned back towards the distant palace.

CHAPTER 22

With luck they would get away. His appearance in the audience room, when he was supposedly incarcerated a mile underground, should be enough to keep Talin Verghese and his henchmen from questioning why he stood there alone. He would be walking into the lions' den, that much was certain, but there was something he must do – a confrontation he must have – and he would have it, come what may.

The men were gathered at the far end of the chamber, poring over what appeared to be a large map. They would need to schedule the attacks precisely for maximum effect, his mind told him. This would be the war room for the coming destruction. He deliberately allowed his footfall to be heavy. One of the men turned to face him, followed by each of his companions. Grayson's entrance gained all the attention he could have hoped. Every one of them stood open-mouthed, staring at him in amazement, but the man who had turned first wore the most ghastly pallor.

Grayson spoke directly to him. 'Have you come to rescue me, Mike? How kind of you.'

For two or three crushing moments, Mike Corrigan said nothing. A clock ticked loudly in the background and several of the men shuffled themselves arc-wise around the Englishman to form a barrier.

'I told you not to come here, Gray,' Mike said.

'You did. And now I see why. Why you were so adamant that I shouldn't.'

'I tried to save you from walking into danger. You were my friend. I would have done anything for you, you know that. I tried to keep you from getting mixed up in this mess.'

Corrigan stepped out of the protective circle of men and faced Grayson directly. His hands moved to clutch at the revers of the loose jacket he wore. He seemed not to know what to do with them.

'Again, how very kind of you,' Grayson responded. 'Particularly as *you* appear to be involved up to your neck. Though "mess" is hardly an apt description. Villainy would seem to hit the right note.'

Mike's gaze slid away. He had no answer to the accusation and it was the Rajah who broke the silence. 'Mr Harte, I am always delighted to welcome a guest, but I regret that you are badly in the way, and will have to be removed. Once more. You should have remained where you were.'

'It may seem strange, Your Highness, but a damp cell holds little attraction for me.'

'Or for your companion?' the Rajah said. 'Where is she?' He adjusted his robes slowly and efficiently, as though an escaped prisoner was the last thing on his mind.

The old man didn't miss a thing, Grayson thought. He would have to bluff. 'She is well on her way to safety, you can be sure.'

Verghese's black brows rose in scorn. 'You expect me to believe such a nonsense? You must do better than that.'

'Believe it or not, it happens to be true.' He became aware of the other men beginning to fan out and move towards him in a pincer movement.

'Then why are you here? Surely you should be well on your way to safety, too.' The Rajah was keeping him talking, while the other men cut off any escape route.

'I have a score to settle. Mr Corrigan knows what it is.'

The Rajah's face expressed utter boredom. 'I'm sure he does, but we are not here to settle a dispute between friends, or even former friends. We have business to do.'

'Is that what business is these days? The business of indiscriminate killing? And you, Mike, what part do you play in this "business"? Are you here to speak for me or make sure the Rajah wins? No, don't tell me, I think I can guess.'

Mike looked pugnacious. 'I'm here to make sure the project succeeds. I couldn't let you spoil it, not after all these months.'

'The project,' Grayson jeered. 'The ultimate euphemism. Have the guts to call it what it is, man – mass murder. What's in it for you? Money?'

Mike's face flamed. 'There's been money, yes. Plenty of it. Unlike you, I wasn't blessed with a silver spoon. You're still young and have the world before you. What do I have precisely? But it's not just about money. I had to take a stand. I had to feel I counted. I've been treated shamefully by people who should know better.'

'Not nearly as shamefully as you've behaved.'

'SIS forfeited my loyalty when they passed me

over for less experienced men. Me! A man who for thirty years worked tirelessly for them. Who risked my life on countless occasions and been so badly beaten that I'll be in pain for the rest of my life. And you expected me to accept such treatment without a murmur, stay docile, and take a second-rate job I thoroughly despise?'

'I expected you to be loyal to the oath you took. Nothing can justify your betrayal, and you have less than nothing. In my view, you've been dealt with fairly. You haven't been pensioned off, you haven't been asked to leave the service. Instead, you've been found another job. And then permitted to come with me to India, despite there being more useful men available.'

Mike's face turned an unhealthy mauve. Grayson could see he was struggling with a consuming anger. 'You thought you were doing me such a favour, didn't you? Mr bloody benevolent, handing out your little perk. A pat on the head for honourable service. What you didn't know was that I couldn't let you come alone to India, to Jasirapur, and your suggestion couldn't have suited me better. You hadn't a clue that for months I've been sending Verghese intelligence on the situation in SIS. He's known every twist and turn in policy, known just how the office back home was responding to the outbursts of violence in Sikaner. It made him sure the project could go ahead with minimal interference from headquarters.'

'That may be true of London, but your plans haven't been smooth sailing, have they? It seems to me that you've suffered plenty of interference from within Rajasthan itself.' Grayson's smile was unpleasant. 'You didn't see that coming, did you, an SIS officer doing his duty?'

Mike shrugged. 'Javinder Joshi has been dealt with. He put himself in the way when our plans were shaping up nicely. And got a little too close to the truth. I couldn't afford for him to contact London and spill the beans. My beans. If he'd told tales, I would have been disgraced, dismissed with ignominy. But I needn't have worried. The Rajah has his ways and means.'

'How charming.'

'And he'd have stayed dealt with,' Corrigan muttered, 'rotting away in that cell, if you hadn't decided to be a hero. But, of course, you couldn't resist the challenge. You had to charge to his rescue. Nothing I could say would persuade you to stay in England. I knew you'd endanger the project the minute you landed in Bombay. So I hitched a ride, and encouraged Daisy to come too. She was an extra safeguard. Not that she's been the slightest use in stopping you – the opposite, in fact.'

From the corner of his eye, Grayson saw the Rajah striding towards them and turned to face the man directly. 'A few minutes, if you will. There are things I need to know, and there's plenty of time for you to do as you wish with me.'

He turned back to his one-time friend who stood, white-faced and rigid, a few feet from him. 'What have you been doing in Jasirapur, Mike? All those hours toiling away in the office?'

'What do you think? I looked for Joshi or I pretended to. Pretended to try and discover something that would help you in your search. It kept you quiet and it kept civil admin contented. And that was necessary. The project had reached a critical stage and I needed to make sure the team at Jasirapur had no suspicions. I fed them little bits and pieces about our search for their lost colleague, and they seemed happy enough to accept what I told them.'

'All the time clearing the path for this sorry band of cut-throats?'

'You can call them as many names as you like. They're my paymasters and have rewarded me well. I've been paid to protect the project by warning them of your intentions. I've done a good job, I think, even though somehow you managed to make it here.'

'Pat yourself on the back. It's the only reward you're likely to get. But a nice long stretch in an English prison will help to compensate. That's, of course, if you're not strung up as a traitor.'

'Look around you. What do you see? Friends? I don't think so. You're a prisoner here and you'll be dealt with. You should have left when you could.'

'I'm not a rat, I don't desert.'

Corrigan flinched but his voice never wavered. 'I'm afraid you'll wish you had.'

'Enough.' The Rajah, clearly out of patience, clapped his hands. 'Seize Harte,' he commanded his minions. 'Bind and gag him. This time we will not worry about the niceties.'

One of Grayson's erstwhile jailors appeared out of nowhere and produced a knife. *Just in case I should struggle,* he thought, as the man grabbed him from behind and the steel's cold tip pricked at his throat. The Rajah stretched his arms wide to shepherd his companions back to the table. Grayson saw the rotund figure of Mr Acharya bouncing from one side to the other, smoothing the map flat and positioning various counters when and where he was told. He'd always suspected it and here was the proof: the secretary was neck deep in whatever evil was being plotted.

'Come, we must mobilise – it's time for the first stage of our war.' The Rajah bent over the table. 'And this is where we will begin, I think, and here, too.'

The knife continued to hover an inch from Grayson's throat as another two of yesterday's heavyweights advanced with a length of rope in their hands. Before they could reach him, though, a voice from the doorway halted them in their tracks.

'Let him be,' the voice said. 'If you harm him, it will be the worse for you.'

Daisy. It couldn't be, but it was. He felt a riot of emotions. Why on earth was she here? She was supposed to be miles away, supposed to be safe. Vexation coursed through him at the knowledge that she'd put herself back into danger. Could she never do what she was asked? At the same time, his heart rejoiced at her courage. And then tore itself apart with fear for her.

'Let him go,' she repeated.

Verghese turned from the table, a sigh of the utmost weariness escaping him. 'Dear young lady, is it really you? It seems that you *and* your companion are living in a dream world.' His voice grew harsh. 'Seize her as well. I had no idea the English were such romantics, but if they wish to die together, who am I to stop them?'

Daisy fought back with her only weapon. 'The army is on its way. Javinder Joshi has gone to meet them and will guide them here. If you surrender now, you'll face prison but not death.'

'A dream world indeed,' the Rajah muttered.

His companions were growing restless. Events were not working out quite as they'd envisaged. The men with the rope were also looking unsure.

'Bind them both,' Verghese commanded. 'She is lying, you fools. How could the army be here? Even if Joshi has escaped, what chance has he had to call up soldiers from miles away?'

'He hasn't,' Grayson managed to say before the men advanced on him. 'But I have. I did the calling before I left Jasirapur. The army are coming all right.'

Mike turned a sicklier white. 'You're bluffing. You're always bluffing. Life is just one long joke for you, isn't it?' he said bitterly.

'That's been your big mistake, Mike, believing I'm never serious.'

The man wielding the knife had become confused by the shower of words, unintelligible words at that. Distracted, his hand wavered for a second while he tried to make sense of the situation. His hold on the knife slackened and the point inched away from Grayson's throat. In those few seconds, his prisoner had jabbed backwards with his elbow and hit the man hard in the stomach, then twisted swiftly to face him and punched him squarely in the face. The man swayed backwards, forwards, then back again and finally succumbed, crumpling to the floor in an untidy heap. As he did so, the knife flew from his grasp and Grayson made a lunge for it.

But he was not alone. Mike had been standing close and threw himself to the floor, scrabbling to reach the weapon. The two wrestled for control: a twisted arm, fingers in eyes, an elbow to the throat, a kick in the groin.

Both had been trained in the art of attack and though Mike had weakened over the years, he was still a strong man. First one, then the other, was uppermost. The Rajah remained at a distance, a pained expression of impatience on his face, while Daisy struggled against her captor to no avail. She was too small, too firmly held, to be of any help to the man she loved. Verghese signalled briefly to one of the servants at the door and a gun appeared from nowhere. She closed her eyes. But the struggling men were too entwined for the servant to take accurate aim and the gun remained pointing into the air. There was a clatter as the knife slid out from between the wrestling bodies. Both men went for it, then the horrible sound of exhaling air and Mike was lying prone.

'An accident,' Grayson gasped. He bowed his head. Mike was dead, he knew it, and he had been the one to wield the knife. But he had no time to mourn before a rough hand latched itself to his collar and jerked him to his feet.

'I think we have seen enough,' Verghese announced in a bored voice. 'Get rid of that–' he gestured in distaste at the body leaking blood over the pristine floor '–and take *them* up to the roof. We have wasted too much time already. When the sun drops below the mountains, throw them off.

At sunset no one will see them fall, except for the vultures seeking carrion. Tomorrow their picked bodies will be a warning to anyone else who might think to interfere.'

Once again, they were on the narrow staircase used by the servants, but this time being hurried to the very top of the palace instead of plunged to its depths. At least they would die in the open, Daisy thought, and not meet a festering end in that dank and dreadful cell. But that was of little comfort and she felt sick at heart. She'd had some wild hope that if she was here, playing a part in Grayson's drama, she might make a difference, and an even wilder hope that she could save him. She'd had no clear plan, except to try to frighten the Rajah into letting them both go. But Verghese had treated her threat with contempt.

And no wonder. It was hardly credible. Mike might have been shaken by Grayson's declaration that the army was already on its way, but the Rajah was a different matter. He'd remained unconvinced and he was right. Any chance of escape depended entirely on Javinder. And even if the young man had managed to find his way into the town and somehow get to a telephone, it would all take time. Too much time. If and when the army finally arrived, the terrible project would have begun its inexorable devouring of people and she and Grayson would be dead. These evil men might be caught, but even that was more of a dream than a reality. They could well have fled by the time the first of the military knocked at the palace door.

Bound and gagged, they stumbled awkwardly up the staircase, their captors pushing and prodding them step by step. Progress was slow and the little party had been climbing for some considerable time before she saw a change in the light. The stairwell was growing noticeably less dim, and in the far corner of her vision she saw a small patch of pink-streaked sky appear above. The patch gradually widened and the glow of a setting sun penetrated the staircase gloom, strengthening all the while, until they were pushed through a stone arch and out onto the flat roof of the palace. Here the light was brilliant, the sun still a great golden ball, though already obscured by the tallest peaks of the surrounding mountains. Beneath its dying lustre, the grey granite of the building sparkled with unusual warmth, making even its embattled ramparts seem less forbidding. Coming at such a moment, it was ironic. She wondered if Grayson shared the same thought.

She'd had no chance to exchange as much as a glance with him. From the instant she'd walked into the audience chamber, there'd not been a moment to think. All she had done was react to the terrible events unfolding around her. Flanked by his captors, Grayson now stood directly ahead. His tall frame was erect, his head high, his shoulders unbowed. Her heart reached out to him. The man he'd considered his best friend, the man who for years had been a trusted ally and companion, had betrayed him so completely. And then had died by Grayson's own hand. It was a nightmare come true and she could only guess at the turmoil he was feeling. But there was no going back. It had happened and they were here together, facing a last trial, facing death.

Their murder was apparently proceeding apace. In single file, they were marched along the roof to one of the turrets they'd seen from a distance, when yesterday they'd driven along the road to the palace. She remembered how happy they'd been just being together. Was that really only yesterday? Such a bewilderment of events ever since, each one sending them a little further on the path towards nemesis. Their captors pushed them roughly into the turret and lined them up side by side. There was some discussion between the men and then their gags were removed.

'At least we can scream as we fall,' Grayson said to her very quietly.

'I'm so sorry,' she whispered.

He cast a sideways glance at the men but for the moment they appeared to have lost interest in their prisoners. 'You've nothing to be sorry for,' he whispered back. 'This is my fault. I should have said a very strong no to you weeks ago when we were in Brighton.' He gave a crooked smiled. 'Not that you'd have listened, of course. And *why* leave Javinder and come back here?'

'I had to. I had to try and help. I know that sounds pitiful but I couldn't leave you.'

'I wish you had. I was imagining you free and safe. And I wanted that more than anything.'

The men had now gathered in a knot a few feet away and were arguing vociferously. Were they growing impatient, she wondered, or would they follow their orders and wait until the sun set? She could see it sinking fast, and even in the short time they had been on the roof, the mountains had been busy swallowing its bright sphere inch by inch. Their execution couldn't be long delayed.

She turned towards him, slowly so as not to attract the men's attention. 'I couldn't ever be free and safe. Not if you died here, alone.' There was a long pause and then she said in a voice that carried on the still air, 'You're my reason to stay alive, Grayson.'

And he was. All these years, she thought, and she'd finally realised that one simple fact. The only fact that mattered.

'It's a bit late to find that out,' he said a little shakily. 'Right now, they're arguing just who is strong enough to heave me over the battlements. You're a cinch, you'll be glad to know. It will happen just as soon as the sun disappears. They're nothing if not obedient.'

She looked out across the immense landscape, the town appearing a pygmy settlement against the vastness of the encircling slopes, shadowed now in the purples and pinks of evening. A broad beam of sunlight shone through the dip where two of the mountains met, like a searchlight, out across the foothills, across the whitewashed town, and came to rest at the door of the palace. Above them, a huge sky sported shades of pink and amethyst and deep purple, with here and there streaks of grey, and a blue that was deepening all the time. Night was coming. The sun was slipping away. Just a small segment flickered above the lowest of the hills.

'I know it's too late to say this,' she began, 'but

if we survive...'

She could not bring herself to finish the sentence. Together they looked down, remorselessly drawn to the drop below. Hundreds of feet below. Immediately beneath them, the jagged rock from which the palace had been hewn sent its spikes skywards. Their chance of survival was nil and they both knew it. She shuffled a little sideways and rubbed her cheek on his shoulder. 'I want to kiss you, but this is the best I can do.'

'In the circumstances, it's pretty good,' he said.

'It means I love you. I've always loved you.'

He bent his head towards her and skimmed her hair with his lips. 'Don't you think I know that, darling Daisy?'

The sun had finally fallen from sight. 'We're together,' he said. 'Remember that, we're together, always.'

The men had resolved their quarrel and were moving towards them. One of them pointed to her. 'You first.'

There was something in those two bare syllables that hit her for the first time with the shock of what was happening. A kick over her heart sent a sharp, frightening spasm through her entire body. Her blood hammered, slamming in heavy painful strokes through head, fingers, throat. They grabbed her by the arms and dragged her to the edge of the turret. She turned frantically to snatch a last look at Grayson, to keep his image in her heart as she fell to her death, but instead she found her gaze riveted on the road below. Surely they were lights that she could see, lights in their dozens, moving purposefully towards the palace.

She tried to focus more clearly but it was difficult. Then she realised. They were torches, torches of fire, and they were coming this way. She stopped dead in her tracks and the man pushing at her almost stumbled. He cursed loudly but continued to thrust her forwards.

'Stop,' she said. And when he took no notice of her, she gestured with her head towards the precipice below. 'Look down there. The army has come.'

That stopped him. He knew the English word. He peered over the turreted wall, then rocked back on his heels, a look of incomprehension on his face and she could see why. Now she was able to make out a line of armoured vehicles, still at a distance but driving between the rows of flame torches, and there were men, small, dark shapes from this height, but massing in their hundreds.

His two henchmen had taken up positions either side of Grayson and yelled across at him. Whatever they said, it made him shrug his shoulders and turn away from the view below. He had his orders and he intended to carry them out. He pushed her up onto the narrow ledge which ran around the inside of the turret wall. From here it was a breath away from extinction. She closed her eyes in readiness, but, as she did so, a great rumbling started up below, the noise loud enough to reach the clouds. The rumbling increased to a roar: engines revved, tyres squealed and a hundred pairs of boots thudded on flagstones. There was a deafening crash, as what she judged was an armoured-plated vehicle smashed its way through a wooden door a foot thick.

The man holding her let go of her arms, leaving her teetering on the ledge. She heard a frantic scuffling behind her and hasty footsteps in retreat. Overcome by dizziness, she dared not move at first. Then very carefully she managed to snatch a glance over her shoulder. The men had melted away. Only Grayson was left in the turret, his hands still pinned behind his back, but with a wide grin on his face.

'Javinder did it!'

Then suddenly there were soldiers, dozens of them swarming across the roof towards them. An officer resplendent in drab olive, a lion badge with two stars on his arm, emerged from the stone archway and marched up to Grayson. He saluted smartly.

'I'm sorry I can't return the courtesy, Colonel,' Grayson said, his arms still strapped awkwardly behind his back. 'A little local difficulty. But perhaps you can help the lady down. She's in something of a precarious position.'

At the commander's signal, two of the soldiers restored Daisy to the turret floor, and then set about cutting both their shackles. Once they were free, the colonel excused himself. 'We must leave you for the moment, Mr Harte. We still have business below.'

Another salute and he had turned sharply back towards the servants' staircase, his men following him down into the bowels of the palace. They were left alone on the roof and, for a moment, they simply stood there in the warm enfolding dusk and looked at one another in a long, long gaze. It was like being born again, she thought. Then they walked into each other's arms.

'Is that it?' she asked.

'That's it,' he said.

CHAPTER 23

Bombay, May 1948

The carriage drew up outside the church at ten minutes to twelve. Daisy craned her neck. Its magnificent spire still kept a benevolent watch on the tree-lined street below, but, after all these years, it was alone in being unchanged. The wall encircling the churchyard was shabby now, its whitewash peeling badly, and its protective railings rusted and unpainted. And the graveyard itself was badly overgrown; she could barely see the memorial stones through grass that for years had rampaged at will. War and independence had left this vanished part of an old empire battling alone against age and decay. Only the spire was still its glorious, tranquil self, its golden delicacy lifting out of the trees to soar skywards.

'Shall we go in?' She felt Grayson's hand on hers. 'It's far too hot to sit outside. The porch should be a good deal cooler and I'm sure the rector won't mind us waiting there.'

She nodded and he came round to her side of the carriage and helped her down. The driver moved his horse further along the road looking for what shade there was.

It was hot, very hot. And she was glad she'd decided on the thin silk dress and the piece of flippant confectionery which sat on her head. Beneath it, she had pinned her hair into a topknot of curls. Like a film star, Grayson had said, and laughed. He had remembered the dress when she'd shown him, and liked it, even though it was old and no longer fashionable. She'd chosen it deliberately. It had been the dress she'd worn ten years ago when she'd married here in this church for the first time. It had been hot then, she remembered, but everything else had been different. She had certainly been different, a bewildered bride, new off the boat from England.

He took her arm and led her into the cool of the stone porch. She glanced through into the church and saw two white-garbed figures at the altar making their final preparations. The scene was uncomfortably reminiscent. But ten years ago it had been Anish who'd ushered her from this porch and down the aisle to meet a drunken and resentful bridegroom. She glanced up at Grayson and he gave her an encouraging smile. He must know what she was thinking. He always did. She felt her hand squeezed comfortingly and the old scene faded away, to leave nothing in her heart but joy for the day to come.

It was to be a true celebration. As she'd wanted. The dress, the church, the carriage, the time of the year, all held the worst memories for her but today would be the chance to expunge those memories for ever, and to make new and very different ones. From this morning, St John's Afghan Church, the silk dress, the hot sun, would mean only happiness. Grayson had been right that coming back would exorcise her ghosts.

The rector beckoned to them from his position at the altar and she had only a minute to smooth out her dress and check that her hair was not about to fall to her shoulders, when the priest assisting him came smilingly towards them.

'Mr Harte, Miss Driscoll.' He shook their hands vigorously. 'Please follow me.'

She was glad that she could go to the altar as Daisy Driscoll, but this time she would be losing that name for good. This time her marriage would mean something. She saw Grayson give a small downward pull to his mouth. 'This is it, Miss Driscoll,' he whispered. 'Any last thoughts? Speak now or forever...'

'None,' she said. 'Except that this is the best day of my life.'

Or perhaps the second best. Her hand instinctively went to her stomach and smoothed the small, barely noticeable bump. From an antechamber, she saw a man approach and stand to one side of the altar. One of their witnesses. Her mouth rounded in surprise when she realised that it was Javinder who had joined them. Grayson grinned at her and she wondered if there were more revelations to come. But the second figure was that of the young man she'd seen him approach at the Victoria Railway Terminus when they'd first arrived from Jasirapur. The boy had come to Bombay for an important interview and Grayson's offer of a carriage ride to his appointment and a hotel room and dinner that night was sufficient to enrol him as a witness. He looked happy, Daisy thought; his interview must have gone well. The boy's smiling face, Javinder's unexpected presence, were symbols of a day where nothing could go wrong.

She walked slowly down the aisle, her arm entwined with Grayson's. The same red carpet, the same black and white geometric tiles, just a little more worn, a little more dowdy. But the stained glass windows were as magnificent as ever and, as the sun reached its zenith and poured itself through a hundred images, the dark interior of the church was dappled with pools of bright colour. It was like having your very own light show, she thought. Ten years ago, she'd hardly noticed their artistry, though the display must have been just as brilliant. She'd been too concerned to hurry to the side of the man she loved, thinking him ill. She'd been desperate to help, she remembered, and then more desperate still when she'd discovered the truth that he was the very worst for drink.

Today the man who stood beside her could not be more different. Despite the crushing heat, he looked immaculate in pale grey shirt and cream linen suit. In the dim light of the church, he made a vivid figure, his eyes a startling blue, his face tanned by an Indian sun. He handed the rings to the rector and the service began. It was brief. No more than ten minutes later they were crowding into the vestry along with their witnesses to sign the register. Then back along the aisle and out into the porch, its stone greeting them with a welcome rush of cool air.

Grayson pressed an envelope into the young

man's hands and wished him well. Then they were in the carriage, together with Javinder, and bowling along the dusty road through Colaba on their way to the port. She remembered the suburb well: large houses, wide roads and overhanging trees. It was a very attractive part of the city. Gradually, though, the roads grew narrower and the traffic more dense. The driver had to pull up at regular intervals, blocked by a cart or a lorry or a cycle rickshaw and occasionally a wandering cow. Vehicles hooted, people yelled to and at each other. The horse twitched his ears and waited patiently.

'Happy?' Grayson asked her, turning from Javinder's congratulations to cradle her arm in his.

'You know the answer to that.'

'I hope I do. But this heat is appalling. It might not have been our best idea – a wedding while we're still in India.'

'We couldn't have done it better. Today has been wonderful.'

'And no ghosts to spoil it?'

'They visited for a while,' she confessed, 'but they're well and truly banished now. And for good.'

'If that's really true, you're forgiven for persuading me to marry in a cauldron.'

'And forgiven for the very private wedding?'

'That's hardly a problem. What man wouldn't want something as modest?'

Javinder nodded his head enthusiastically. 'Indeed Miss... Mrs Harte. But yes, Mr Harte is right. The big wedding is not a good idea.'

'Javinder,' he exploded, 'how many times have I told you to use our first names?'

'I forget ... Grayson,' he said carefully. 'Things are so different now. With independence, there is no barrier. We can use names. We can be friends.'

'Weren't we always? I'd hoped we were.'

'Yes, yes, of course. But that was because you were not as the others. I have had many British colleagues over the years, but never a British friend – except for you.'

'And I'll stay one, I hope. I want you to visit us, once Daisy and I are settled.'

She leaned forward and clasped Javinder's hands. 'You must promise to come to London very soon. I intend to take you to every one of the sights.'

'You are very kind. I would like that. But first I have a most gigantic mountain of reports to write.'

Grayson wrinkled his forehead. 'I've left you a lot of work and I'm sorry. If the justice system could have dealt with Verghese and his entourage more swiftly, I'd willingly have helped.'

Before they'd left Jasirapur, they'd signed witness statements concerning the events at Sikaner. She knew that Grayson was hopeful that these would be sufficient and they would not have to return for the trials to come. There was plenty of other evidence both in Jasirapur and Sikaner of what had been going on, paper evidence and evidence on the ground. And, of course, Javinder's own testimony.

'Don't worry. It will be a very big pleasure for me to make those reports. Every word that I write will be one more to condemn them.' She had never heard Javinder sound quite so ferocious.

They were approaching the port at last and the scattering of carts dwindled, while the lorries increased in number and size. Then they were alongside *The Arcadia,* the liner that was to carry them to Southampton. And only just in time, by the look of it. Their journey from the church had taken far longer than they'd expected. The ship's hooter sounded three urgent blasts; sailors were swarming around the gangway, ready at any moment to roll it back across the quay. Porters appeared out of nowhere to unload the small amount of luggage they'd brought and were soon squabbling over their right to do so. The driver shooed them away, waving his whip, but it did nothing to deter the arguments. Somehow they managed to clamber up the gangway with only two porters alongside, each carrying one small bag. It was comical, but this was India and this was the way things were done. At the top, they waved a final goodbye to Javinder and saw him jump back into the carriage. He would be on his way now to the railway terminus and Jasirapur.

'I've ordered tea,' Grayson said, as they flopped exhausted on to one of the narrow bunks. 'I thought we'd have a quick drink and then go up on deck to wave Bombay farewell.'

She looked around the cramped space, deciding where she could stow her few belongings for the three weeks they would be at sea. He saw her looking and said quickly, 'I'm sorry the cabin is so small. It was the biggest they could find at such short notice.'

'What's a small cabin, when you're happy. *And* when you have an electric fan?' The fan was doing little more than churning warm air, but nothing was going to spoil her delight in the day. 'Short notice or not,' she said, 'you've managed to get us a berth on the best side of the ship.' She saw him smiling. 'It is starboard on the way home?'

'It is and you're getting quite the traveller. Listen, that's the steward outside. Tea is what we need most right now.'

They were on their second cup when she felt the first thrum of the engines, then a jolt as the liner cast off its moorings and began its slow progress out to sea. She put her cup down.

'Come on,' she said, 'we should be up on deck.'

'You go ahead and I'll join you in a minute. I need to find the purser's office. There's a telegram I must send.'

The air was still solid with heat when he emerged from the companion way, but the beginnings of an offshore breeze fluttered hopefully at the ship's flag. They were already gliding smoothly out of the shelter of the main harbour, the blue waters growing wider and the flat roofs of Bombay's whitewashed buildings more distant. There were bright sails everywhere, dozens of small craft looping a pathway in and out of the many small islands that studded the bay; and the small tug that had pushed and pulled them from their berth was turning in a lazy arc and heading for its mooring. He looked back at the quay disappearing from view and thought how very different was their departure today from that of ten years ago. No noisy troops clumping in pairs up the gangway, their *topis* and kitbags slung over their shoulders. No military band playing farewell tunes, no singing or shouting, or throwing coloured streamers from ship to quay. And no crowds gathered to wave goodbye to the lines of troops on their way home to England. The last of the British soldiers were long gone and somehow it felt better for that.

He needed to feel better. The business with Mike still weighed heavily. He would never understand what had made the man a traitor. He understood his grievances all right, in many ways he sympathised with them, but to have betrayed the service, to have betrayed his country, for that's what it amounted to, that he couldn't understand. He'd suspected for a long time that all was not well, but he hadn't wanted to believe the worst. And then he'd heard Mike's voice, seeping from that audience chamber, a final miserable confirmation. But Corrigan's guilt didn't make it any easier – his death was a wound that would take many years to heal. It had come out of nowhere and was the last thing Grayson would have wished. It was murder and he was responsible. He might comfort himself that it had been pure accident, that he could as easily have been the one to slip on the knife at a deadly angle, but the fact that he had killed a friend would always be with him.

He braced himself to meet Daisy. He didn't want to burden her with his darkest thoughts, not after all she'd been through. She was standing at the ship's rail, shading her eyes against the sun, and watching the vessel carve a majestic passage through the calm waters. To her right, the tangle of docks was receding rapidly and in the streets beyond, coconut palms, mango trees and tamarinds were no larger now than matchsticks. On a slightly raised strip of land to her left was all that remained of the earliest British fortifications. They appeared and disappeared within minutes. But she didn't notice. She was looking neither to left nor to right but steadfastly ahead, as though willing the ship to travel fast and true to the home for which she'd searched for so long.

He looked at the small, erect figure standing at the bow of the ship and his heart was filled with such a fierce and possessive love that for a moment he felt physically shaken. That they were here together as man and wife was little short of a miracle. Months ago, he'd accepted the hopelessness of loving her and set out quite deliberately to kill his feelings. Or so he'd thought. But then they'd been thrown together in this adventure, and he'd known within days, within hours even, that his emotions burned as brightly as ever and possibly always would. Somehow they'd come together again and somehow he'd made Daisy his own. If he had any say in it, that's the way it would stay.

CHAPTER 24

The ship was passing the great white arch that marked the Gateway of India when he came up beside her. 'Do you remember the last time we stood watching the Gateway slip into the distance?' he asked, then answered his own question. 'Of course, you do. How could you not?'

She smiled up at him. 'Neither of us were quite sure then what we were returning to. And you had no idea that within months you'd be back in India again.'

'With luck, that won't happen this time. The Rajah made no attempt to hide his tracks. He's left behind enough evidence in the palace to hang him and every one of his fellow conspirators, including Adeep. At the very least there'll be enough to ensure that prison is their final resting place.'

'But not Ramesh Suri's.' She pursed her lips at the thought.

'Not at the moment,' he agreed. 'He's been a lot more calculating and a good deal more clever in covering his wrongdoing. But the police are on his trail. He'll have slipped up somewhere – greedy men always do. And I'm pretty sure there was something else going on, something that can provide more evidence. He wasn't just chasing money. Once the project was launched, I'm certain he hoped to implicate the Rajah, but escape scrutiny himself. Somewhere he'll have locked away the documents he considered incriminating. But an expert prosecutor should be able to use them against him as much as against Verghese.'

'You're saying that money wasn't his prime motive?'

He saw her expression and didn't blame her for the scepticism. 'His game was certainly to make as much money as possible, but then I think he intended to shop Verghese. And that has to be pure revenge. When the Rajah's son wrote to his wife that he was leaving her for another woman, he dishonoured the Suri family and, in Ramesh's eyes at least, made a whore out of Parvati. So what better revenge than to make money from Karan's father and then see him land in jail?'

'He couldn't have anticipated that his own son would be part of the crime scene,' she said thoughtfully.

'He was unlucky in his timing. Until that last day, he'd always managed to keep his distance from the action, and if it hadn't been for the Rajah demanding Dalip's presence in Sikaner, there wouldn't have been a family member in sight when the project kicked off.'

'But Dalip is certain to be charged, isn't he?'

'They'll both be charged eventually, father and son. Like I say, there'll be stuff that can be traced back to Ramesh. And, of course, the Rajah is more than happy to spill his own beans. There's no love lost between them. It was a business arrangement that suited them both, until it no longer suited them. Suri senior had a legitimate business selling Indian antiques around the world, but a somewhat less legitimate one doing deals in secret for people who didn't want publicity. Dalip has been learning the trade. He's thoroughly implicated in the shadier aspects of the firm.'

'I still feel a little sorry for him.'

'Well, don't. He was more than ready to take over after Ramesh retired with his ill-gotten pile.'

He noticed the slightest shadow pass across her face. 'He was brought up without a mother,' she said. 'That has to be some mitigation. His father's say has been everything. Dalip was his clone and has done exactly what he was told.'

'So you don't blame him?'

'Only partially. And Daya, not at all. He seemed a sweet boy bullied by his family.'

'As far as I can see, Daya is a complete innocent. He's at Delhi university, a law student, and has no interest whatsoever in his father's business. With luck, the authorities will leave him alone.'

He broke off and waved towards the headland which lay at the extreme south of two parallel ridges of low hills. It was the harbour's last protective arm. 'Look, Colaba Point.'

'We're there already? We must have picked up speed.' She swivelled round to face in the opposite direction. 'I can hardly make out Malabar Hill.' The highest point above the flat plain on which most of Bombay was built had all but vanished.

'We should say our last goodbyes then.' He put his arm around her shoulder and hugged her close. 'Talking of Dalip Suri, I never reported him for the hit and run. I didn't tell you before – you've been a little preoccupied. I was going to add it to the charge sheet, but then I thought the incident might be better forgotten. I didn't want to give the authorities any reason to detain us or bring us back here. Right now, I think you've had enough adventure and possibly enough India.'

He was right. She had had enough. And he was right, too, to say that she'd been preoccupied. There had been almost too much to grapple with. At last she knew the name of her father, but it was a knowledge that disturbed as much as gladdened. Somewhere deep within she'd never expected to uncover the truth and now she had, there was joy certainly but tinged with a profound sadness. She'd found her father, only to lose him again. She would never know him, never even know about him. His father, her grandfather – and her mind still stuttered at the fact – would be in prison for what was left of his days. There would be no touching reconciliation between them, no stories of her father's early years. But, and it was an amazing but, she had not been abandoned as she'd always imagined. Knowing that truth had brought her a new-found peace and brought, too, a fresh confidence.

And that mattered. Her self-esteem had never been more than fragile. She'd fought against being a victim, told herself there were plenty of others orphaned as she had been, others raised in harsher conditions even, and she'd refused to be downtrodden or exploited. But the struggle to believe in herself, to make any kind of life, had often been lost. When Gerald arrived in her world, she'd thought naively that, after all, she might be special, only for her hopes to crash to earth when she'd found herself special in the worst of ways. Special because she'd married a man who, for his own mean ends, had not hesitated to thrust her into danger. But she was through with that. What Gerald had done was no longer important. What Anish had done was not important either. Instead, she would remember him as the friend she'd loved. A friend and a brother, her own flesh and blood, part of a family she had never known she possessed.

Her quest was over. She knew who she was and she knew where she wanted to be. Home. She was going home. She looked out at the sea and saw not the broad expanse of ocean but a powerful road speeding her to her destination. It was carrying her towards the new family she and Grayson would make. No fairy tale this but far, far better. Fairy tales, as she'd learned to her cost, could too easily crumble, but this story would stay warm and stay solid. It would be the building of a life together.

'Did you send your telegram?' she said, pushing her thoughts aside. Grayson was still on duty and she must remember that.

'I did. And managed to confirm that it arrived safely.' He paused for an instant. 'It was about Mike.' She knew it was difficult for him to talk about his friend, but it was best they did. From now on they should have no secrets from each other.

'The service will make the arrangements?'

'He's to be brought home for burial. In Ireland, I believe.'

There was another pause, longer this time, and then she asked what had been on her mind ever since she'd heard Mike's voice in the palace. 'Did you never suspect him?'

'I came to, but only very gradually. I kept hoping I was wrong.'

'And Javinder? Did he know anything of Mike's activities?'

'He told me he'd become suspicious months ago. But I was the only one at headquarters he could talk to and as I was Mike's closest friend, he felt it impossible.'

'He couldn't go over your head? Send his report to a more senior officer?'

'He wasn't going to write to London to tell them they had a spy in their midst, if that's what you mean, though he was pretty certain that was the case.'

'I don't see why not, if he was so sure. Anyway, how did he come to that conclusion – about the spying?'

Grayson looked ahead, his face stern. 'Apparently he alerted the police force in nearby towns several times about possible trouble – he has his own informants in and around Sikaner – but each time the troublemakers, or rather the killers, got away before the police arrived. There had to be someone tipping them off and since Javinder was sending advance information to London about the police raids, the tip-off had to have come from headquarters.'

He stopped talking for a while and began to drum a tattoo on the painted railings. Daisy waited quietly beside him. 'Several things pointed him in Mike's direction,' he said at last, 'but he couldn't be definite and he didn't have proof. Without that, to accuse an SIS man of treason would have been death to Javinder's career. That's why he went to Sikaner to find out for himself who was behind the violence and who was helping them in London. But he found out more than he bargained for. The project in all its grisly detail landed in his lap, and he landed in that dreadful cell. At least he's fit again now and he'll get promotion for what he's done – not as much as he deserves, but still a promotion.'

'All that planning,' she said wonderingly. 'All the money the Rajah must have spent, and all for nothing.'

'Splendid, isn't it? Not a single injury or death that day. Instead the project died.'

'Thanks to Javinder. And to you.'

'And you, Daisy. You're in there with us.' He was smiling now, she was relieved to see. Mike had been temporarily forgotten. She hoped that, as the months rolled by, memory would grow kinder.

'What will happen to Sikaner now there's no rajah, and no son and no grandson?'

'Do you fancy offering your services?'

'Don't tease.'

'I mean it. You should be the next in line, though you might have a little difficulty convincing the authorities that the palace is yours.'

'More than a little difficulty. Think of how shocked they'd be at the prospect – mixed race, illegitimate, and a woman.'

'Possibly their worst nightmare,' he agreed companionably. 'There's a son of the Rajah's cousin somewhere. Strangely, he's in the Indian Army too. I imagine he'll resign his commission and take up the reins. And bring Sikaner into the

Indian union.'

'So it's like I said. The Rajah's plotting was all for nothing. Look, Grayson.' She tugged at his arm and pointed at the land, now only the faintest of outlines. 'Don't miss our final view. There she goes, the last of India.'

'For a while at least. And, to tell the truth, I'm looking forward to getting back to London. It may be grey and damp and the city may have been battered to the ground. But it's home. And it's where we'll make a fresh start. That has to be good.'

She was silent for a while, and then blurted out, 'How will your mother feel about the marriage? When you tell her.'

'She'll be delighted. She's always liked you. You know that.'

Daisy hoped she knew it, but she also knew that Mrs Harte had come to doubt her commitment to Grayson and she might not be quite so willing now to welcome her new daughter-in-law.

Grayson seemed unbothered. 'I had a letter from her a few days ago,' he went on. 'Something else I haven't mentioned. It took an age to get to Jasirapur, but arrived just before we left. It was full of notes on how to keep cool and how to be careful of the water and the food. Full, in fact, of utterly useless advice. But she did say she was delighted to hear you were with me and hoped that when we got back, we'd take tea with her.'

'Taking tea with her doesn't mean she'll be happy to see us married.'

'But you don't know what her postscript said, do you? That if I possibly could, I should try to persuade you into a church.'

'I'm sure she never said that,' Daisy protested, imagining the words were wishful thinking on his part.

'She certainly did. She's always known you were the right one. She got quite cross with herself that she never managed to sort out a wedding for us. Now we can tell her we've done it all on our own.'

'It seems unfair to spring it on her. We should tell her the news before we go to any tea party.'

He considered the matter for a moment and then said decisively, 'You're probably right. I'll telegram once we get to Port Said.'

Port Said was where the east would finally be left behind and where they would set their face westwards towards a new life. Grayson, it seemed, was following the same train of thought. 'She's already talking of finding a different flat for me. She doesn't think Spence's Road is the right address to welcome a respectable young woman. And, if I know anything of my mother, once she gets that telegram, she'll be growing wings to fly around London. There won't be a stone or a room that stays unturned. Prepare yourself – she can be exhausting.'

'I won't mind as long as she's happy for us. We'll go and see her as soon as we reach London – unless you have to report to Baker Street straight away.'

'I'm sure I can wangle a few days' leave. And you're as free as a bird. Brighton is but a distant memory. I wonder if your old matron is still fulminating.'

'Quite possibly. She was a good fulminator.'

'To little effect though. You'll have the pick of

the jobs in London, and there's plenty of time for you to look around and choose something you're really set on.'

She didn't say anything and she felt him glance quickly down at her. 'You are going back to nursing? You're not going to let one spiteful woman hound you out of the profession?'

'No,' she said a little uncertainly. 'Not for ever. I'll go back eventually.'

'You'll soon find a hospital that won't care whether you're married or not. So why not now?' He was looking puzzled. 'You've always loved nursing.'

'There's something I shall love more. Make sure your mother looks for a two-bedroom flat. The second room need only be small.'

She could see his mind working rapidly. There was the click of recognition, then the most joyful smile spread across his face. His arms went around her and he jumped her up and down. Several of their fellow passengers smiled at his exuberance.

'Hush, Grayson. Put me down this minute.'

He set her gently on her feet, then stood with his arm around her waist, as they watched the enormous golden circle of sun slip inch by inch into the vastness of the ocean. With its disappearance, the air freshened and he hugged her closer.

'We'll come back to India. And we'll bring him with us.'

'Yes,' she said, 'we'll bring her with us.'

'We'll bring them both,' he laughed.

'But all in good time.'

A shoal of flying fish chased across the bow of

the ship, scattering small droplets of water. They watched as the sea gradually regained its glass-like surface. He bent his head and she felt his kiss skim her hair and brush the nape of her neck.

'And time is what we have,' he said. 'Do you know that from the very first moment we met, we've never had the chance simply to be together.'

She cuddled closer. 'Think of it as another adventure. And the best one by far.'

The publishers hope that this book has given you enjoyable reading. Large Print Books are especially designed to be as easy to see and hold as possible. If you wish a complete list of our books please ask at your local library or write directly to:

Magna Large Print Books
Magna House, Long Preston,
Skipton, North Yorkshire.
BD23 4ND

This Large Print Book for the partially sighted, who cannot read normal print, is published under the auspices of

THE ULVERSCROFT FOUNDATION